ATLANTIC
BLACK

A. S. Patrić is a bookseller and teacher of creative writing. He is the author of two short story collections, *Las Vegas for Vegans* and *The Rattler & other stories*, and a novella called *Bruno Kramzer*. His debut novel *Black Rock White City* was published to critical acclaim in 2015 and won the Miles Franklin Award in 2016. *Atlantic Black* is his second novel. Alec lives in bayside Melbourne with his wife and two daughters.

A. S. PATRIĆ
ATLANTIC BLACK

transit lounge

MELBOURNE, AUSTRALIA
www.transitlounge.com.au
First Published 2017
Transit Lounge Publishing

Copyright © A.S. Patrić 2017

This book is copyright. Apart from any fair dealing for the purpose of private study, research, criticism or review, as permitted under the Copyright Act, no part may be reproduced by any process without written permission. Inquiries should be made to the publisher.
The moral rights of the author have been asserted.

Cover image: Stephen Carroll/Trevillion Images
Internal image: Detail from "Beneath the Vortex" by Ray Collins
Author image: Bleddyn Butcher

Cover and book design: Peter Lo

Printed in Australia by McPherson's Printing Group

A cataloguing-in-publication entry is available from the National Library of Australia: http://catalogue.nla.gov.au

ISBN: 978-0-9954098-2-8

for my father

We inhabit a world of unfinished stories, and echoes,
the repetition of age-old horrors and miseries.
David Malouf

RMS AQUITANIA, *31 DECEMBER 1938.*

Katerina Klova walks out onto the sun deck. The air is sharp enough to force a lightly dressed passenger back into the soft warmth of the interior. The porthole glimpses she had coming up from one of the lowest points on *Aquitania* allowed her to hope for pleasant sunshine. The weather yesterday was brilliant. She saw flying fish in the afternoon, at the prow of the liner, their sleek silver bodies skimming and lifting into the air, often for two hundred metres or more before diving back down into the water, easily outpacing the ship at full speed.

Her mother remarked that it must be an incredible liberation to break free of ocean depths and find that kind of drift through the air, scattering the weight of water in droplets, floating over the face of the waters. Anne used that expression and it reminds Katerina now of the first verses of the Bible, about how the earth was without form, and void. Darkness was upon the face of the deep and the spirit of God moved upon the face of the waters.

Anne was speaking French and there were a couple of Parisian dandies nearby who took the shared language as an invitation to converse. Anne refused to turn her head towards them. Katerina would have enjoyed the conversation but had to return her gaze to the flying fish as though utterly mesmerised, lest she offer the two men any more of an invitation.

The chap with black opal cufflinks remarked that these fish seemed to breathe air, yet that had to be an impossibility, didn't it? So each was holding its breath. A desperate interval rather than a liberation. The fellow wearing a lilac felt fedora said these flying fish wouldn't fly at all if they weren't trying to evade a predator below the water, eager to eat them up like sardines—he'd seen newsreel of a fish with a monstrously large mouth that sucked them up in their dozens.

The waves are slight but the water is not flat today. "Choppy" is the word for the irregular, broken movement. Electric restlessness in the water. A noiseless rain begins to fall, contributing to the frantic surface in billions of lightless sparks.

Below deck it is all rooms and corridors, secondhand air, stagnant and compressed around the many moving bodies—bodies sweating, coughing, farting, sneezing—the stop and go of bodies passing here and there.

The liner moves with glacial steadiness and Katerina feels as though she's sitting atop a snowy mountain peak beginning to avalanche down a cliff face at a gradually increasing speed and there will be an imperceptible transition to freefall—then a drop into vast submergence. They will sink and sink. Her mother will sleep and sleep.

Katerina finds an umbrella in a metal amphora near the bulkhead hatch and walks the damp deck. She falls. Gets up quickly. Almost slips over again. Her skirt is wet and continues to gather drops of water up to her thighs. She keeps the umbrella low but doesn't turn back. Small steps. Careful of her balance, she gathers her hair with her left hand and winds it around her forearm and wrist, pulls it down her neck, tucking the cord of it into the cardigan she's wearing.

The deck is the height of an eight-storey building pushing through the water far below. She gets a sense of a level plane from looking at the horizon. That bending line where sky and ocean meet. But they never do meet. Vision stops at a sickle cut across the world.

A crewman strides over the deck as though it is dry. Rubber soles on his long red boots. Katerina thinks that perhaps he is going to warn her or direct her in some way—tell her that anyone who doesn't need to be above deck should keep well away from slippery tilting surfaces.

He passes Katerina with barely a glance, spits out across the rail with a brutal expression around his mouth, disappears from the deck a few moments later. Passengers rarely walk with that kind of purpose. Destinations aboard ship don't have the urgency they would on land. Passengers dawdle and amble. When sitting, they cross their legs and swing a foot around as though to create a pendulum free of time.

Odd to see the deck empty today except for one man leaning over the rail. Three thousand passengers and almost all kept away by light rain. He wears a long slick black jacket but is bareheaded and his hair drips rainwater at his collar.

Bright flashes near the horizon, lightning so distant there is no sound of thunder. The weather has been cold; bright and clear up to now. Ice and snow won't stop passengers coming up for fresh air in a few days. More than the open skies, there will be desperation for a glimpse of the wider world. To be free and clear of the turbulence of other people, who even when calm exert pressure on others saying hellos, commenting, staring. Better is a crewman spitting over the side of the ship or that bareheaded man leaning over the railing, pulling his collar tight around his neck, needing nothing from anyone.

Katerina closes the umbrella and tilts her head back to feel the rain on her face. Silly to avoid the rain on an ocean liner. Isn't it incredible that a person can cross the Atlantic, over six thousand kilometres of open water, and never become wet? Seems bad luck; to encourage catastrophe in an act of petty hubris. She opens and lifts the umbrella above her head again; feels for a moment a pleasant sensation—the frigid wind from the ocean across her wet face, the way it freezes her eyes, her cheeks, her nose and her mouth.

Gulls tear around the air above, frantic for food. Yesterday morning the ship sighted Haiti, mist-blue hills in the distance, and they might already have passed by Puerto Rico, out of the Caribbean Sea and into the Atlantic. Soon there will be no more scavenging gulls. The desperate sounds they make, a species endlessly squawking from a ceaseless hunger.

The man in the slick leather coat, hand at his collar, steps away from the rail. He is about to walk across the deck to the hatch but halts because of the raucous gulls hovering around them both.

"The rats of the air. Revolting birds, are they not?" His English is nearly perfect despite the heavy German accent. "On a previous crossing I saw a whale passing near the ship. It was summertime. She lifted her majestic tail in the air as if she wanted to wave to me. The whale is a sublime creature to see breach when you are moving in her own water—that she exists, as incredible as a dinosaur. Every time she surfaced, these gulls would land on her back to peck out meat for their breakfast. Yes, they are carnivores. Her flesh was pockmarked from their attacks. Could be that it was not pain for her."

"I'm not sure how far seagulls can fly across the ocean. There must be land nearby. One of the Virgin Islands maybe?"

"Would you mind if I lit a cigarette?" he asks. She looks at him, confused by the question. Why would he need her permission?

"Beneath your umbrella. So I can use the matches." She nods and he steps closer to her than she expected. She can smell the odour of his body, not sure whether she finds it pleasing or repugnant. Perhaps both, as she has found some men: repellent and welcome at the same time.

He opens his long coat and from an inner pocket removes an engraved silver cigarette case and matches. His fingers are wet enough that they glisten.

"Would you like one?" he asks and she nods though she's never been able to draw on a cigarette without coughing.

The flash of light and the smell of phosphorous are lovely. He lights both hers and his own with the same match, two cigarettes in his mouth. One more intimacy she didn't know she had agreed to. His mouth looks dry yet they're close enough to kiss. He breathes out an exhalation of tobacco smoke. She has always enjoyed the smell.

She draws back on the cigarette expecting to cough it out but she doesn't and is relieved. He buttons up his jacket with fingers that continue to tremble. His hair is dripping cold water onto her hand as she holds the umbrella. A warm, red glow for them both from above. A floral design—the red of poppies in the umbrella. Left behind by a passenger, perhaps years previously.

"How did you know I speak English?" she asks.

"I have seen you out here the last two days reading your

books. I was surprised at such a young woman keeping company with Henry James. Mine own English is not so good to read Henry James without translation."

"Sometimes I think I'd like to read him in translation myself."

The German laughs. Katerina is surprised to have made him laugh. She wonders whether he is mocking her or perhaps trying to ingratiate himself. Yet a moment later he says *Wiedersehen* and walks away.

When he has disappeared through the bulkhead hatch and she is alone on the sun deck Katerina takes a cherry-wood box from her shoulder bag. She thinks of it as a jewellery box even though Audrius Klova used it to store cigars for a few years in Warsaw. One day it was empty and Katerina began to use it as a place to keep Amelia, her favourite doll. Putting Amelia to bed every night in the box until she saw Grandfather Mikelis in his casket at her first funeral and understood that the bodies of our loved ones are put in boxes when we want to bury them, so Katerina started using her father's cigar box instead for flower heads and autumn leaves and acorns and pine cones, river stones and seashells she found while exploring when they moved to Lisbon, and then later, for letters and her diary. She throws the box over the railing the German stood at a few moments before and watches it open on its loose hinges, spill its contents, and barely cause a splash in the restless rush.

Contemplating suicide. It hasn't occurred to her until this moment. She is sure of it. The way he was leaning over the rail. Trembling, not from cold, but from how close he had wandered to the edge of his life. Hearing her slip and fall, a slight squeak with every step across the wet deck, unfolding her umbrella, folding and unfolding it again. The noise of the gulls and his memory of a previous crossing when a whale had waved. Majestic. A desire awoken, for the warmth of smoke and air in the lungs, and the thought of being so close to another their breaths might mingle. Leaning over the rail. Without form and void. Darkness on the deep. Faceless.

Katerina sucks at the dead cigarette and realises the ember has been blown away by the sea breeze.

❖❖❖❖❖

"If ever I get up to heaven, you see—I'll only have hell, only have hell—bringing the fires up with me." A man is singing, playing his guitar in a lounge down the corridor from the bulkhead hatch. There are a few other passengers seated around him and they have instruments as well but they wait, listening for now. Perhaps they take turns because they do not know each other. *A motley orchestra*, thinks Katerina, liking the phrase for the sound of it more than for its meaning. It would make a good title for a Fritz Lang film.

"Only have hell, only have hell," the guitarist sings, picking the strings with his fingers as Katerina has seen Spanish players do when they play.

Her teeth click together as she trembles through her jaw, shivering up and down her spine—the coolness outside most keenly felt when she steps back into the warmth of the ship. She had carried that heat out with her onto the sun deck and lost it gradually, feeling the cold as a fresh release until it reached deeper, past blood and flesh, into organs and bones. She pulls her cardigan closed at the neck. Movement will get her warm so she walks quickly.

She moves along a passage to the main entry stairs and down to the first-class foyer, passengers on Deck D heading towards dining tables or away from finished meals. She bumps into a doddering woman on the wide landing, a busy intersection of bodies bustling up and down and through to port or starboard, bow or aft, hearing the crone exhale all the air in her lungs as though she crashed into a pillar, smelling the wine breath, a stink of urine on her, the noise of air knocked out of her body.

"*Oof,*" the old woman says but doesn't fall. Neither of them gives an *excuse me*. Too many bumps aboard a ship to apologise for every single one of them. No, it is the smell of urine that makes Katerina want to keep her mouth closed and hurry on.

She heads through a door and along a corridor to a narrower set of stairs and down again to Deck E and a very long passage to the kennels. Passes many passengers and crew, keeping her gaze down, her long hair a curtain around her face. Amazed at herself, that she can manage to navigate her way about a ship that only three days ago was a labyrinth she got lost in twice looking for the Palladian Lounge.

The three borzoi are in a locked kennel that would be a large enough space for one of them. They prefer close company over different kennels—sisters never separated from their litter. Katerina is assured that her father's borzoi are walked every day on deck, as promised before the trip. Yet Katerina is not convinced by the way they scramble and whine, all three at the door, pushing and climbing over and snarling at each other, and biting, to be at the door when Katerina opens it. *Another two weeks of this*, thinks Katerina. *Another two weeks!*

It's too late to get them separate kennels now. The hold is full, not only with dogs but animals that are being transported from Central America to a zoo in Belgrade. There's a jaguar on an iron chain at the end of the hold—the single creature here that is calm and still. Beside him on his straw mat is half a cut cow carcass, showing ribs and spine, the meat crimson and bright pink. Untouched by the jaguar's massive jaws. The cat watches the movement of the room as if the rust-flecked links binding him to the metal hook in the deck are a nuisance; a temporary impediment.

"I was about to feed them breakfast, Miss. Maybe you can help," says the steward.

"Breakfast? This ship confuses my sense of time."

Katerina isn't sure when her mother was carried to the infirmary on a stretcher. Every porthole and window they passed on the way was black. Empty corridors, cabin doors shut. All quiet. Silence but for the sound of the engines getting louder the lower they went in the ship. The humming of the generators. The thrumming steam turbines, ploughing fifty thousand tonnes through the Atlantic.

"Might be lunchtime, for all I know," Katerina says.

The steward doesn't look at her. Busy with the many animals in his care. "Open these cans if you like. They'll enjoy being fed by someone familiar."

The label on the can shows a picture of a horse, the way that a can of beef might display an image of a cow. The label also says *Vitamin Enriched Mineral*, though she's not sure what that means. These rooms were loud already—the volume increases to the point of hysteria.

A rattlesnake sound comes from wooden boxes by the entrance. There are three stacks of four and each might contain a different species of snake but that particular rattlesnake warning noise has to be part of what's causing the general uproar. The steward shoves wriggling white mice through sliding panels at the ends of these boxes.

Katerina gathers her hair and ties it into a loose knot at her neck and then takes the can opener and places it on the raised metal rim of the can and begins to turn the lever. The smell from within gets stronger as she opens the can. An awful odour. Amazing how terrible a smell can be without indicating rot. And of course the dogs won't mind. Perhaps it is an appealing aroma to them.

Sweat is trickling down her ribs. She needs a bath. She hasn't yet managed to have a bath on *Aquitania*. Her mother has required too much attention. Katerina has been able only to clean herself with a wet towel in their cabin. She opens another two cans of horseflesh for the dogs.

She walks to the borzoi's cage and opens the little hatch through which she reaches in and turns the can over. She jiggles the can, the dogs go into a frenzy. One of the bitches bites her on the wrist. The bite doesn't make her drop the can. The meat slides out of the can a moment later. She withdraws her hand and doesn't mention it to the steward. Maia, Electra and Alcyone are her father's dogs; Katerina has never been able to tell them apart. Beads of blood rise from the imprint of teeth in her flesh.

"If you wait half an hour we can take them for a walk."

It's hectic and the steward is shouting as he deals with feeding time. "There's only so many leashes a man can hold on his own."

"I'm sure you'll manage well enough," she tells the steward, not sure whether he can hear her. She has to get away from the brutal noise of hunger.

Thinking of the steward holding as many leashes as he can fit in his large hands reminds Katerina of her fourth birthday—the day her father bought her forty helium balloons. A couple of weeks into their first move, walking a cobblestone street in Warsaw with forty strings in her own hand.

Until then, Leningrad was all she had known, and there were many ambassadorial moves to come. The balloons above her head bobbled and strained to be let loose as her small feet negotiated the cobblestones.

Audrius Klova stopped and entered a shop while she waited outside because she wouldn't fit through the door with the wonderful celebration of balloons above her head. And then Katerina let them go and was ecstatic as the bright colours separated, and drifted higher and were blown away.

Flakes of snow blew horizontally across the Warsaw sky, over the city's buildings aglow in the late autumn sunlight. The reds and blues, dotted greens, pinks and yellows, silver and gold stars, among the high flurries of white. The loveliest thing she'd ever seen. When the balloons were out of sight her exuberance vanished and she felt a vicious change in emotion.

She cried for her balloons, gone so soon after they were presented to her by her beaming father. He was smiling in the store, happily chatting with the man behind the counter putting his order into a wooden box. She could see him through the amber shopfront glass. Paying for the wine and whisky while she waited for him out in the street. She lied and told him the many strings had slipped from her fingers.

He slapped her across the face. Said he saw what happened through the window. Slapped her across the face again and told her to stop crying. And she did—she stopped crying after the third time he slapped her. He had a cigar in his mouth as he was slapping her, not looking particularly upset. A grim duty and then a puff of smoke.

He'd removed the leather glove from his right hand when he came out of the store and knelt down before her as he'd often done affectionately and she'd felt that gloved warmth in his palm as it struck her exposed left cheek. Perhaps she had been rosy pink from the cold. She was scarlet red on the way home. She felt the glow of the slapped check, and everyone they passed must have known why only one side of her face had such vivid colour.

Flakes of first snow catching in everyone's hair and dissolving moments later from body heat. Her father puffed on his cigar and she blew smoke out into air rapidly getting colder as evening fell. The snow continued to drift across the city and she hoped there had been a few others who lifted their heads and noticed her birthday colours flashing among the white flurry.

Katerina walks towards her cabin with the perverse thought that Audrius Klova, who had bought forty balloons for four years, should have slapped her four times, one for each year of her life. He made up to her during the evening with kisses and songs that tasted of tobacco and whisky.

❖❖❖❖❖

She is near her cabin, picking her way around boys playing marbles in the corridor, a chalk circle drawn on the floorboards. Ship movements rolling the marbles might be accepted into the game as an element of luck. "Norwich," the boys call. One of their surnames, or it is part of play—might it have something to do with the city in England? "Norwich," they call out again. She has turned a corner and is out of earshot before she can decide what the word might mean to them.

Through an open door Katerina sees a woman sitting on a stool at the vanity, painting her fingernails. Dressed in so much black she might be in mourning. The bottle of nail polish is a festive shade of rose. She's up to the index finger of her right hand and awkward—the unwieldiness of a right-hander using the left for a task requiring precision.

These views through cabin doorways are so quick they appear to Katerina as paintings, the framed images a constantly changing exhibition.

She saw a man yesterday morning in pyjama pants and only his undershirt sitting on the edge of his bed carving slices of a green apple with a bright knife. His left leg had been amputated below the knee, the faded, striped pant leg rolled up. A veteran of the Great War. The expression on his face, photographically sharp, said something of ordinary isolation that would be covered up when out on the promenade or in a dining room.

No windows in some of the cabins, yet even portholes give little relief from a caught and trapped sensation; imprisoned despite possessing the keys to the cell. Quiet acts such as reading with the door open are common because privacy isn't required. A small cabin oppresses so much that the passing of other passengers is an acceptable nuisance, as flies buzzing overhead are a fair trade for open windows at the height of summer.

Perhaps these glimpses are less gallery images and more like the recovered frames of film from a camera damaged in a house fire. There's the same arbitrariness to what is preserved by random chance. Usually an image of no real consequence, yet circumstances can focus perspective. The loneliness of travel reveals loneliness everywhere else. Isolation amid the crush of people aboard an ocean liner—isolation in every frame of every moment.

Katerina read a quote from a Yugoslav poet called Aleksa Alimpich in a letter from her brother. The poet said that it is possible to live for years in a burning house. A fascinating idea without the slightest plausibility, which she understands is precisely why it continues to tease her. She finds herself wishing it was an image photographed or painted so that she might relieve her own imagination of its impossibility. A home on fire and yet mother and father, uncles and aunties, grandmothers and grandfathers, the many children, all go to sleep in their beds every night, wake up in the morning, eat meals at the dining room table, and occasionally members of this family burn.

She comes upon an officer standing next to another open door. Unusual to see crew looking so idle. A midshipman. Maybe as young as she is.

"Hi," he says, as informal as kids meeting on a playground.

"Hi," she says, and stops. On the sun deck she felt much older than her years and now the opposite. Through the open door she can see part of a bed, and on it the bottom half of a man's body. Supine and naked. Withered white shanks on the blue sheets, mottled grey pubic hair and a pale glimpse of his genitals, mustard nails on gnarled feet splayed out.

"Sorry," the midshipman says. "I should have closed the door. He's been cleaned up but there's still an awful smell. Not sure how long he's been dead. In bed when they found him, cozy under the covers, so he wasn't disturbed until the smell gave it away."

"I don't smell anything." There is a vaguely unpleasant odour in the corridor—nothing she would have noticed walking by. There are books on the bed and the floor. "Was he reading when he died?"

"Not the kind of books you'd find in a library. Pornographic." Speaking the last word as though it is a profanity. Katerina's face does not respond to the word. She waits for him to continue.

"Pornography from Japan and India and I don't know where else. Things I've never seen before. Images with animals and humans in there I don't even count as pornography. That old man was sick in more ways than one."

Looking into the room, Katerina is not sure whether the books lying open and scattered across the floor were left by the man on the bed or the men who found him. She takes a step towards the doorway and peers into the room. No magazines. No cards or any of the other cheap ways to reproduce pornography. Painted images hand-bound in leather and top-end photographic books filled with black-and-whites. That was all she could tell from where she was standing.

"Did you want to come in?" the young man asks dubiously.

"Are you here to guard the door?" she asks, watching the expression on his face change and change again. "To make sure nothing is disturbed—or stolen?" The Norwich boys around the corner and along the hall would sweep straight into this room after their game of marbles, pause at the spectacle of the old fellow on the bed, dead and naked, yet no doubt fall upon the open books like kittens to saucers of milk.

"They could have locked the door for that. I'm not sure why they asked me to stay in the room with him and wait. It's been two hours. I didn't want to leave my post." He turns his palms towards her, arms hanging uselessly at his hips. "I had to get out of there."

"Keeping you alone in a room for a few hours with a dead man—it sounds as though it might be an initiation. Maybe a bit cruel. I've heard of worse from my brother. Kornél is an officer cadet in France. See what you're made of, that sort of thing.'

"I was so … I felt … I didn't even think of it in terms of training."

"Best thing you could do is order up room service. Let them find you eating steak and kidney beans when they come back for you. Have a glass of wine as you consider the rare books of the collection."

"Are you …?" He points to the cadaver on the bed inside the room. "You are joking. A few days ago this Yank was in Mexico and he walked onto our ship with a ticket and his suitcases. The matron had to clean the shit and piss from his arse and legs. Who could eat a meal in there?" He glances into the room, his palms on his thighs, bending forward at the waist. Straightens up and looks at Katerina again. "What kind of girl are you?"

"My father has a large collection of pornography himself. We're carrying it over to Europe for him. Well, we're taking his whole library. There are crates and crates of books. I could show you the pornography if you were interested. There's no bestiality so you wouldn't need to worry about being repulsed."

"You look at pornography?" he asks.

"My parents complain that I'm not interested in anything or anybody. That I spend too much time reading. I love books. There's nothing that offends me in books but it's different when you see the same things in life. Then I feel like absolutely everything offends me. I can look at a woman in a picture and wonder whether she is really enjoying what the man is doing to her, and I think that she is, and that she isn't. That there's a balance in every moment of feeling disgust and pleasure." They hear the feet of the boys running along the floorboards of the corridor—closer and then further away.

"You're smart." It came out of the midshipman as much an accusation as a compliment.

"Not really. Just have a way of remembering interesting ideas. Bits and pieces of genius, but nothing comes from me. It's torn-up pages from books in my head."

"I would like that."

"To see my father's pornography?"

"I meant, get to know you."

"Maybe both?" she asks and he nods.

"What's your name?" he asks.

"This is yours." She touches the name embroidered on his uniform at the chest. "Gerard."

"My name is Gerard Cypress. No-one calls me Gerard. I used to be called Junior at home and here they mostly use surnames. Which is fine by me. Never liked Gerard. Call me Cypress."

"OK. You can call me Klova then."

Katerina looks into the room again. She notices that the man has hives all over his body. Perhaps that's the reason he's naked. So that he could scratch himself. Are hives a condition that itches? She had hives once when she was very young but it knocked her out for a couple of days, nearly killed her, and afterwards left her with very little memory of what had happened. She can't remember whether she itched. Even if the old fellow didn't need to scratch, the feel of fabric on the skin would have been painful or maybe too warm if he was feverish.

"Is he contagious?" Katerina asks, because it might not be hives. "Some terrible disease from the jungles of Mesoamerica?"

"The doctor said it was an allergic reaction. Anaphylactic shock."

"Something he ate?"

"Nothing on his record. It could have been a kissing bug. That's what Deering thinks—the boatswain. Bugs that got into his luggage when the old codger was in Mexico. Deering has seen them at work. He's been around the world a hundred times and he's seen a great deal. These things suck blood, a lot more blood than a mosquito, waiting for a person to be asleep before they climb into the bed. They're attracted to the smell of a person's breath, it's sweet to them, so they bite near the mouth. That's why they call them kissing bugs."

"Really don't blame you now."

"Excuse me?" Leaning forward.

"For standing outside in the corridor." Leaning back. "For allowing yourself to appear such a forlorn child."

❖❖❖❖❖

Sedation was all the doctor could offer Anne Klova this morning. There was a quiet room to herself but it was hardly a hospital. Two weeks away from port. Only a few days clear of land before Katerina's mother, who'd always had trouble sleeping, couldn't cope any longer. Unable to sleep at all for three nights in a row, she'd begun imagining an octopus, dripping black ink, wound around her limbs, her chest and neck.

"Imagining" was the word the doctor used. Her mother had fallen to the floor to writhe, gasping for air, passed out before the doctor could reach their cabin on Deck B. After the hallucination had passed, the bruises on her arms, on her legs, from her thrashing and falls, the bruises around her neck from her own hands attempting to release the grip of a tentacle, could not be explained as marks of self-violence. Even free of the hallucinations she believed the strings of bruises, resembling the sucker marks of tentacles, were proof she was being attacked by an octopus. This had gone on for nearly twenty-four hours. Few moments of apparent clarity where she could see that of course no such monsters of the sea had managed to creep onto the ship to grapple with her—in order to weaken and to strangle her.

Her mother said that it was well known that an octopus

could climb onto ships to steal crabs from fishing barrels, that couldn't be denied. Yes it was true, the doctor said—from fishing trawlers, not from world-class ocean liners. The deck was well over ten metres above sea level and there were steel hatches, and there were doors and there were flights of stairs and mazes of corridors busy with people, over four thousand in crew and passengers, and any one of them would raise the alarm if they saw a horrible sea creature creeping along. He was grinning as if he'd explained a joke.

Anne Klova was blinking and shaking her head and blinking again. Of course they can climb and they can squeeze through fist-sized holes. "Look at my arms and look at my legs and my neck look at my chest if you don't believe me." And her mother even lost her sense of modesty and opened the front of her dress and exposed her breasts so the doctor could see the bruises crossing her body.

So, sedation and a clean bed in a room to herself. The doctor told Katerina her mother would have a good long sleep and she should be much recovered. There's not a person who ever lived that could manage without sleep. It's as vital to the mind as oxygen is to the blood, the doctor explained to Katerina and suggested she go back to her cabin. It would all settle down.

Was the doctor telling Katerina that her mother was drowning, that dreams would give her the air she needed? How was she to understand what was happening to her mother? She was afraid to ask the doctor whether perhaps it was the culmination of years of pressure, and that something was permanently broken; that from now on Katerina would only ever be able to see crumbling fragments of her mother—afraid to ask because she had the sense that asking might make it true.

Maybe it was as simple as a good night's sleep. She sat beside her mother and wanted to read her something to help her dream pleasant dreams. There was nothing pleasant she could find in the Bible she pulled out of the bedside drawer. A horror story from start to finish, as far as Katerina could see. God was a monster. And the men and women of the book—either his victims, or baby monsters desperate to grow up big and strong.

Katerina sang a lullaby her grandmother had sung to her when she was a child about a ladybird princess helping an injured soldier on a battlefield. Didn't leave the tiny sick room for an hour. Her own fatigue made it excruciating. She was able to get only snatches of sleep in the lulls of her mother's hysteria. The chair had an uncomfortably low back so she dragged it to her mother and lay half across the foot of the bed. Fell asleep. Dreamless; obliterated for a time.

When she opened her eyes she heard the sound of her mother whispering. The words didn't make sense. Her legs and arms began to thrash beneath the blanket as though she was again contending with the long ink-black arms of a horror of the deep. "It's all right, it's OK," Katerina said with a series of soothing noises. All the lights had been turned off except for a dim light bulb above the mirror. In the darkness Katerina could almost see those lithe tentacles reaching, gripping, constricting. She reminded herself she was not afraid of an octopus. Below the blanket—the frantic movement—only the limbs of her mother.

She wanted to tell her it was all a ridiculous idea in her head. A foolish fear grown too big, a nasty illusion yet still a trick of belief come over her in the darkness of her mind. There were predators like the shark which might be something to be fearful of, those rows of razor-sharp teeth, and whales that could leap out of the water and be frightful through size alone. What was there to be afraid of in the form of an octopus? Laughable, really.

Katerina had seen drawings in Father's books, and Mother had surely seen the pictures as well—black etchings from long ago of tri-masted ships being hoisted into the air by an octopus ten times the size of the vessel about to be crushed to splinters. No-one had believed in such a thing, had they? Perhaps only the most ignorant of people who spent their lives in villages beyond the immediate influence of science. And yet the ocean was immense. The Atlantic seemed to be a definite shape on a map, a certain place, but it was just a word, an abracadabra denoting an actuality so vast it was beyond imagination and deep beyond reckoning even with the most advanced scientific tools.

Katerina called for Doctor Blackshaw. She pushed her chair back against the wall. Stepped aside, both hands up to her chin, thumbnails pressing her bottom lip hard against her teeth. Doctor Blackshaw and the nurse strapped Anne Klova down with wide white straps rolled up from underneath the bed, duck-cloth straps that might be useful in stormy weather to keep sick patients in bed. The doctor decided to give Anne Klova another injection to help her sleep. *More* help.

Her mother's eyes opened a moment when the needle pierced the flesh in the crook of her arm, her eyes, a lovely clear-sky blue that Katerina didn't inherit, going under the waves of hysteria one last time. Unable to keep up the fight, she said. "Sorry, I'm so sorry, Kitty." Not opening her eyes again as she spoke. Began to murmur, "My apologies, my apologies, my apologies," as the sedation dragged her back down into the abyss of herself. A thin line of red lipstick, remnant at the very edges of her lips from crazed preparations to see the ship's doctor hours before crumpling to the floorboards of their cabin.

Katerina waited until she didn't know what she was waiting for. Leaned forward and wiped the saliva trickling from the corner of her mother's mouth with her own handkerchief. Laid it on Anne's pillow beside her knocked-out face. Katerina left the cabin knowing her mother couldn't reach for it. More immobilised than if she had been put into a straitjacket.

There was a young nurse outside at the nurses' station who would no doubt ignore the handkerchief. A Glaswegian girl called Flora with an accent so thick that Katerina struggled to decipher her English. She was too young for her job and as careless as a poorly disciplined schoolgirl. Only a few years older than Katerina. Maybe the nurse thought they were the same age. Katerina turned seventeen in May, often thought to be older because of her height.

Flora fondled her white nursing cap and the hairclips that held it in place as she talked with giddy enthusiasm to a young man from America about their plans for the evening—for the New Year's celebration. Katerina found the same chatter and eager preparation in much of the activity on *Aquitania*. So many bustling bodies and smiling faces ready to break open in cheer. Noise that'll thump and clang. The cheering and singing throughout the ship as 1939 was rung in. All of that clamour would mean another needle. More sedation for Anne Klova.

The next time her mother rouses from her sedation and

begins struggling against the straps holding her down, the doctor could be busy with a patient on another deck in one of the hundreds of other rooms and this nurse would not notice until Anne Klova started to scream. Then it would be a question of how long it might take to find the doctor and bring him back through the many corridors, down or up the stairs, hurrying along more corridors, while Anne Klova imagined that ink-black tentacles were reaching around from beneath the bed to crush her.

❖❖❖❖❖

Katerina stops at the locked door of her cabin—puts her head to the wood and closes her eyes. She needs some sleep. She needs to cry. She needs it to be quiet and still for a few minutes. Lifts her head away from the door as she hears footsteps walking down the corridor. She doesn't want to be asked if she is all right, whether she needs any help.

The cabin key is in Anne's handbag. The thought of returning to the infirmary is paralysing. She can't go back to her mother, writhing under those duck-cloth straps. Closes her eyes and shakes her head. Clenches her fists but doesn't lift them from her sides. A trickle of sweat down her ribs. She smells unwashed. Soon she'll begin to stink.

She hears the Norwich boys, a stampede of footfalls bustling up and down the wood of the halls. They go from room to room—two or three of them with family cabins on this deck.

"Good day, Miss," one of them said to her yesterday in passing. "It's a good day. Happy day … when a tug comes into Bristol Cities." The last part as she was heading away.

She was surprised that they'd said nothing when she passed today. Unless "Norwich" was slang for something else as well. They are on the move again. Around the corner.

She can hear them arguing about football—Matthias Sindelar's decision not to play for Germany in the World Cup. They will soon come thumping through her corridor. She can't continue standing here before her cabin door. She'd smiled at the boy saying "Bristol Cities" yesterday and they guffawed before she was out of earshot. They had all said *bonjour, Mademoiselle* before that, sweet as puppies. Today, so absorbed in their game, they didn't even turn their heads.

An unlocked door is an impossibility. Anne often asks Katerina to check that a door is locked after double-checking it herself. Katerina reaches out a hand and puts it on the door handle and pulls it down. Her mother is careful about the door being locked. She can't be careful about anything anymore.

Food for two is waiting in the cabin. Dinner from last night. Forgotten in the storm of hysteria tearing through the room. The trays pushed aside. Steak gone cold on the plates under the metal covers—gravy formed into a skin that looks as if it has been half peeled from rotting flesh.

Katerina and her mother ate lunch and dinner in their cabin, venturing out in the morning for pots of tea and freshly baked pastries. Being in the room and all its hectic mess is awful, worse for the absence. The clothes her mother put on and took off and put on again and the jewellery and hats and shoes across both beds, the tables, scarves and shawls piled and hanging from both chairs, the various components that used to make a pleasing image for Anne Klova in the mirror now jigsaw pieces in disarray across the cabin.

The lamp was left on when crew carried her out. It is still switched on. Katerina's dress is damp from the sun deck drizzle. She unties and unbuttons and lets her dress fall to the ground with all of her underclothes. She wants to get away from the smell of her own sweat soaked into the fabric, the mildewy aroma of the rain. She kicks the whole mound away as though it is a small body.

There are baths on one of the lower decks, a pool to swim in. She's not sure where but she can find it if she can work out what to wear. She hasn't brought a swimming costume. She crawls beneath the covers of her bed. Naked and cold, on the verge of shivering for a few minutes, until her own warmth is gathered in by the bedsheets. She tries to recall whether she locked the door when she came in.

Anne's gowns, skirts and shirts are draped across her and Katerina can smell her perfume in a silk scarf near her face. Her mother brought six bottles of perfume for the trip across the Atlantic. She said that's how many she needed to still be able to smell them, since wearing only one all the time loses it to the sense of smell. And she'd always hated the smell of the sea and fishes. She didn't want to get off the liner in Calais smelling like the sea or fishes.

Katerina can hear the sound of running feet outside the door. A moth fluttering around the lamp, bumping into glass with a *tink, tink*. The running feet gone, and perhaps that will be all from the Norwich boys for a while. Katerina tries to remember whether she locked the cabin door. Her eyes open and close, open and close. The moth goes *tink, tink* on the glass, and then fluttering, fluttering about the light.

She falls asleep too quickly. Her whole body jerks as though she's dropped into bed from a height. She pats herself on the chest as if to say *there, there*. Opens her eyes. Closes her eyes. Falls asleep.

❖❖❖❖❖

Katerina wakes, aching. Her wrist is pulsing pain. Half-asleep, she lifts her arm out of the bedsheets to look at her wrist and finds bruises beginning to grow around four puncture points. Teeth marks. She thinks about what type of insect could leave such a large bite mark. Or what kind of person. Cypress's story about kissing bugs from Mesoamerica is playing on her dozing mind. She remembers that these are the marks left by one of her father's bitches.

How long has she been asleep? Light comes from the jadeite glass boudoir lamp fixed to the dresser. The two portholes in their cabin are behind drapes so she can't see from her bed whether it is day or night. She might have slept through the New Year's celebrations. Clearing her head isn't easy. She feels drunk with fatigue.

Closing her eyes to get more sleep makes it worse—a vertigo that spins faster and faster every minute she stays in bed. What is the time? It would help to know. A folded travel alarm clock was usually on the table beside the bed. Not there now. She sits up, back against the headboard, and gazes around the dismal cabin illuminated in seaweed green.

She dreamed that the ship was sinking and that no-one was alarmed. The midshipman was standing at the open door of the same room but wouldn't talk to her. Her panic was growing into hysteria and she yelled at him that they had to get off the ship. Cypress was at attention, as expressionless as a palace guard.

The German emerged from the room and explained that no-one was panicked because the ship had submarine technology and there was nothing to worry about. The intention had never been for the ship to simply cross the Atlantic yet again, but to locate the largest octopus ever born to the ocean. Which was quite something, the German said, considering the millennia of ocean life.

He couldn't or wouldn't explain why they were going in search of this creature and what would happen when they found it. The German's calmness and the midshipman's steadfastness only roused her desperation to get off the ship in any way possible. There was a blurred sequence of attempts to find a hatch that would open onto air.

The clearest images and the last from the dream are still raw in her mind and continue to agitate her imagination. *Aquitania* was upside down and Katerina was lying with her back against the sun deck, buoyancy keeping her there—but barely. She felt as though she was in a bubble and the slightest twitch would see her bead of air slide off the smooth wooden surface. She'd be lost quickly, her bubble popping in the plumes of air escaping from the ocean liner. She was motionless, trying to blink and breathe in minimal movements.

The ship was descending into a darkness getting thicker every moment until there were points of illumination below her that grew into circular patterns of light. These discs were arrayed on a vast ridge, and appeared to be cities embedded in gnarled black stone. Emerging from the gloom, the circles were revealed to be the octopus's suckers, all getting closer, until her bubble of air slipped away from *Aquitania*'s inverted deck and she awoke blinking away the black water of the Atlantic.

Katerina gets out of bed and puts Anne's dresses away in the two suitcases she brought with her and she packs her hats and scarves and replaces the perfumes in their travelling case and keeps cleaning until all traces of her mother and her struggle with the octopus hallucinations are gone.

She eats a banana that is spotted brown but not quite inedible and a small bag of brazil nuts. Afterwards finds herself ravenous for food—for a proper meal. She tries to remember when she last ate. Two soft-boiled eggs with buttered toast. Yesterday's breakfast. If she had lunch she can't recall what it might have been. She opens her suitcase and puts on clean underwear and a new dress, one she was going to wear for the first time at the academy in Saint-Cyr.

Thinks about the dream and shakes her head. Such a horrific leviathan living beneath the Atlantic—a brief glimpse results in a spasm of fear—the bubble slips and bursts. Drowned like millions of people before and multitudes after. She should have kept her calm and at least seen something unique before she died. The face of the deep. An embrace from the lord of the underworld. Nothing of the sort, and such a mediocre death after all for Katerina.

"What's the point of the monster if I die by drowning anyway?" Her voice is harsh and loud in her ears.

A night previously, Anne knocked on the panelled wall behind the dresser and then the wall behind the bedhead. She asked, "Are the walls metal? Not all of them are, I'm sure, but listen." She knelt on her pillow, resembling a distressed child who needed an answer from an adult. "It's unbearable, the way every sound resonates, every noise vibrates. Every word I say is tolling on the inside of a church bell."

Katerina hasn't noticed how hard her voice could be, she has spoken so rarely to Anne in the last three days.

"And when you sleep, Kitty, you grind your teeth."

The portholes are bright, two shades of blue divided into sky and water. Not raining outside anymore. She finds the small folding clock on the wooden floor beside the bed. It tells her it is twelve-past four. Can that be true? She puts it to her ear and hears nothing. She shakes it and it begins ticking again. Thirteen-past four. It can't be the next day. If she'd slept through the afternoon and evening her dress wouldn't still be damp. She separates the bundle of her clothes and hangs her undergarments and dress up to dry. She gets the other key to their room and locks the cabin door. There's a peach-coloured ribbon in her luggage she can use for the iron key. Hangs it around her neck.

It has to be afternoon. Maybe it's midmorning. Her sense of time is off. She might have slept half an hour. It is rare to have such a vivid dream in so short a sleep but it has happened before. She has had to take her sleep when she can get it: her mother going down the hall to the toilet, or going to see a woman on Deck C who said she had some herbs that would make a great tea for calming the nerves. Herbs called skullcap, valerian, passionflower, St John's wort. A witch's concoction to

Katerina's ears. To her nose as well. While Anne was gone for whatever length of time, Katerina would sleep.

With her mother in the infirmary time has opened up, become strange and uncharted. How she will fill two weeks alone on *Aquitania* baffles her so much she finds herself standing in the middle of the now tidy cabin, blinking, breathing, not knowing what to do even with the next hour. Yet that sense of time losing its predictable *tick-tock* through the day, the feel for the progress from breakfast, lunch to dinner, waking and sleeping at either end, might be expected—perhaps a common phenomenon for passengers crossing from one time zone to another.

Soon the New Year's Eve party will begin and Katerina wonders what that will be like on the ship. Had her mother not been in the sickbay they would have stayed in their cabin and waited out the celebration as though it were bad weather they had to endure. Her mother would have drunk the awful-smelling witch's brew and tried to keep herself calm, hoping for just a couple of hours' sound sleep.

Katerina is already wearing her best dress. She'll venture out later so she takes it off and puts on her pyjamas. She's been looking forward to wearing the dress for months. Sent by Father when he was in Paris, recalled now to Moscow. Yes, she'll wear it tonight. She finds a bottle of burgundy nail polish. She is left-handed so she does her right nails first. It'll take a little while to dry. The kind of nail polish that annoyingly never feels enamel-hard. Should be fine by the evening. She has a lipstick that goes well with the nail polish called Black Cherry, though Anne says it is much too dark.

Her brother's dress uniform is on the wardrobe, the coathanger's hook over the top of the door.

She picks up a slim book by Mina Loy, careful to keep her nails clear of the paper. Gets back into bed to read, leaning against the headboard. Finds words she underlined in a poem she can't remember reading: "Since the black lightning desecrated the retinal altar", and "How this expressionless 'thing' blows out damnation and concussive dark". She tries to read "Der Blinde Junge" again but finds her mind wandering away from the page. A gift from her brother. His inscription on the title page. Waves her fingers in the air like she is shaking off water to help dry the nail polish.

She hears the sound of laughter, two men, maybe three, in the corridor passing by her door. Harsh working voices. The kind of men who would as easily throw abuse as a greeting.

She looks at her brother's cadet uniform again. With the troubles Kornél is having at the academy, she is sure the laughter would have bothered him. He's never been one to laugh easily but when he laughs it doesn't sound as it should for a full-grown man. Twenty-one years old yet his laughter is that of a child and he's helpless to change so natural a sound. His time at the academy has been violent. His vision in his left eye has been blurred since April because of a fist fight. So he doesn't laugh at all if he can help it.

Maybe the eye has cleared. The last she heard from him was an October letter. He has been burned on his arms with cigarette embers. His ears ring constantly because one of his roommates woke him one morning by firing a rifle out the window above his headboard. It makes sleeping difficult, the noise in his ears, and the malevolence of this roommate.

Her brother has sent her letters about everything he is experiencing but he tells their parents none of it and expects

Katerina to keep quiet. Even when he tells her that he has failed in an attempt to poison himself. He promises Katerina that it has merely made him want to see it through—to graduate.

Most of his letters from the academy are hidden in crates in the hold, among Audrius Klova's voluminous letters and journals and his official documents, which Anne would never touch. "I'd be turned to stone through sheer boredom," she'd said. She was more than willing to hunt through Katerina's suitcases and has continued to read Katerina's diary more or less secretly. She sometimes confused what Katerina had told her and what she had written down, responding to either without considering how she was giving herself away.

The diary has become a fiction over the last year, the "Katerina" within it only partially resembling its author. The pages are intended to confuse her interloper, sometimes to torment her, though it began as nothing more than teasing.

She would note in her diary how Anne has started to have a faint odour about her. Days later, among other observations, Katerina would write of her mother's odour again and in yet another entry wonder why that subtle whiff of decay continues to follow Anne around. It is there even after she's bathed. What would that odour become on the long journey across the Atlantic when bathing would not be as easy? A stench? Did Anne not notice it now? She would certainly notice it by the time they disembarked in Calais.

On another page it reminds Katerina of the time Anne hadn't understood she needed glasses for a year before going to see an optometrist—prior to that, the world going hazy was put down to stress and exhaustion. Using the word "decay" repeatedly, knowing that it would hit a nerve. And always using her Christian name in the diary because there was a sting in taking away the word "mother"—*Maman*, as Anne preferred.

Or Katerina would sketch out snatches of poetry her mother could only assume (since she read nothing but newspapers and magazines) were Katerina's attempts to write:

Black creeps from root to root,
Each leaf
Cuts another leaf on the grass,
Shadow seeks shadow,
Then both leaf
And leaf-shadow are lost.

Which was from a real poem, "Evening" by H.D.

Katerina keeps the last letter Kornél sent her within the pages of a Russian translation of Antal Szerb's novel *The Pendragon Legend*. She hasn't read the novel so has been able to use one of the uncut pages in the middle of the book as a secret envelope.

I am sure, in years to come, these experiences will do me good! Don't you think a person has to be pushed past their limitations for a chance to grow? A man can very well stay a child all the way through to old age. How many old fellows did we see when we were growing up, as foolish as they ever were. I can't help thinking of Mazzanca when we were in Lisbon. All those shoes! Do you remember that old idiot? Or Uncle George, come to think of it. Fourth wife and you know it is only a matter of time before there will be a fifth aunty for us to welcome into the family. We never do the opposite when they leave …

they simply disappear. No, I thought, this will not be what I write in stone. Failure. Such total failure! I felt that what is essential is to survive in a bitter winter, flourish when the seasons change. I have been thinking about it ... Unusual for me to continue to think. Aren't we all so distracted for so much of our lives? Rarely do we ever focus for a few days of continuous thought upon a subject of vital importance. How to live? That's too easy. How not to die before actual death? That's a harder question. Impossible ... eventually. What it comes down to is a tolerance for pain. To accept fear as well. Pain diminishes and fear corrodes. I put the poison in my mouth and tasted both on my tongue ... diminishment and corrosion. I spat it out and nearly died anyway. When I was in hospital (it was put down as food poisoning, so nothing to go on my record and shame Daddy) I thought about how a human being comes from an invisible seed. As I got close to the edge of my life, utterly unable to move, mute, blind, barely capable of breath, I could feel how despite my flesh and bones, thoughts and history, I was yet the invisible seed. First in the womb and then in the brain. I could feel it as much as know it, but it was very distinct ... A seed. One so small it was as made of particles of light, and it could flicker like a candle flame near an open window. I take this to be my soul, but I disagree with the religions. It didn't seem eternal, celestial, God-granted. Rather I was struck by the opposite ... How feeble, how vulnerable, how of the earth, as ordinary as an acorn, as mundane as a pumpkin seed. Do you recall the way Granny loved to eat pumpkin seeds? Crushing them between her teeth to get to that small soft heart. Funny the things you think of, the absurdities that go through your mind when you are stuck in a hospital bed for a few days!

Following his own words was the long quote from Aleksa Alimpich, a poet he'd discovered recently. Kornél wrote at the bottom of the page his first initial in lower case and a full stop. Something he's been doing since he learned to write. For all his learning he has yet to see the need to use paragraphs. Every thought rumbles into another, tumbling down on paper as soon as it arises in his mind. At the top of the page: *Saint-Cyr, 11.15 p.m., 16 October.*

Katerina looks at the clock again. Quarter-past four. She lifts it to her ear and it isn't ticking. She turns the key until the spring inside is tight, closes the face and puts the folding travel clock beneath her mother's pillow. She folds the letter and places it in the pages of the Szerb book. She looks at the author picture on the back cover.

A heavy wool suit with overly broad lapels, a generic white shirt and a tie he might have received as a birthday present when he turned sixteen. He has a high forehead, emphasised by hair combed back in a rather vicious manner, and a gaze that is perfectly neutral, almost at a place of zero, not solemn or jovial, withdrawn or convivial, expectant or dejected. For that reason, Katerina finds the image of Antal Szerb beguiling. It is as though this one person in this one photo has been caught in a moment when everything—future and past, hopes and fears, life and death—found a precise balance.

It was interesting reading *Journey by Moonlight*, another Szerb book. Her brother read it before her and there were marks in the margins and lines of prose underlined, yet rarely a comment. Not in this gift, of course. The other book she plucked from Kornél's shelf for the title, which she mistakenly thought was a romance.

She preferred reading with his lines and asterisks. The author and a reader, the presence of one reminding her of the presence of the other. Katerina could forget, for chapters at a time, that there had been a person who put each letter to paper in the first place—then her brother might underline a sentence: *Italy he associated with grown-up matters, such as the fathering of children, and he secretly feared it, with the same instinctive fear he had of <u>strong sunlight, the scent of flowers, and extremely beautiful women</u>*. Was it as odd a combination of humour and beauty for him as well? Perhaps he found it merely a jarringly discordant list. An asterisk or an underlined phrase indicated neither approval or disapproval.

… *<u>what was really unendurable was the silence in which they sat, the silence when one man tells another that he stole his gold watch and then neither says a word.</u>* She might not have noticed that line had her brother not underlined it. And then there was a question of what caught one person's eye and left another wholly unmoved. Something could bring tears to her eyes and it wouldn't be at all memorable to another person. It isn't especially important when it is a book, but she has the feeling that there are fundamental events in her life that would not merit an asterisk from anyone else.

"Don't tell *Maman*," he wrote in the postscript of the letter from Saint-Cyr.

❖❖❖❖❖

The lock is turned and her door is opened. A priest stands there looking around the cabin. Eyes glassy, blinking, he takes a step inside. Notices Katerina in one of the two beds. He looks at the number on the door again, makes an expression with his mouth, a twisted mixture of confusion and annoyance, backs up and closes the door again. *Elephant's trunk*, as Uncle Georgie or one of the Norwich boys would say. That was clear from the difficulty the priest had taking those backwards steps. A cigarette in his mouth, not much left of it apart from the glowing ember. Is a priest meant to smoke on duty? Maybe he isn't on duty, but then why is he entering her cabin without knocking? Katerina hears the lock click into place. She is alone in her cabin again. She sees herself from the chaplain's perspective, one of those doorway snapshots in *Aquitania*'s corridors.

"I will let my body flow like water over the gentle cushions." A seductive fragment of Sappho's poetry which now makes Katerina feel as though she might dissolve into her pillows and sheets and leave nothing but stains.

She moves to the edge of the bed and drops her feet to the floorboards. Her bare soles feel how thin the rug has been worn, her toes can distinguish where the sides of each plank of wood were joined. She's been in this cabin long enough to know which two creak—when Anne was trying to sleep, creaking floorboards became very noticeable. She reaches out a toe like a finger over a piano and presses down a floorboard and hears a squeak, and then presses the other she knows will make a similar noise.

The tobacco smell lingering in the air reminds her of the German up on the sun deck. She wonders whether he might be up there again. Certainly, he'll be there tomorrow. It is a pleasant smell, tobacco smoke, especially only a waft of it. A parlour aroma that would go well with breath that smells of brandy, though the German's breath didn't smell of alcohol. She didn't get quite that close. Close enough to see he hadn't shaved for a couple of days and to wonder how rough that would feel on her face, on her neck, between her legs—on the soft parts of her thighs. Would he kiss her down there?

Katerina stands up to smell the tobacco smoke the priest left behind when he mistakenly opened her door and then withdrew without a word of hello or goodbye, any kind of acknowledgment, let alone apology. As if speaking to Katerina wasn't necessary. The kind of behaviour that Katerina experienced when she was a child often ignored by adults. Must have been because she was still in bed, tucked up under a blanket. She walks to her brother's uniform and places the officer's hat on her head.

Did she appear a child to the German in the drizzle on deck? No, he had come close and offered her a cigarette. The way he spoke to her showed that he understood what she was. She turns and sees her reflection in the mirror of the dressing table, wearing her brother's peaked cap. Her expression at zero. She grimaces, bottom teeth sticking out, a childish monster. She tries out gleeful surprise and even then a ghoul appears in the reflection. She lowers her head and levels fury at the reflection. She's reminded of the mouthful of bile, that gargoyle expression of the crewman on the sun deck before he spat over the rail. Perhaps he had talked to the German a few moments before. Stepping away. Disgusted by the weakness. Choosing not to restrain the passenger from finding fathoms of oblivion below.

She tries the door handle to make sure it is locked. Pushes her mother's two suitcases in front of the door. She takes off the cap, pins her hair up and puts it back on, then walks to Kornél's uniform. She takes the jacket off the hanger and puts it on. Fits well enough.

There is no magic in the world anymore of course. That ends with childhood but a uniform possesses a clear, direct mythic power. It is a heroic costume, the officer's uniform. Enough to make a person want to endure any degree of suffering, and to make others suffer, though the latter did not need a ceremony.

Not knocking because it was a dead man's room. It seemed such a random event. Was the priest sent to perform last rites? Or if that is something that can be administered only to the living then a drunken blessing for the body—a shove for the departing soul in the direction of paradise. Confused when he saw the corpse in bed and when the body moved he could only back up and leave wordlessly. Frightened in his befuddlement, and inebriated enough to feel his own soul shoved away, even if not in the direction of paradise.

The pornography will be spread around the cabin for the priest. All those open books he will have to close—impossible for him not to see the many images of fucking. Katerina can't help but wonder whether the crew have left the pornography out for the rummy chaplain to find because maybe they are not dissimilar to Kornél's fellow officer cadets.

Soon Kornél will graduate at the academy, top marks despite all the trouble with other cadets. Perhaps the laugh he has, which sounds childish to his own ears, is nothing remarkable. Every man reveals traces of the child he was for anyone who is really looking: a particular expression of sadness, an unexpected grin, a spontaneous face never seen in the mirror.

Maybe what Kornél doesn't understand is that the kind of barely directed havoc, violence breaking out at any opportunity, comes from a source of mayhem without which there wouldn't be a Saint-Cyr. And the suicide attempt was an effort to eradicate the child who lingered, giggling and glorying in costumes. Failing to bear the truth yet brave enough to peer through the reflections of war.

The quote from Aleksa Alimpich in Kornél's letter:

It is possible for us, at times unavoidable, to live in a burning house, for years at a time. We will become desperate of course, to write on things which survive flame a little better at least than paper. The first efforts will often be ink on the end of needles—words pushed into the flesh. It becomes necessary to carve into our own bones and then whatever survives combustion will be collected. We'll call it history. Until the next fire.

On the uniform breast is embroidered the one word: *Klova*. Katerina stands to attention. Lifts her chin. *I will* not *let my body flow like water*. The buttons are made out of gold, each one sewn on by Anne. She buttons up the jacket and the metal throws off a chartreuse glow near the jadeite lamp.

❖❖❖❖❖

Katerina has finished a 5th Avenue by the time she's made her way down to Deck E. She should have bought two of them. Hungrier than she should be to enjoy chocolate, eating it as if it were part of a meal. She tucks the wrapper into her sleeve. The women's ward isn't far away now.

Perhaps she'll go back the way she came and buy another 5th Avenue. She has found that there is a main route to get anywhere on the ship, and there's always a lesser way as well, shabbier or more hectic and it is not quicker in terms of point A to point B, getting waylaid or misdirected common enough. Katerina has begun avoiding the main routes the better she knows *Aquitania*. The useless wandering, the ambling, directionless pace of passengers is intolerable. Crew have a bustle. Not the kind of anonymous push on the streets of a city or the hustle and stop of commuters on busy transport; rather, a quickstepping gait—the companionable nod and move.

She might have thought to buy chocolate for Anne as well. No bouquet of flowers either, which she would enjoy. There have always been flowers wherever they lived, however temporarily. Standing orders with florists near or far from the embassy. Every Monday morning and every Friday morning and never the same kind of flowers week to week. Yet Katerina has arrived empty-handed. About to step through the doors, stopping at a dustbin to throw away the 5th Avenue wrapper from her sleeve.

On Deck C, the shoeshine boy played a ukulele as he waited for customers in a corridor used mostly by crew. He didn't have a hat, either on his head or before him on the floorboards, so the ukulele wasn't for passenger coins, though he was proficient enough to be able to busk. Perhaps it isn't permitted. He might have to wait to get to Paris for that. On the trip across he earns his money by polishing shoes. Crew need to have their shoes polished but passengers need not worry about a shine for now. Some wear slippers and most are in a careless holiday mood. Later on in the evening the boy will no doubt move to service partygoers making their way to the various New Year's festivities.

When she was about to pass him, the country song he was singing stopped abruptly and he bellowed, "All of Me". A cappella for the first three words and then accompanied by his ukulele. The plaintive singing had a playful force and was very sweet from a twelve-year-old's mouth.

"Take my lips, I want to lose them.
Take my arms, I'll never use them.
Your goodbye left me with eyes that cry.
How can I go on, dear, without you?
You took the part that once was my heart,
so why not take all of me?"

The shoeshine boy wasn't sitting in the leather chair; that was reserved for the next customer. She didn't want to sit and put her foot on the wooden box with its raised iron pedal. He played his ukulele, cross-legged, sitting on the hard, dusty floorboards. There are carpeted halls in the better parts of the ship. He was a beautiful tow-headed boy with a long fringe but cut very close at the back and sides. Cowboy American when he was singing, coal-mining English when speaking freely.

She listened to the rest of the song instead of walking away— lifted the hem of her dress to show new patent leather boots with an apologetic look on her face. And then found that he sold a few things from the box below the iron pedal. Chocolates, small bags of opium as well. She bought the 5th Avenue and the boy played "All of Me" again when she walked away, not singing the lyrics this time. Perhaps he played it for every girl or woman who came by his corridor. It was still sweet and funny.

Katerina walks through the doorway leading to the infirmary. Before she can take a step towards the nurses' station, she is blocked by the boatswain and a nurse conversing in the corridor. They stop talking and look at Katerina. She lowers her head and takes a step, knowing that they will move aside for her to pass. They don't. She halts, raises her head. Uses both hands to push her hair behind her ears. Doesn't say anything because she's found that it's not necessary to talk at all walking *Aquitania*'s passageways.

She might walk around them, but the boatswain takes off his cap and runs his hand through his sweat-damp hair, puts it back on his head. At the same time it represents the doffing of a hat to a young lady. His voice is overly loud for the quiet corridor the three of them are standing in—telling Katerina she needs to back up, step through the door, wait in the hallway. Low-burning, contained anger in his face. No question that he is to be obeyed. Cypress said the boatswain's name was Deering—perhaps the man who had ordered the midshipman to stay in the cabin with the cadaver.

"Haven't you already said all there is to say?" the nurse asks Deering. She was relieved by the interruption and is nonplussed that it was merely an intermission. She gestures with her hand to Katerina, indicating that she should be allowed to help a passenger in need.

"No." He looks back at the nurse—takes a step nearer and does not talk any quieter for the proximity. "So far, I've made the situation clear to you. I am about to outline the ramifications should you fail to fully understand the first part of the equation. I will fix it for your dancing eyes."

The nurse shakes her head and nods in an exasperated movement. She is looking only at the boatswain as though she's forgotten that Katerina is still in the hall; holding her tongue for the time being. The way her bottom lip is drawn over the top, the tight expression makes the young nurse look like she was scolded enough when she was a schoolgirl that being berated by the boatswain makes little impression on her.

Katerina apologises with a sharp nod, turns and walks through the door again. She can hear the boatswain talking, his anger making it difficult for him to control his volume, yet his tone of voice is no more than insistent as he tells the nurse that not only will all medicines be checked off, by him personally, before and after the festivities tonight, but that from now on, Monday morning every week will be an inventory inspection by which the nurse will be held to account. And yes, he will be talking to the matron and the doctor as well if need be. She is to go back to her duties immediately. There's a murmur and then the boatswain's voice utters one last word before silence. "Stop."

Katerina takes a few steps from the door and stops as though the boatswain is talking to her. She has the absurd notion that she should throw away the opium she has in her pocket—as if he might come out and pat her down. She waits and Deering soon leaves the nurse, passing Katerina in the corridor without looking at her, saying, "You'll excuse me, please, Mademoiselle," after he's already begun walking away.

Flora does not recognise Katerina when she arrives at the nurses' station, either from the morning or just now in the corridor. She tells Katerina that Doctor Blackshaw is not in the infirmary at the moment, as if that's the only reason she could have possibly come.

Katerina tells the nurse that she has come to visit Anne Klova and makes out from the heavy Glaswegian accent that it is not possible. Flora is looking at the door as though expecting Blackshaw at any moment.

"Not possible?" asks Katerina.

"No. Not possible." Flora does not look at her.

"She's my mother." Katerina doesn't know what else to say.

"Yes, of course." The nurse looks down at some paperwork. She has to fill it out, tick a few boxes on the sheet before her. Not raising her face. "Do you think I've forgotten you? You were here only an hour ago, for God's sake."

Katerina lifts her hand and brings down her palm on the papers before the nurse.

"What are you talking about? I'm asking to see Anne Klova. Why can't I see my mother?"

Flora can't push the hand away and is forced to look up at Katerina, to meet her gaze. Flora and Katerina might have been schoolgirls together. There is little of the separation that a profession in medicine should draw between two people. As much fear as anger in the young nurse's face.

"You would not want to see Mrs Klova in the state she's in. We've had to restrain her for her own safety."

After a moment Katerina says, "Yes, I know. She was already restrained in her bed when I left."

"No, not in the bed. We've had to put her in a straitjacket."

"How is that necessary?" Katerina lifts her palm from the nurse's paperwork. "She was in bed, she had those white straps across her body, holding her down."

"Those straps are to keep a patient in bed during a storm. Not a restraint for the psychotic."

"Psychotic! What are you saying?"

"I went to attend to her, tried to feed her some breakfast, and she clawed my neck." The nurse unbuttons her uniform and opens it enough to show three scratches crossing her clavicle. There is a smear of iodine across the marks but they aren't deep enough to warrant a bandage.

"So you put her in a straitjacket! Because she scratched you?"

"No, of course not. It was because she tore an eye out of its socket."

"What? You look fine. You've even got your nails done for tonight's big celebrations."

"Not my eye," Flora says, incredulous at Katerina's stupidity. "Her own eye."

❖❖❖❖❖

Mixing a bowl of lather in his hands, Alder Gideon pumps a jack with his foot and lifts Blackshaw. A white sheet covers the doctor from chin to shinbone. When he's satisfied with the mixture, the barber pushes a lever to lower the back of the leather chair. Blackshaw is almost horizontal. His jowls are covered in shaving cream with very few strokes of the brush.

He only stops talking when Gideon covers his mouth with foam.

The barber cleans Blackshaw's lips and around his nose with a hot towel in small, sharp movements, leaning in to focus on his own bit of surgery. Leaning out again and taking a step towards an ashtray and his cigar. Enjoys a few puffs before stepping back to the chair. The doctor has resumed talking. The possibilities and probabilities of another war in Europe, the potential belligerents and their developing military technologies. Speaking from a supine position—neck open to a capricious slash of the straight razor.

The doctor is able to see over the crest of his own belly into the silvered-glass mirror covering the wall and from this perspective can take in the whole room. Another man sits on a low stool, supplying hot white towels when required. Katerina knows the man is deaf from the noises he makes, random sounds arising from his glottis. Blackshaw watched Katerina walk into the room but didn't say hello or otherwise acknowledge her.

The affable doctor offers an estimate of the fatalities such a catastrophic turn of events could result in. Forty million lives, maybe as many as seventy million lives. The deaf man, down on his heels, leans forward onto his hands and for a moment glares up at Katerina like a well-trained hound, not knowing how to respond to her presence; waiting for a command to attack or settle. Burbling noise from the bottom of the deaf man's throat.

Katerina is quiet. Watches as the barber brings down the straight razor—first to the doctor's left cheek, then his right. Gideon cleans away all the bristled foam and when he's done he applies a hot towel. The doctor's entire face is covered in a series of folds as precise as a turban, which leave nothing but his nose exposed. The barber walks to the side of the chair, to a strap attached to the wall, and runs the blade up and down ten times. Holds up the bright steel and returns to the ashtray and his cigar before going to the doctor.

Gideon brushes lather onto Blackshaw. The same process follows while Katerina waits. She stands by the slow-turning helix of red and white, a barber's pole attached to the wall near the door, barely audible yet needing oil to stop the clank and squeak as it revolves. *Alder Gideon* in gold leaf on the door, and below the name, *The Proprietor*.

Katerina doesn't leave the room. She needs to know what happened in the infirmary between the time she left her mother and when she returned. Only a couple of hours later. It wasn't long enough for a disaster. Then again, how long does a disaster need? Usually fast. A rush of misfortune. The disaster had already happened, she simply didn't see that it might progress, that worse was in store. The disaster seems to be without limit now that Anne has plucked out her own eye. No resting point, let alone a rock bottom. Katerina shakes her head. What an absurd expression to use while steaming across the Atlantic. Getting to rock bottom here would be an end, not a resting point.

There is a large light above the barber's pole. It was once white but the glass has gone sallow. The bulb inside is weak, the filament growing dim rather than burning out as they sometimes do. Within the opalescent sphere are the black marks of insects that found a way into the light, and no way out. They must have made that *tink, tink* sound the moth made in her cabin. Those black marks would have been brutal for something as small and fragile as an insect. Difficult to imagine a human being throwing themselves against a wall enough times, and hard enough, to leave a stain. The barber's hand is too thick to slip into the thin neck of the sphere and they aren't worth the bother so the black marks will stay for years.

Katerina's right hand comes up to her forehead, her left hand lifts to her neck. The eye would not have come loose like a cherry pit spat from the mouth. An eye is connected by nerves behind the socket so the impulses of light it registers can be transmitted to the brain. She must have reached into the socket with her thin forefinger. She has long nails. The nurse will have cut Anne's fingernails to the quick since the mutilation. It should have been done immediately after Flora was scratched. Anne has always had long painted nails, ever since Katerina can remember. Unpainted nubs now. She has such small hands, they must resemble the fingers of a child with a gruesome nail-biting habit. Those long nails, nothing but pretty all these years, finding a practical purpose. Severing the connection between eye and brain. The illusions of her eyes, mistakes made in the deceptions of her mind. Unable to stand it any longer. Not for one moment more. The lies were the only things she could get her hands on. So what else could she do other than destroy, tear and pull? Was that what she was thinking? Katerina puts the heels of her palms to her eyes. Presses until she sees stars. Takes a few short breaths. Drops her hands and opens her eyes wide. Mouth agape until she collects herself a second later.

The kind of thought that leads to tearing out one's own eye

is likely beyond reason, a chaos of pain and fear precluding any one clear idea. Future and past obliterated. Just the eternally opening, deepening, sucking vortex of the present moment—within which, utter confusion and desperation, disorientation and despair, spinning and drawing one in. The eyeball a plug on a chain at the bottom of the bathtub. Thoughts should rush away with a gurgle.

"Don't look at me," Flora said and shoved Anne's handbag at Katerina. "It shouldn't fall to me to deliver such news." She had a tray of plastic cups in rows of two—one with water and the other with pills. "Stop looking at me. I have medicines to give patients. That's my job. It's the doctor's job to give such news to the family. And I didn't want to have to talk, did I, Miss? But you forced me to talk. Don't think I don't know how bad that was. What else can I give you? You need a shoulder to cry on but I'm not made of stone. More like Lot's wife, me. A pillar of salt afraid of the next breeze." Her hands went up to her nurse's cap to make sure it was in place.

"Horrifying how a person can be walking around, all fine, all proud and fine, a pretty lady at that, and then … I don't know what happens. What happened to her and what might happen to any of us. Something terrible, and there's no medicine I can give her that will fix the trouble, and I can't help it but I worry about myself. Could such a calamity occur to me? Happens to everyone eventually, some awfulness, and all you can hope is that it's not too soon. And maybe it will be quick when it does come. That it won't destroy dignity. You see, Miss Klova, you should have waited for the doctor. He's at the barber's. Getting his cheeks nice and shiny again. I've been a dull knife for a delicate job. Go and tell him how awful I am, though he already knows it, of course. Just please don't look at me. Let me go my own way."

Compelled to wait for Katerina's permission. Katerina nodded twice, very slight, almost imperceptible movements up and down of her head, her body mannequin-stiff. The nurse picked up her tray. Katerina could see how much Flora was trembling from the water spilling from the small plastic cups, seismic shakes of her hands.

The men in the room talk. Every few minutes their eyes return to her, standing in the hallway, the way she stood, motionless and silent, at the nurses' station. None of the men says hello. There's no question, clearly she's here for Blackshaw and the doctor's business is his own, yet he goes on talking about trouble developing on the Continent.

Katerina walks to a waiting chair and sits, her mother's handbag on her knees. *Not many can imagine their own deaths, and I wonder how few can imagine seventy million lives*, thinks Katerina. She opens the handbag. Anne's cigarettes. She finds the lighter and inhales. Or seventy million cigarettes? Seventy million fish in the sea? Seventy million grains of salt for a pillar in the shape of a woman? Katerina exhales smoke.

Anne didn't take the handbag with her. She wasn't able to, yet she never went anywhere without it. So Katerina held it to her own chest as they walked the halls, passing a steward finishing his nightshift, yawning, so tired he didn't lift either of his arms to cover his mouth, and a chef in uniform hurrying up to the kitchens to begin breakfast preparation for hundreds, his hands busy with his neckerchief.

She left the handbag on Anne's bedside table as though her mother might sit up after a little nap and search through it, maybe light up a cigarette. A bottle of perfume, the cabin key, red nail polish, papers which included both their passports were also inside. Her make-up and a compact mirror, something she was prone to pull out every half-hour she was in public.

In the handbag are keys to the house in Mexico that they might never see again. Audrius had been clear in a telegraph: *Do not sell. Do not leave.* He'd been away for two years. The next telegraph that came through was even clearer: *STAY.*

Perhaps Anne kept the house keys because she wants to carry the option of return, or maybe the keys have always been in her handbag and belong there beyond reason. Anne Klova is not able to sell the property without the consent of Audrius Klova. He made sure of that before leaving for Europe.

In the barber's window are a sheep, a donkey, a cow, a baby in a crib of hay, three men wearing crowns, a shepherd holding a staff and a lantern, another shepherd holding a lamb, and an angel with an unfurled length of silk with the words *Gloria in excelsis Deo*. The crowned men bear their gifts for the baby: gold, frankincense and myrrh.

Of all the figures, the most useless is the baby's mother, caught in some act of blessing or adoration. Jesus doesn't need her milk. Hard to imagine God's son sucking on a woman's tit. Well, at least in this nativity scene in the barber's window, leftover from Christmas. Mary Magdalene's breasts are a more believable need later on in a carpenter's life. The figurines in the barber's window are about half a metre tall. Any smaller and they would look like a child's dolls.

Katerina has forgotten to smoke her cigarette and a long cylinder of burnt tobacco falls onto her skirt. The ash keeps its tubular shape. She gives her skirt a shake and draws back on the cigarette. The ash cylinder disintegrates when it hits the ground. Katerina is sure it will be the mute's job to come around with a dustpan to brush away the scattered ash. She looks into the handbag again, cigarette between her teeth.

Among Anne's papers there are letters addressed to Katerina from Kornél. They are open yet she hasn't seen any of the letters before. They are postmarked November. One early December, about the time Anne booked passage on *Aquitania*. All of them were sent after the last letter Katerina received from him in October. Perhaps Anne was not unaware after all of the letter she had hidden in the uncut pages of the Antal Szerb book. She simply made sure that Katerina got no further letters from her brother.

Alder Gideon has contented himself with a few words here and there, happy to encourage the doctor to talk himself out. Part of the service, Katerina assumes, is to allow a man to speak his mind without argument. The deaf assistant looks at the two men and stares at Katerina for a while with a series of awful expressions she can't read. She draws back on the cigarette and while she doesn't enjoy it, she's as surprised as she was on the sun deck that the smoke doesn't make her cough as it used to when she tried it with girls at Liceo Franco.

when you look up at night, you will see
preferably with the benefit of some altitude
that the stars are easy
much easier than the dandelions at your feet

A poem at the end of one of Kornél's letters, in the postscript, after he wrote, *I thought you might like this*. Katerina isn't sure what Aleksa Alimpich meant by *easy*, and wonders if the word lost something in the French translation from Serbian. Perhaps it was a fragment from a larger poem. Katerina has read that a dandelion is a perfect creation, requiring no birds or insects for pollination—disseminating itself worldwide, crossing impassable obstacles, easily floating over the Alps on a breeze. Kornél was right, she does like it. *The stars are easy.*

"Yes, yes," the barber says, nearly finished with the job at hand, "yes, of course." He has said that a number of times during the shave. "Of course. We had the Great War. Brothers, fathers, sons, of course. Gassed and shot. And we all know that was enough. More than enough. Of course there will never be another one, thank God. Armageddon deferred. Thank Christ."

Doctor Blackshaw might as well have been relating the premise of a science-fiction horror film he saw recently while ashore in the Americas. Gideon's response is that he has already watched such a movie and it wasn't for him. A detectable sneer on his face that a man as intelligent as Doctor Blackshaw should take such projector flickers to heart. Fine if the doctor enjoys such amusements, of course—if he can be diverted from sense and reason, more fool him. The white sheet is removed. The lever on the chair is pushed and the doctor is returned to his feet.

Blackshaw walks towards Katerina. He puts a cigarette in his mouth and searches his pocket for matches. The deaf man is quick to light the cigarette for him with a lighter that was in his hand before the doctor pulled the brass cigarette case from his pocket. There's no thankyou for the assistance. The doctor plucks a fragment of tobacco from his lips. A deep inhalation as he watches Katerina reading. He exhales. He looks at the deaf man, bemused that he's now waiting for the girl to acknowledge him.

I'm reading The Iliad. *Required reading here, of course … I'm enjoying it in any case. And I'm reading* Journey to the End of the Night *at the same time. Not recommended by the academy, to say the least. Homer says, "Let me not die ingloriously and without a struggle, but let me first do some great thing that shall be told among men hereafter." Céline, who has indeed managed to produce some great thing despite a paltry soul, says, "You can lose your way groping among the shadows of the past." I wonder if you've ever thought about how interesting it is that when we read, we will often as easily read the words of men who are dead as the words of men who are alive? It doesn't matter … and yet there's an inkling I have that it does matter. Somehow we never feel the bones of literature below the pages … we do not taste the blood when it is licked up off the page. I once thought that there was a kind of immortality in pursuing a life in letters, but Katie, don't you think the opposite is also true? I have begun to think death is allowed in. We allow rats as black and wet as the inkwells they've emerged from to eat out our minds sentence by sentence … even so, I find myself writing and writing, feeding them every scrap of my love that I can find. Love is sweetest yet they thrive on the meat of pain and fear. Those two things most of all … but where are the rats? Why do I say rats? I'm sure you're asking yourself. I don't see any rats. I haven't gone insane. I don't feel any kind of gnawing at all. I find that I nevertheless behave as though I do feel them gnawing when I wake in the mornings and my roommate tells me I have been driving him crazy grinding my teeth during the night. When I lie down to sleep, I startle as if there's a horde of rats beneath my bedsheets. And then there's the dreams I ...*

The deaf man claps loudly, twice, the way a hypnotist might to wake someone from a trance. Katerina raises her head, blinking.

The doctor says, "Hello." He finds another fragment of tobacco to pluck from his lips.

"I've been bitten," Katerina says. She pulls her sleeve up and turns her wrist to him. The deaf man steps in to have a look. "There are four puncture points. I have noticed bruising. Some swelling." Looking up at him, she adds, "Occurred about an hour ago."

After he's washed his hands Alder Gideon walks over to a bench, where he has a plate covered over with a cloth. There's a sandwich beneath the muslin and he takes a couple of mouthfuls, standing, waiting for the next customer. Deaf to the conversation in his store as he chews. Eyes unfocused, uninterested in the reflection of himself in the mirror. A bite between customers. He's a thin man. Draws the cloth back over the plate and uses a clean napkin for his mouth, leaning in to a mirror to make sure there are no crumbs in his walrus moustache.

"I didn't think much of it at first," Katerina says. The doctor lifts his hand, palm up, flipping the row of fingers twice, indicating she is to stand up. "It might be infected," she says as she gets to her feet.

Blackshaw takes her arm and lifts the wrist. Puffs on the cigarette between his teeth. There isn't enough light. He moves Katerina a few steps to a lamp by the barber's counter and inspects the wound. He has a lovely smell about him—fragrant foam and the lotion the barber splashed on his face and neck. The shaved flesh is flushed and smooth. It reminds Katerina of her father in the mornings, though Audrius Klova would never consider using a barber for shaving.

"Is this a dog bite?" It's an exclamation as much as a question.

She nods. "Yes. A dog bit me." Feeling very young and foolish.

"It's not a dog bite," he says. He lifts his gaze from her wrist and looks at her, examining her face now. As if she's lying. She shakes her head once and nods again, feeling even more the idiot child.

"How in the world … did you ever … get bitten … by a dog … on a boat!" It is over-pronounced, and again, not really a question. Shaking his head with a smile spreading across his clean cheeks. The deaf man is smiling as well. When Blackshaw notices the grotesque expression he drops Katerina's arm and it falls to her side.

"We need not go back to the infirmary for this. Nothing broken. Fairly certain of that already." He leans his head in the direction of the basin. "Come with me and we'll have a look at what we have on our hands, excuse the pun." He lifts her arm again to take another look. "Almost at the pulse point." He gestures for hot towels and a leather bag placed next to the chair he was sitting in a few minutes ago for his shave.

"Not pierced on the outside of the arm so I suspect the dog didn't intend you any serious harm. Didn't get a hold and didn't shake. Four puncture points on the inside forearm; radial artery only a millimetre away." The deaf man fetches hot towels and then the bag. "Not deep enough for a real worry."

Blackshaw doesn't thank him. Words would be wasted. The deaf man stands by the doctor's side and opens the medical bag which the doctor carries everywhere he goes on *Aquitania*.

"Roll up the sleeve to the bicep." He takes out a small bottle and splashes liquid onto his hands, watching the barber's assistant work the sleeve up her arm.

"You'll excuse me," he says to Katerina, lifting her wrist and squeezing the area around the bite. "We'll encourage you to bleed."

His tough fingertips find her veins and trace them along the soft of her forearm. Beads of blood form at the four puncture marks and run down in thin rivulets, into her palm, between her fingers, and drip into the basin. She could cup the blood as you might to drink from a tap.

Two men have entered the barber shop and look over at the odd scene by the basin, do not pause as they move, one to a leather chair for waiting customers, the other hopping into the barber's chair. The barber walks over with newspapers from London and New York. They're waved away. More than three days old. Nothing new until they reach Calais.

"A dog's mouth is a filthy place." Blackshaw's fingers are firm and continue to work the flesh near the puncture wounds, pushing for more blood. "Have you ever thought what a dog's mouth does? Not only will it eat and drink with its mouth, but a dog cleans itself with its tongue, itches the pelt with the teeth when the dog has to scratch, and being handless, it's also the only way for it to manage anything, so a dog's mouth is in effect its hands, for whatever it might want to pull or toss or rip. Or in this case, to rebuke you, for some error the dog has perceived in you."

Blackshaw has been as interested in Katerina's face as he has the wound. Katerina shows him none of the pain. She does not allow a tremor in her voice. Concentrates on an even tone.

"So 'encouraging me to bleed'—that's in an effort to clean the dog bite."

"Squeezing out bacteria with the blood." Blackshaw nods and the waiting deaf man brings a hot white towel. The doctor cleans the wound. "We'll use penicillin if it gets infected. Keep an eye on it for me."

The barber calls out, "Tomalin!" and the deaf man springs to his side at the raised chair as though he hears the call. Tomalin would have seen both doctor and patient turn their heads to the noise. The client is covered with a sheet. Gideon is voluble with the new man, talking about Don Budge, who has become the first player ever to win all four grand slams in a single year, possibly the greatest tennis player of all time, and if it is too soon to say that for certain, then there is no doubt that he does indeed have the best backhand ever seen. The barber had the great, great pleasure of watching him destroy an Englishman at Wimbledon, Henry Austin losing 6–1, 6–0, 6–3, and Budge, at six foot one, has a serve that will go down in history as one of the most devastating weapons of the game.

Alder Gideon has spoken little and is so subdued she hasn't heard him clearly enough to pick up that he is Australian. She assumed he is English, same as the doctor. Why there was "great, great" satisfaction in witnessing an Englishman being demolished doesn't make sense to Katerina, as it would have had the barber been American. Blackshaw removes a bandage from his doctor's bag and begins winding it around Katerina's wrist. He nods at the comment, bottom lip pushed out—otherwise unaffected.

"You'd be surprised how many bites I treat aboard ship in any given year. Not dog bites, of course."

Tomalin makes his throat noises, growing excited by the talk of tennis, or perhaps dogs, hopping around the shop fetching towels and illicit magazines from Paris for the two American customers, ready to swap seats since the barber has finished the first, much faster than he was with the doctor, maybe because of how coarse Blackshaw's facial hair is. Just one pass of the blade was necessary.

"But which kind of bite do you think?"

Tomalin gurgles and mouths unpleasant sounds. Katerina is no longer sure that he is deaf. She can't determine from his animated face whether he is ecstatic or furious. The barber points to the low wooden stool and Tomalin sits. Subdued easily. Face returned to calm, attentively waiting.

The man in the barber's chair saw Budge play even more recently, only in September, in fact, at the US National Championships, where he beat Gene Mako easily. He then played with Gene Mako to win the doubles title as well … and then he played with Alice Marble to win the mixed doubles! "Winning becomes a joke at some point, doesn't it." The customer in the chair laughed, as did the barber.

"Insects," says Katerina, thinking of how the pornography collector had died, according to Gerard Cypress. She watches Blackshaw's hands working the bandage around her wrist, distracted by the gentle care after the pain. Kissing bugs. "Or rats. Rats bite as well, don't they?"

"Yes, they bite. Not the most common type of bite I treat."

He fixes the bandage in place with a pink safety pin designed for a child. He raises her arm to inspect his work. And then lifts her fingers to his mouth, takes her index finger between his incisors. Releases her and smiles.

"Human bites," Blackshaw says. "Men, women and children. All have cause to bite another person on occasion. And really, a human mouth isn't all that different to a dog's mouth when it comes to bacteria. So watch out for that infection. The wound might weep or you might begin to feel feverish."

❖❖❖❖❖

The weather has improved. Katerina stares out at the view from the salon windows in the packed writing rooms on Deck A. There are no unoccupied seats. She will read Kornél's letters later. For now she needs to keep moving. To open her mouth wide and suck in air. To make noise. Wanting to run. Wanting to push people out of the way. Shove and swear and spit. Walking. Face up, shakes her head twice, face down. Not to the infirmary. Not to the cabin. Where? She went down to see her father's borzoi and was repelled by just how vicious it could be, this snarling need to run.

A great many passengers have a similar intention—open decks, open air and the open sea. Katerina chooses corridors and stairs that lead away from the press of people and their happy noise. It's New Year's, that's the reason for the pervasive bonhomie. Hundreds and hundreds of them will soon be loosed in celebration.

Forced again to slow and to stop and to ease her way past people loud in laughter and conversation. They have stopped to talk. Clusters of strangers exchanging pleasantries. Boisterous in the early days of their trip across the Atlantic. The adventure of it all apparent in their buoyant faces.

Katerina finds herself in a part of *Aquitania* she's never been to before.

Three soldiers turn when she passes them and follow her along, trying to get her to stop and speak with them—to find them amusing or charming. British officers in jodhpurs. A lieutenant with ruddy cheeks takes hold of her hand. She's able to pull it away and take a few quick steps to outpace the bustling company. Ducks through a doorway and slams the hatch behind her.

Her right arm is throbbing at the wrist and in her left hand she's holding a hair comb that she might use to put her hair up. She wonders how clean it is.

As she was walking away from Alder Gideon's shop she heard feet pounding along the wooden floorboards of the corridor behind her. A frightening sound, but then Tomalin couldn't call her back. He would have to touch her to get her attention. When she heard his footfalls she turned around. He reached out a hand. Touched her shoulder with his fingertips and then even more gently the injured right arm.

"Tomalin!" The barber's voice was clear enough down the corridor though he hadn't left the shop. "God damn you, man, where the devil have you gone? Tomalin!"

The spasm that went through Tomalin's face and down his body indicated that he could hear. No doubt of it anymore. It was as if a leash had been tugged. He wanted to scamper to heel. There was something he needed to do first. Katerina took a step back and Tomalin shuffled with two tiny steps forward.

The same noises rose from the glottis and she could see into his mouth. Or see enough to feel appalled at the absence—the loss of words and taste. Standing face to face with him, watching his mouth forming odd shapes that had nothing to do with words. Like watching a blind man's eyeballs roll around in their sockets. The ragged base of the tongue was still in there, flipping about, the dorsal fin of a fish attempting to wriggle down his throat.

Tomalin reached a hand into his worn grey cardigan and pulled a woman's hair comb from the breast pocket of his shirt. An item that would have been retrieved from a lost-and-found box when she walked in. Perhaps he presented a gift to any woman on the rare occasion one strayed into the barber's. It was warm with his body heat when he gave it to Katerina.

The decorated comb is old; the celluloid a blond colour with a black overlay picking out highlights in the design. Flower stems like reeds lend a Far Eastern impression. Within them there's a constellation of star-shaped flowers. The flowerheads growing independently of the stems. Five-pointed flowers that resemble the Tudor rose yet not English in aesthetic. She is surprised by how much the comb pleases her. She looks at it again and it seems clean enough to put in her hair.

She finds a water closet and sits down on the toilet seat to read more of her brother's letters. The light is too poor to make out the words clearly. Kornél's handwriting is difficult to decipher at the best of times. She lifts her skirt and releases a surprisingly hot gush of urine, washes her hands and cleans the comb—washes her hands twice more with soap. She opens

Anne's handbag and takes out the bottle of Shalimar. Not a lot left. Katerina removes the lid; pauses because Anne isn't one to share her things.

Blackshaw said he might visit Katerina tonight but no word of Anne. Only then, in the privacy of her cabin, could they talk about her mother's true condition. A disease might need to fully manifest before anything could be said or done. Patting her hand as he held it. Some kind of assurance. She wasn't certain. And then he offered her a cigarette but she shook her head and left the barber shop.

Katerina feels pain in her wrist. The result of Blackshaw's hard-pressing fingers and thumbs. Maybe it's infection from the dog bite. There are two tins of Blackstone's aspirin in the handbag. She opens them, finds both empty. Hard to gauge for herself how feverish she is. Perhaps by the time the doctor comes to her cabin she'll know better if she has an infection. And she is sure she must stink by now. A touch of Shalimar will help. She dabs, accidentally spills a little down her neck.

Katerina feels the sweat trickling down her ribs again. Shivers. She has found her body temperature to be erratic. She often feels chilled and moments later might feel the closed-in warmth of a greenhouse.

She can rarely tell what is behind the walls on the ship. There are engine rooms down below but there are generators for the electricity and they might be anywhere on the ship. The four funnels of *Aquitania* rise through each deck to tower above the uppermost deck. A wall can be hot to the touch, or cool. The insulation on the ship fluctuates. Maintenance crews are busy during winter with pipes freezing and bursting.

The wall is beading with condensation. She extends her

arm. Cold. The immense volume of the ocean beyond—water surging across the thick metal walls. The cool of the morgue where the man of pornography is kept now. The kitchen's huge refrigerators, stacked to the ceiling with the provisions that will get everyone across the Atlantic. She can only imagine what's beyond the walls the same way as she can only guess at the intentions behind a freely given gift or the doctor's offer to visit her later in her cabin.

❖❖❖❖❖

Katerina finds her way to the enclosed third-class promenade, a sheltered area aft on Deck D open to the Atlantic. Much nearer to the water than the sun deck. The sound of the ocean opening up the largest space a human imagination can take in at once yet she's too tired to look out across all that blue water, heaving even when placid. She closes her eyes, opens them again and takes a few steps. There are wooden benches along the gunwale that remind her of a train.

Strange to think of *Aquitania* as akin to public transport. Cunard's advertising, all the company brochures, proclaimed a grand history, not to mention an incredible safety record, with figures spread out over decades of steadfast service. A passenger like Katerina might be persuaded she was safer floating in the middle of the ocean than she might be with her feet on the ground anywhere in the world. An ocean liner is a different species of transport—a steel skyscraper laid horizontally for those who have only ever moved in and out of houses of wood.

Aquitania directs attention to its elegant drawing rooms, salons, dining areas, lounges and smoking galleries, frescoes on the ceilings, hung as they are with chandeliers, punctured everywhere possible with ornate skylights, as though it is a vast floating palace with a multitude of rooms for all, an aristocratic welcome for every one of its temporary guests.

The third-class promenade is stripped of these pretensions. Public transport indeed. Katerina wouldn't be surprised to find graffiti on the walls yet the passengers here are decent enough, resembling those she sees in corridors and decks everywhere, if not exclusive onboard destinations like the Louis XVI restaurant or the Palladian Lounge.

So what now? Saint-Cyr gave me a world and beyond that world I find none. I suppose you'd call it Life, and my next goal must be to find a way to shrink Life down to a world again. When we were children we would look at the globe and talk of the world as though the planet was the same thing and we could keep it in our minds, complete and full, in fact about as empty as a soap bubble. The world that politicians talk hot about is not much better, more colourful, yet nothing but bubbles blown from their circus mouths. Living in Paris is a possibility. Daddy isn't in Moscow as we thought ... he's living here. I hesitate to go to him. He's aware, I'm sure, of my expulsion by now but I'm afraid to see my disgrace in his eyes. I might take passage for London ... I know a painter who needs someone to share the rent, as artists always do ... that'd be a world that might welcome me and my spectacular failure.

She closes her eyes. Folds Kornél's letter and slips the

envelope back. Holds the handbag to her chest, arms around it. Sways on the bench as a wave of fatigue sweeps across her. Puts her head to the rough painted metal of the strut beside her bench. One of a row of benches and bracing, the struts sweeping through the deck and beyond the ceiling. Her skull against one of the ship's ribs. She opens an eye, the old white paint covering the iron, closes the eye. White raindrops. Drops that move like those on the window of a car. These drops of white caught in their slide down steel. Hardening. Tough now. Tiny beads she can feel against the scalp at the side of her head. Pleasing.

She feels a whirlpool open up to swallow her mind—a deep drain of exhaustion swirling at the bottom of her thoughts. Dizzy. Letting her head press against the painted white rib of *Aquitania*. She has no sensation of the ship moving. *Aquitania* often feels motionless despite her blood registering thrumming and shifting energies.

"I will fix it for your dancing eyes." His voice had the force of violence, the control of one used to brutal discipline. The way the boatswain's body was drawn to a stop, halted before the soft, spoilt face of a girl who'd rarely known the touch of a man—and on those occasions Flora had, only in caress, only with a kiss—made Katerina wish that she had uttered another petulance, dared the release of those coiled energies. It was a voice that rose from the bottom of Deering's stomach, the weight of his whole body behind each word: "I will fix it for your dancing eyes." Katerina feels that sonorous voice through her organs like the hum of *Aquitania*'s engines.

A family with three children. All five of them with colds, coughing in chaotic chorus when they get going after brief interludes of conversation. The family is close, also sitting on the benches of the promenade. Sharing an early lunch. There are bologna and cheese, peanut butter or blackberry jam sandwiches and the choices are creating divisions among the children and negotiations have become necessary, which might be amusing if Katerina didn't want so desperately for them to shut up.

"Shhh," she says, more in an effort to return herself to calm and quiet. The ambassadors of the third class are parents distributing their homemade meals. Another round of coughing breaks out among them. "Shhh," she says again, through habit. The almost silent shoosh she made a hundred times in the last three days for Anne when nothing could bring her quiet. Shhh. The soft noise of an ocean moving across metal walls. Shhh.

Her hands are on the bench beside her and her fingertips explore grooves cut into the wood. Some are deep, some feel as shallow as wrinkles in fabric. She opens her eyes. The other benches have words scratched into the wood. Blue paint covers most of the messages, which are half-submerged; she would guess many are fully submerged. Others have been cut into the benches since that last coat of blue paint.

SOPHIE
–N–
HADRIAN

It looks fresh enough that Sophie and Hadrian might be aboard the ship now. Or maybe they are divided by the ocean and are drawing nearer. Perhaps further apart. All capitals. Letters could be more easily made with straight lines. She likes that instead of "and" a letter has been engraved with those two long slashes either side.

I ♥ KRISTINA!

The heart, all curves, done with great difficulty. A simple message might have taken an hour or two. That could be why they are mostly messages of love. What else has enough ardour to want to be carved into a wooden bench? What else is as stupid to need to be carved into a bench?

FARE
THEE
WELL

No name. No date. Each word singular, on three successive back beams of the bench.

The eldest child approaches Katerina and offers her a clementine. "Hello, Miss. Are you hungry?" The boy speaks with an American accent. He coughs into the crook of his left arm.

"Stephen! Leave the woman alone. She need not be bothered by you more than absolutely necessary."

The mother is reaching out an arm but is unable to lean forward. She has a fourth child sleeping beneath her shawl. Katerina can only see the minute fingers of the infant gripping the edge of the shawl. The mother drops the outstretched arm and grimaces at Katerina, a smile in her eyes.

"I didn't get a chance to eat breakfast this morning,"

Katerina says. "You know what that's like. You get lightheaded; don't feel yourself." She leans forward and Stephen gives her the clementine.

The boy goes back to his bench and returns with a basketball.

"Watch this," he says as he spins the ball on his finger for half a second. "I'm not allowed to bounce the ball but I can still do some great tricks." He lifts the ball in one hand and then lets it roll down his arm. The goal would be for it to roll over his shoulder and up the other arm. He can't manage it. The ball bounces a couple of times. Stephen gets a reproving glance from his father.

"You've got some great tricks for such a little basketballer."

The boy looks perplexed. "Where are you from?" he asks. He must have met people on *Aquitania* from more places in the world than he knew existed before his trip.

"Let that woman be, Stephen. You saw she had her eyes closed, didn't you? Perhaps she's seasick."

There's a pleasant surprise at being called a woman, not a girl. Stephen's mother attends to her daughters. They are fighting over the last clementine. The older one has pinched the other and now the younger punches. Their father walks away for a few minutes to himself, and to have a cigarette, coughing as he inhales.

The father has a heavy way of putting down his feet. They can hear his footfalls as he goes to a rail down the promenade. His son has a lithe way of moving—his own footsteps barely make a noise. One of Stephen's shoes has a much thicker heel than the other. He must have been trained to be quiet, unlike his father, so that no-one in the family would have to hear the scrape and thump as Stephen moves about because of his short leg.

The orange jacket of the fruit is very loose, easy to peel away. She lifts it to her face. The lovely smell of a clementine.

"I'm from everywhere," she says. Stephen moves closer to her as though that were only the first part of an answer. It's enough information for most people asking that question. He sits beside her on the bench. He leans in and smells Katerina. Fills his lungs with Shalimar.

"I was born in Shangri-la. Have you ever heard of it?" she asks.

"Uh-uh." Shaking his head.

"It's a city in a valley near the tallest mountains on earth. I didn't grow up in Shangri-la. My family has never stayed in one place too long."

Stephen has a coughing fit. Katerina eats a piece of clementine. The first food she ever had beyond mother's milk was sucking the juice out of a piece of clementine. Anne has told her the story many times. The point was her milk. Her life substance feeding Katerina. She eats another piece of clementine. Doesn't tell Stephen about being an infant as young as the baby hidden by his mother's shawl.

"What was Shangri-la like?" asks Stephen.

"All year round there was a wide and surging river of ice flowing past my nursery windows. Even when the fields were green and the warm wind was gentle with the swaying heads of a billion daffodils. Hundreds of dandelions. I saw a pack of grey wolves devouring a deer with immense antlers of over twenty points, snow spattered about the stag in red—all of them just outside my windows, moving along on top of that white river. My mother and father didn't believe me when I told them— none of the palace servants believed me either. Maybe I dreamt it, I know I used to have very vivid daydreams when I was little like you, so that's what it was, probably. Nothing but a daydream. And yet the antlers were distinct—immense, sharp and silver. I thought it would be wonderful to have that deer's head on my nursery wall. Right above my little bed. Now that seems mean. What do you think?"

"At Christmas you could hang tinsel and shining stars from the silver antlers." Stephen coughs again. When he stops he asks her where she grew up, if not by the river of ice.

"I spent a few summers in Xanadu where Kubla Khan lay down his crown. He was an emperor destined to rule the entire world, to bring a hundred generations of peace, but Kubla Khan lost his only daughter when crossing the great oceans, and then lost his heart. All his love drowned with this most beloved child. Princess Narantsetseg was a gift from paradise. When she played her dulcimer she would dispel all sadness. She could mend the broken and crippled with her songs. She brought celestial light to the souls of the greatest of kings and showed how the world might be illuminated. The grown-ups cried for days when Narantsetseg drowned, while the children played in the wild as if we had no parents anymore. We wore grey wolf fur and ran through the woods howling for blood. Every creature fled from us, even a black bear that had never run from a thing his entire life. There must have been two hundred of us, all in a screaming blood fever and reeking of brimstone. We all slept under the stars and when we woke up we went home and forgot we had ever been such wild animals. Since that summer I've been taken here and there to the home of one emperor or another, none anywhere near as grand as Kubla Khan in Xanadu."

Stephen slides off the bench to his feet. "My father has

promised he'll take me with him on safari when I'm old enough. He's already been to Tanganyika and Kenya. We had a lion rug but my mother said he bought the lion rug and didn't kill the lion himself. And then my dad sold it anyway because the lion scared everyone. I think it's because we lost most of Grandad's money in the Peru mines. But he did shoot the lion, he just didn't kill it. He says that's why you don't go on safari all by yourself. I can have a rifle for my next birthday, he says, but I don't know if we'll be able to afford going to Africa. Maybe when I'm a grown-up."

A man dressed in a fawn duffel coat is walking the promenade with a black pug. The dog comes nosing around Stephen. The boy has half a sandwich in his hand and the pug is wondering if it can have the rest. Stephen lifts his hand above his head to keep the bologna and cheese away from a dog that would barely reach his hip if it could jump. The man in the duffel coat calls the dog back, using the name Pogo. The dog is not on a leash so the owner reaches down and tugs Pogo back with a finger in its collar, then goes down on his haunches and pats the dog on the head.

He tells Stephen that Pogo won't hurt him, that Pogo is very young also. In fact, he's been alive just six months. Stephen says his brother Robert is also six months old but can't walk or run like Pogo or do anything much more than cry and sleep and eat. Pogo's owner explains that dogs start more quickly in life, and they also don't live as long. For Pogo, his six months is more like our five years. Pogo is about as old as Stephen and he's only interested in making friends. So if Stephen wants to, he's welcome to pat Pogo. Stephen is not sure he wants to touch the small black dog. His sisters slide off their bench to come and have a closer look at Pogo.

Katerina throws the clementine skin away in a nearby rubbish bin before she leaves the promenade. Stephen walks after her, a quick shuffle that disguises his limp. His mother calls him back. Called to heel.

Our dog years, thinks Katerina. The compressed time of history is somewhere in a child as well, even if he doesn't see it.

"Goodbye, Miss." He offers Katerina his hand for a shake.

"OK," she says, feeling odd, play-acting though the boy's face is serious. Tiny fingers. Dimples where his knuckles will one day emerge.

"I liked your story and I think you're pretty," he says, a formal manner about him.

Such a sincere boy. "Fare thee well."

Katerina thought the promenade might be a place to sit and read her brother's letters. Perhaps all that matters, for now, is that he's written the letters—that he's put paper into envelopes, licking them shut before placing them in the mailbox.

They've been travelling together since they were children, one embassy to another, in many countries and cities, surrounded by different languages to the one they spoke between themselves, friends and relatives passing through their lives briefly and rarely. So it has always and only ever been Kornél and Katerina.

Katerina has written Kornél many letters while he's been at Saint-Cyr. There is one she regrets sending him. Military training was about her brother finding purpose and committing to a path. Instead he has been pushed along in the same dire direction he was already heading. The letter that came back from the barracks infirmary after he found a bottle of poison was an answer to a letter she had sent him. It began with a question.

Have you ever known a moment, perhaps you are walking beneath the branches of tall trees in a garden, or you are running your fingers along the spines of books in a library, and you feel in an open instant that death is nothing but a passing thought? When it flitters through your mind, your wish is to fly away with it—leave body and mind behind. Gone with the passing of a thought. You pick a book from the shelf and put it back without opening its pages. Or you continue to walk through the garden and return to your room at nightfall. A day has passed which will never be remembered by anyone. A book opened, never read. The sun did nothing more than pass through the leaves of a tree. When you lie down to sleep, that sunlit thought returns. It is as easy to forget everything as it is to let go of your mind and sleep, your mind can be released that easily. Forget that today the sun moved through your mind. How loud, how loud is our exploding sun? Your ears roar as you settle down into bed. Everything is dark and very quiet. All that you are, all of it, will be silent.

Katerina pulls up her sleeve and finds a couple of blood spots have risen through the bandage—one large and the other small. The bigger stain is the result of three puncture marks and the smaller stain will soon become a part of the other if she continues to bleed. She pulls down her sleeve. Might need only one more change of bandage. Soon she'll stop bleeding.

❖❖❖❖❖

The restaurant chamber rises to the height of two decks with a vaulted ceiling and is loud with voices, plates and crockery, choruses of laughter from different tables. "What? When?" Words loudly exclaimed in anger. Deep-chested coughs. A plate is broken. *The overwhelming murmured chaos of conversation*, thinks Katerina, overwhelming at least when you've been quiet in a cabin so small you can hear your own breathing coming back from the walls.

Birdsong flitters through all the human noise. Red canaries are singing in a seven-foot-high wrought-iron cage near the entrance of the restaurant. In the centre of the room a pianist plays Chopin's *Fantaisie-Impromptu*. His hands work on their own, eyes dull, barely needing to read the sheets of printed music. He is not a physical player, the kind to make a show of the power it takes to play an instrument the size of a grand. His fingers wave the music into being, as if touching the piano is a dreary obligation. A cigarette hangs from his lips. Ash falls but not on the keys. He closes his eyes as he leans back on his stool to take a deep drag of tobacco into his lungs. The smoke emerges from his lips in trickling ribbons rather than one cloud of exhalation.

Balloons float over one of the tables. They are tied to a centrepiece with fishing line. From a distance the bright colours look to be hovering in a cluster, liable to rise to the skylights far overhead at any moment. There will soon be a cake with candles. There will be a birthday song as well. Either the pianist will stop performing his own repertoire or he will play for the party. Katerina can't imagine him singing, "Happy birthday to you, happy birthday to you, happy birthday, dear …"

A gentleman calls across the room when he spots the table his friends are sitting at and drags his giggling wife behind him. In her progress she knocks a hat askew with the frilled hip of her ball gown. Faces in the restaurant turn to them, not with annoyance as they normally would; today it is with smiles that excuse the exuberance of newlyweds.

One of the birthday balloons pops. The noise is amplified by the height of the room. It's loud enough to startle. Audrius Klova enjoyed such moments. He said there was a brief pause which revealed the fight-or-flight response—the depilated ape still in his cave despite hundreds of years outside conquering the globe.

A giggle. What wonderful acoustics! Just a balloon popping. A chuckle. The shadow of silence afterwards. Nothing in the pianist's face suggests he hears any of the noise, playing not for an audience but for the shadow.

Katerina walks as if the ship is passing through turbulent waters. Swaying as she makes her way between the tables. All the seated diners making her feel too tall for high heels. She has the sensation of wearing high heels for the first time in public, having practised many a night in her bedroom.

She wears yellow chiffon—one of her mother's dresses. Short-sleeved with a delicate floral design in sweet shades of red, pink and purple, all tastefully balanced. Smelling of the Shalimar she spilt, with more than one perfume already caught in the fabric of Anne's gown. She'd like to reveal the dress but is still wearing her coat. Overly warm. It's a fur that reaches down to her knees, too long to place on the back of a chair, though no-one is gauche enough to do such a thing in the Louis XVI anyway. Perhaps she missed the cloakroom when entering the restaurant. She flushes at the thought, tells herself it should be easy enough to get a waiter to take her coat.

Katerina notices the Parisian dandies, dressed even more exuberantly than they were yesterday on deck. She asks the waiter leading her through the tables if she can sit at the empty table beside them. Today they can talk about flying fish or whatever takes their fancy. She lifts a hand in greeting. Both nod at her. Smile. Turn away. They leave Katerina to herself though they are close enough that they wouldn't need to raise their voices.

The pianist finishes playing Chopin. Takes the glass of whisky sitting on the piano and drains it. Asks a passing waitress to refill it for him. Lights up another cigarette. Rolls his shoulders, settles and begins playing adagissimo, a piece by Erik Satie. Katerina doesn't know the name of the song. She's learned enough Chopin but it is Kornél who plays Satie in a brooding mood.

She sits at a table in the centre of the room yet no-one approaches to ask her what she wants to eat. To see if she wants a drink. To take her coat from her. She waits. Keeps her hands interlaced in her lap, hidden by the overhanging tablecloth—a screen that allows a small space for her to writhe despite the interlacing. Her face is as dull as the pianist's expression though he has the benefit of whisky; enough for the numbness to flow through his blood and into his brain, not so much that it will affect the alacrity of his fingers.

The pianist says "Thank you, my sweet girl," when the waitress places another glass of whisky on the piano. He is able to use his right hand to pinch her while his left hand continues to play the melody. The waitress walks away and Katerina wishes she could see her expression. The pianist closes his eyes and he might be finding pleasure in the music he's playing or it could be the tobacco smoke or the thought of a firm arse.

Soon someone will notice Katerina and come to ask her what she would like to eat and what she would like to drink. To take her coat. All she can do for the moment is gaze upon the pianist as if he is the sole reason she has come to the restaurant.

She's not sure the maître d' will allow her to drink scotch but she would love to allow that numbness to spread all the way through to her fingers. She'll ask. Let them say no if they must, remind her that she's a minor.

She wants her mouth to burn, for her tongue and throat to feel heat and for everything within her to settle to a simmer. She unclenches her fists to stop her fingernails pushing into the heels of her hands. She has pushed deep enough to break the skin in the past. Places her palms on the table.

Her father would ask her how it was that women find such a fashion graceful. Her long nails, painted deep red. A capitalist refinement declaring hands not used for labour. A political attitude that is habitual. What he finds more interesting is how women wear their claws out, paint them the colour of blood, and see none of the brutal animal. And men like him can't help but find it elegant in a restaurant of spotless white cloth and polished silver cutlery, and especially when caressed at the neck as Anne has often done after dessert. "Use your nails, my darling woman."

She's close enough to hear the dandy with black opal cufflinks talking. They are eating an entree of fish stew. They have already complained that the soup is cold. Really, barely warm. Should call it vichyssoise and avoid expectations of heat. In all seriousness, ceviche in Peru is a delight.

"There's an article from Peru. Did you read about this?

Happened in May. A story about a girl who gave birth to a healthy baby boy in Lima. The girl's name is Lina Medina. No? You'd remember the name if you read the story. It's a real grotesque. Lina Medina is five years old. Yes. That's right. Five! And it's all scientifically substantiated. X-rays and the rest of it. I've seen a picture of the doctor in his white coat, and the mother and child. The doctor is standing side by side with the five-year-old. She's barely over hip height. She's smiling. Her infant is in a pram. Awful as that is, I'm glad they didn't print the X-rays along with that picture. Can you imagine?"

Must have cut it out of her, thinks Katerina.

She raises her hand and a waiter sees her on his way to the kitchen. She's not confident that the harried expression on his face is a promise to return when he has a moment. Katerina might not be sitting in his area of responsibility. She remembers she has cigarettes in her handbag and pulls one out and lights up. She suppresses the cough she feels on the first inhalation.

"Is the wait long?" she asks.

The fellow wearing a black velvet smoking jacket with a quilted silk shawl lifts his hand, his bottom lip pushed out, an expression that asks what is a long wait given the circumstances?

The other dandy, astounded by the Lina Medina article, is reminded of a story of his own, from a Buenos Aires trip he took in '32. He isn't sure who the author was because the story was passed about as pages—not bound in a book. Maybe it was written by a passenger on the ship. There are books, letters and manuscripts in various states of abandonment or completion, left over from previous trips, that people find, forgotten at the bottom of a wardrobe, slipped behind a couch or below a mattress. Perhaps it was one of those and all the more interesting for the mystery of its origins. While reading he thought the story was factual. The dandy pushes away his bowl and lifts a napkin to clean his mouth before continuing.

"The story begins with a woman sitting on the edge of her bed not knowing what is happening. There is almost total silence in her house. The birds haven't begun singing. The only thing she can hear is the sound of a man breathing hoarsely, somewhere near. A nightmare? She has been awoken so abruptly she doesn't understand anything, who she is, or where she is. She can barely open her eyes. She's in pain. Indistinct for the moment. And then it is an overwhelming agony that obliterates her in waves. She can't tell where the pain is coming from. She sits on the edge of her bed, waits for her memory of who she is to return. That's the worst of these few frightening pre-dawn seconds—that she has yet to return to herself from unconsciousness, as though a person is able to forget their soul in the abyss below when returning to the world. Her waters break and everything comes back to her. Her hopes for a baby boy. She has four daughters, all of them adored. Even so her husband runs a vast trading company, of exotic spices and fabrics, of opium as well, and this beloved man needs a son to take over the company. Outside her bedroom window she notices a very bright star shining in the night sky. She doesn't believe in omens but her husband will: 'Look at that star, my love.' He wakes in the bed beside her and when she tells him it is time, he leaps out and wakes the servants and has them bring fresh linen, a bucket and mop, sends another servant with the coach to bring the midwife. The local doctor would still be drunk from the evening, if he was even home. When her husband returns to their bedroom, she tells him he should put on some clothes. In his haste he hasn't noticed he is not wearing a scrap of clothing. Her laughter is cut short by a painful contraction. The house is a hubbub. She is happy when she produces a boy. It seems an innocuous start to a story. It's not long though before this hopeful woman, full of love, has smothered the infant when they are alone in the evening on the first night."

He leans back and then pushes out his chair as if he might stand up. Looks about for a waiter.

"Why?" his friend asks. Katerina almost asks the question herself but she isn't meant to be listening despite the proximity of the tables in the crowded restaurant. "Why would she kill her newborn?"

"Do you think it's too late to change my order? That stew was so very disappointing. And now I'm not sure whether I should have asked for chicken from the same kitchen that produced that cold entree." He raises a hand and clicks his fingers twice. "The worst pain I ever experienced was from food poisoning. Have you ever found yourself banging your head against a wall from agony?" A waiter arrives to take away their plates. Another waiter arrives to fill their glasses with wine. The dandy gazes at both waiters with distaste.

"Does the story need an intermission?" the other asks, adjusting his plaid cashmere bowtie.

"They smell. Not quite a stink. Surrounded by water and these men might not have bathed since Mexico. What will they be like in two weeks?" he asks before the waiters are out of earshot.

"Go on. Why would a mother kill her child?"

Katerina coughs when she next draws on her cigarette.

"The infant can speak. Just a few hours old and his eyes are clear and his voice is small because of his undeveloped lungs, yet he forms perfect syllables, distinct and clear words, despite the milk on his lips, remnants of the life he has taken from her body."

"What kind of motivation is that?" His friend laughs. "The mother could make a fortune in the circus with such a child!"

"The story moves back and forth in time. Her husband is inconsolable. Of course he is. The boy he has wanted. For years. That he needs. Dead. I wish I had the story to give you. You should read it yourself but I'm sure it's never been published. It's gone now, unless you count the memories of a few travellers who thought it novel enough to pass around. It reminded me of Heinrich Von Kleist. Who knows? Maybe it was Kleist."

"I haven't read Kleist. It's a bit after his time, isn't it?"

"Don't be silly. I wasn't suggesting he was travelling aboard that ship in '32. Must say, I adore the notion! Kleist, the poor fellow, lived a shambolic life so I imagine he left stories strewn all over the place, people picking up bits and pieces of his work here and there, losing them along the way."

"I wouldn't care if it was a story reminiscent of Kleist or if it came directly from his arsehole, even if not quite a fresh turd after all these years!" Exasperated by the denouement's delay. "Fabron, have you forgotten how the damn story ends?"

"I do apologise. Incredible how the whole thing was woven together, a lyrical yet realistic depiction of life from a mother's perspective, giving birth to a talking infant. A son who tells her that he is the Second Coming and the end of the world will happen as soon as he can stand on his own two feet. 'I am the apocalypse.' She can feel the truth of his words in her bones,"

Fabron says, tapping the table with his index finger. "She has never known insanity and has no fear that she has now lost her mind. She was sleeping in bed before waking at midnight to feed her baby. The infant's body will cool quickly. Her bed will still be warm. She walks about her house, one she and her husband built from humble beginnings. She peers in on her four daughters, each in her own room, sleeping soundly. Lovely descriptions of their bodies in flickering candlelight, mouths open and limbs askew, faces crumpled into the pillows and delicate fingers sleep-twitching. One of the girls, Angelina, is always uncovered. The mother must pull up the blankets to cover her youngest, thinking her body must be warmer than everyone else's—so she can't help but kick off her sheets. When the mother was a girl she slept in the same bed as her mother and father and sister. They shared the warmth of their bodies. No heating otherwise. Her daughters don't know how lucky they are, how rare and precarious success in life is. Or perhaps the author used the word 'happiness' rather than 'success'. She joins her husband in bed, and before she goes to sleep she thinks, no, we are not ready for the end of days. Happy that she was able to smother baby Jesus before he could say another word about his Heavenly Father and the celestial kingdom."

A woman near Katerina's table is eating quail. Two of the small birds lie on rectangles of hash brown, bedlike. The quail are wrapped around with belts of lightly fried bacon. Small round white potatoes that resembled a clutch of eggs, a big dollop of cranberry sauce and a mound of peas. A generous plate of food but the woman is distracted by conversation— listening to a man describe the trouble he's been having with his hernia.

There is a tear in his abdominal wall that will never heal, not if he lives for another forty years. Surgery. It is an unpleasant prospect. It isn't what worries him the most. There is the prospect of chronic pain that might result even from successful surgery. That is the unfortunate situation with a nephew in Bruges. And then of course it might tear again or he might find his abdominal wall rips in a different section. His intestines will spill out if his hernia gets much worse. There would be emergency surgery, as opposed to the elective kind.

When he stops to eat, the woman begins to eat as well. She uses her fingers to pull away a quail leg from its body. There is a bowl of perfumed water on the table for her hands. She uses a napkin to clean the grease away and then picks up a knife and fork until the time comes to break open the second quail's body. A task she can only manage with fingers.

Doctor Blackshaw is walking through the restaurant. He halts with a broad smile for the diners he knows, a robust good cheer that is used to ward away the nervous chatter of symptoms and illness that people are prone to in his company. The fellow with a hernia waves at him as well. They don't converse. He was reminded of his condition at the sight of the doctor.

Katerina puts her palms to her eyes, then her fingertips as her elbows rest on the table. Takes a breath.

Blackshaw has the kind of voice Katerina has only heard in the theatre before. It lifts heavy tones and carries them lightly across the room. Even the pianist is put in shadow. Whoever the doctor talks to is an undistinguishable murmur yet his own voice is deep, clear and expansive. In the barber shop Katerina thought it was the boxy room itself, the mirrored walls creating unusual acoustics, or her own sensitivity to what Blackshaw might say to her. In the Louis XVI restaurant it is apparent that he talks for the back rows as much as the front. It turns many a diner's head with a pleased expression. Katerina can't help but think of the word "gift" when listening to the voice, it is so striking in the opulent atmosphere.

"Are you alone?" Blackshaw asks. Katerina moves hair behind her left ear as though she needs to hear him better before responding. The forceful good cheer Blackshaw directs at every passenger pushes her back into her chair.

"I'm alone," she says. "As you see me."

"Of course you are." He puts down the leather bag he also had at Gideon's, then pulls out the chair opposite and tells her he will join her, as if there is no question that she would want him to sit at her table. He has the air of a man used to doing women favours of this kind. To being of service. He'll lift her spirits.

When the waitress comes a moment later to take his order, Blackshaw places his hand in the small of her back. Katerina has seen ostlers caress the flanks of horses in the same way. The hand would settle a creature and direct her to his purpose. Blackshaw orders scotch and a steak.

The waitress turns her face to him. "Rare, of course."

"Rare," he confirms, his hand resting on her hip now. She turns to Katerina and asks what she wants to eat.

"What the doctor's having." Katerina hasn't been given a menu. "That'll suit me just as well."

"Well done," the waitress says.

"Thank you," Katerina replies.

The waitress cocks her head. "No, Miss. How would you like your steak? Well done?"

"No, I said 'rare', didn't I?" Katerina looks at the doctor, a smirk on his face. She busies herself cutting and buttering a bread roll the waitress placed on the table a moment before. "And we'll have *two* glasses of scotch," she adds. Blackshaw nods and the waitress walks away from their table. It has been a dramatic morning, he says as he strikes a match alight and brings it to his cigarette.

"I would have taken you for a girl who might spend half an hour on a salad. Dabbing at your lips with a monogrammed handkerchief after every nibble of lettuce. Adventure in a crunchy crouton! Satisfaction in a cherry tomato!"

"It's been a long wait."

Blackshaw is disappointed. No response to his wit, not even a smile. He looks about the large bustling room. So much laughter. Smiles everywhere but not here. He had hopes of better company.

"They serve a big piece of meat. Especially when you're sitting at my table."

The dandies have paid for their meals and a waiter has cleared after them. A second waiter puts down new cutlery and glasses as the first waiter returns to seat a family at the same table.

"Are you always this tight-lipped?" he asks.

Better to be tight-lipped than to come off a fool. She nearly remarks on the coincidence that it is his table, assuming that he sits in this very spot every day for his lunch. Of course it would be the doctor's table anywhere he decided to sit. She flushes, appalled that she came close to making another gaffe so soon after thanking the waitress for saying well done. Shakes her head once. *Well done*, for what?

"Felt like hours," she says.

He draws back on his cigarette. No longer smiling.

"Maybe it was just minutes, but minutes on this ship seem longer than anywhere else in the world." The cutlery is replaced on their table, an extra-sharp knife for the meat. *Cuchillo de carne*.

"It might be different for you since you're an employee. You have your work hours," she says, after the pressure of his silence forces her to continue speaking.

"They're awfully busy at times. You can't imagine life in the kitchens." His left hand reaches around the back of his neck to scratch or ease out a knot. "Passengers spend an inordinate amount of time eating. Common enough for passengers to gain ten pounds on their trip across the Atlantic."

"I didn't think they were ever going to serve me." The expression "serve me" strikes Katerina as pretentious. "I would have been happy to have gone into the kitchen myself and scrambled some eggs. Toasted some bread. A little butter to spread over the top. It didn't need to be anything fancy."

"The kitchens are a chaos only Hades can fully appreciate. Cuts and burns are as nothing. Daily inconveniences. Disfigurement and mutilation are not uncommon. I've sewn more than one finger back on after an improvised amputation. A whole hand came off in the first month of my service." Shaking his head. "First time I'd seen an industrial meat grinder."

A long cone of cigarette ash is knocked off against the edge of the ashtray. He offers her a cigarette as an afterthought. She waves it away. Her mother's cigarette has already burned down to its filter in the ashtray after two inhalations.

"Easy to be invisible on this ship. I've been ghosting around all morning."

"Likely the maître d' thought you were being joined by someone," he tells her.

She mumbles that she might have been waiting for the Second Coming as the doctor pulls out a small case from an inside pocket of his suit.

"There are occasions when you need to put your hand up. Because you don't look hungry. You don't look as though there's anything you need. Or want."

"Shouldn't they assume I'm here for a reason?"

"The world in general, my girl, is too busy and too involved with personal dramas to assume, to wonder, in most regards and particularly about your whims, fancies or desires." He takes out his glasses and begins cleaning them with a small cloth from the case. "Not unless they pertain directly to the whims, fancies and desires of another. And yet there's a kind of woman, often young, who makes an art of looking as if she wants absolutely nothing."

Katerina is trembling with hunger. Blackshaw's words take a few moments before they mean anything. *I did raise my hand, didn't I?* She would sound like a child if she asked that question. Maybe that's why she was ignored. Or it wasn't that she was merely young. Served forthwith when the doctor came around. A man full of consequence. Her hunger and displeasure are nothing. There'd be ramifications to Blackshaw's hunger and displeasure. "Ramifications". The word Deering used with Flora.

I am only the result
Even so, even so
I am empty of result

A fragment of poetry she found in a book with missing, burnt pages in Prague. Many of the books survived the Great War and Czechoslovakia wasn't affluent enough to cover the damages a decade later. She left the dismal leather-bound book behind and picked up instead poetry by Sappho, unread and discarded by a university student. A last-minute choice that Katerina didn't realise would also be filled with fragments.

Kornél loved second-hand bookstores but this was a rough place near the university. It was also a key-cutting and shoe-repair store. Kornél bought tobacco there every week. He said later it was like wanting a nice fluffy companion, a pet with a pedigree, for your little sister and taking her to the pound to find it, where everything was mongrel and brutal.

"Even so, even so, I am the result."

Blackshaw has leaned over to talk to the pianist. To compliment him and ask him to play George Gershwin's "Summertime". Blackshaw is interested in hearing how it ought to be played; he can't himself quite get the right rhythm when he plays the piece. Gershwin is a common request and the pianist says he can play "Rhapsody in Blue" in two minutes, thirty seconds—normally it's fifteen to seventeen minutes long! He laughs at Blackshaw's befuddled expression. The pianist doesn't play the entire song at four times the speed. It's a clever version, all the essential elements of the song intercut and abbreviated. Perhaps the glee of the playing is also malicious, it's hard to tell—hacking up the song in this manner—yet the doctor is certainly enjoying it, hands clapping along fitfully, as if he can't wait for the appropriate moment for applause.

A woman is breastfeeding a child at the new table. Katerina knows she must never have left South America before if she thinks she can expose a breast, even if it is to feed a baby. She has two older children with her at her table and a man opposite, father to her offspring. A fat butcher dressed up for church is what he resembles. He could just as well be a banker who has grown as rambunctious as a gorilla with the kind of clambering success they have in South America.

The breastfeeding woman is angered by one of her boys and leans forward to clamp her thumb and forefinger around his mouth, presses his cheeks to his teeth tightly enough that he might taste blood, and then she shakes his head left and right. She speaks a few words and is quiet. She doesn't release her grip on her son's jaw until she sees the submission in his eyes. He will be silent. The other son is silenced as well—it is apparent he knows what it feels like to have his cheeks pressed inwards against his teeth in the manner shown him across the table.

The baby breaks away from the woman's breast, a white bead on the nipple, a tiny rivulet running from its lips, satiated on mother's milk and ready to drift away into the deepest slumber. The fat butcher or banker father leans forward and with one long finger extended, pokes his chastened son in the rib, a prod as much as a tickle. It rouses the boy following his mother's discipline. His father is smiling. The boy chooses to imitate the smile. Just a few seconds later it seems genuine. The baby burps, bubbles of milk forming on its lips.

Katerina takes a mouthful of whisky. Closes her eyes and breathes in air that feels cold because of the spirit. And another sip. Flaring heat down the back of her tongue and settling in her oesophagus, unbearable until the lovely fade of heat.

"I'm surprised you're wearing the hair comb Tomalin

gave you. There's no telling where it came from, I hope you understand that. The man is known to wander *Aquitania* and finds the damnedest things. Feathered hats and compass cufflinks that spin with every movement and point north whenever he's still. A Knights of Malta medal, which he's been known to wear on special occasions." The doctor laughs at the notion that such a man might have a special occasion. "There are others like a moa necklace, which he rarely dons while on deck, thank God. Perhaps he wears it in his cabin as if he's a Maori warlord. He might have a costume and face paint to go along with the bone necklace."

The comb is above Katerina's right ear. The right side of her face open to Blackshaw's gaze. It's more than she'd normally show. She ties her hair back or puts it up in a bun only when she is alone, and it has never been cut short. Below her shoulderblades normally, all the way down her spine at the moment. She has good hair and she is proud of it; more than anything it's embarrassment over her left ear. That ear doesn't sit flat against her head that way her right does. A doctor's metal forceps when she was born, having to haul her through the birthing canal into a nurse's waiting bucket. The forceps had bent her ear and then they'd gone deeper and put a depression into the side of her head.

Blackshaw is proficient with a knife, lifting the first piece of meat from his plate before Katerina has touched her cutlery. He leans back in his chair and unbuttons the top button of his trousers so that he'll have enough room for his lunch. He's already finished his scotch. Lifts the empty glass for the waitress, as though toasting her as she passes, a few metres away, scuttling along with a load of dirty dishes for the kitchen.

Katerina finishes her glass of whisky. The taste revolts her and the burn is that of an acid, not the kind of heat she wanted at all. Medicine, in the end. Maybe harsh, *doing her good*.

The pianist walks away from the piano; he's older than Katerina thought when seeing him play. Age evident in the way it bends his legs and makes him limp. Making his way through the crowded tables, past the large birthday table and all its hovering balloons, patting the birthday boy's head and saying happy birthday. Stealing a piece of bread from the child's plate.

"My father's bitches would love our lunch," she says as she cuts into her steak. Half-finished already, Blackshaw tilts his head with a dissatisfied expression for Katerina. Disapproving without wanting to be fatherly. Perhaps it is the word "bitches" he doesn't think acceptable for mealtime conversation. Is the word to be used only in the derogatory when speaking English?

"That's where I got my bite. The three of them are down in the hold. They'd be done with their slabs of meat in seconds. They'd barely chew. It'd be wasted on them. Can't help thinking that. Wasted. Not on us. We can savour each mouthful. There's no savouring in a dog's appetites. They gobble everything they want as soon as they can. As happy with tough old horsemeat that's been in a can for a year as a piece of flesh taken from a cow just a few days ago. Isn't it nice to think of a lovely green meadow? See our cow wandering aimlessly along, munching on fresh clover, straying a little too close to the butcher. And then it's over to Hades's kitchen so it can be cooked to perfection. Placed on these spotless white discs. I do enjoy a little red in the meat, even if I do feel queasy when I see a whole animal on a plate, like the quail the woman is eating over there. Or a fish, when the kitchen hasn't removed the head, leaving it for you to manage with the cutlery on the table. It's the eyes. A creature's eyes remind you they have seen the world. If they weren't dead they'd see you coming. Or if it's a body like a quail, that perhaps they'd flee if they had the chance. And for all that, it doesn't bother me seeing blood in the cut."

Her habit is to slice meat into pieces all at once, then put the knife aside and eat her whole meal with only a fork in her right hand. Anne tells her she needs to start eating like an adult. That woman who pincered her son's mouth now leans forward to brush a lock of hair out of his eyes. Proud of her boys, it's clear.

The pianist stops before the large wrought-iron aviary. He crushes the piece of bread he took from the birthday table and puts his hand into the cage. Rubs his fingers into his palm, sprinkling crumbs for the red canaries. There are fifty birds and most have flown to the roof of their cage, hanging upside down, tough little claws gripping the black iron lacework. They are waiting to see what the pianist intends to do with his hand. The mass of red feathers drops down to the floor of the cage to eat before he has withdrawn his arm. He keeps crumbs between the fingers of his fist and enjoys how the birds peck at him to get at his bread. The pianist turns his palm over, birds on each of his fingers, all of them singing.

The waitress brings over Blackshaw's scotch. He instructs her with a raised hand, a movement to the side indicating a cut, not to bring another for his table companion. Katerina can imagine he makes similar gestures with his nurses; the patient would not need any more medicine for the moment.

She doesn't notice until she sees the gesture that perhaps

she is drunk. When she closes her eyes this time, her head spins as though the entire ship is being sucked down into a drain like a toy ship in a bathtub. A disorientating image in her mind connected to a memory of Anne pulling the plug. "Bath time is over," shouted afterwards from another room, leaving Katerina to tremble in the emptied tub. Katerina could enjoy the draining away, the hot water flowing away from her flesh in an incremental line. The feeling of weight returning to her limbs. Weight in her head and her hair sucked through the grate and down the drain until she couldn't move and the cold air made her body feel hard and brittle, shivering as if shivering might break her apart.

She opens her eyes when it feels as though the spinning might topple her from her chair. They eat for minutes without speaking. She looks at Blackshaw and thinks it odd that he's sitting at her table. A stranger. What's his first name? It's likely he doesn't know her name either. He rests his gaze on her face but she doesn't lower her eyes to her food as he might expect. She has a drunken notion that if she drops her gaze and lets him freely look at her he could cut her down to pieces. She would rather be quail and stare back at him. If she had the courage, she'd wink. She blinks until he is the one who must look away. Blackshaw doesn't see her smile. It fades from her face and she could as easily cry in the next moment as laugh.

I could be torn up just like "Rhapsody in Blue". Every moment I've been alive played out in a minute. Not even a song—an amusement to be played for any mood. She picks up her glass and puts it down when she sees that it is empty.

"Apologies for rambling. When you mentioned Tomalin I couldn't help thinking of a dog. The way he scampers at beck and call, not able to make an intelligible sound. The noises he makes. Awful!"

He has been sucking the marrow out of the bone. Audrius enjoys doing that as well. Blackshaw's plate is empty otherwise. Katerina has left the bones and strips of fat. Never in her life has she felt tempted by the prospect of marrow. Audrius wouldn't chew and suck a bone in a restaurant, only at home. It occurs to Katerina that for the doctor this *is* home, the Louis XVI little more than his dining room.

"Tomalin is in possession of a Bible, a very old one. He found it somewhere or other and no-one laid claim to it either on that particular voyage or since. A nineteenth-century tome with pages falling out, but which Tomalin nevertheless reads every morning and every evening." Blackshaw has pushed away his plate. As he talks he dips his fingers in the scented fingerbowl on the table and then uses a fresh napkin.

"We had a Belgian scientist aboard in '33, the year after I began service, and he took an interest in Tomalin's Bible after a shave. Following an examination of the book, he established that this Bible so dear to Tomalin was bound in skin. Not leather. Not pigskin or any other regular sort of animal hide used for such purposes. No, it was the skin of a man." Blackshaw has brought his own toothpicks and is so efficient at dislodging fragments of meat caught between his teeth he barely needs to pause between sentences.

"We were assured that this was not so uncommon as any of us might have supposed. And we really were all in disbelief. The Belgian, who'd seen the kind before, said no, the book was not proof of a barbarian ritual or exotic punishment. Not at all. It wasn't sanctioned by the Church but some monks nevertheless wanted their flesh to be put into service, in just such a way, after they died. To consecrate themselves. God's word made flesh!"

The woman at the table beside them has finished eating her quail. Katerina notices her legs are patterned like loose-fitting socks about to roll down to her feet, yet this is flesh. Veins swollen, working their way through the blues and blacks of rotten fruit. She is surprised the woman doesn't wear stockings. Most women wear stockings anyway, let alone with such horrendous legs. When Katerina glances at the older woman—short hair, pert nose, upraised face—she is glad she doesn't wear stockings. And it's all below the table, below the crisp, clean, white linen of the tablecloth anyway.

"Yes, that man has found strange things over the years. He's been on *Aquitania* for well over a decade already. And who knows where and when he found that pretty hair comb you are wearing."

After wiping his mouth one last time, Blackshaw throws the napkin down, pushes out his chair and turns it to an angle so as to lean back with his legs extended. The waitress steps around the doctor's feet to bring him another drink and he takes a sip.

"I'm surprised Tomalin can read. I thought perhaps he was damaged." Katerina taps her temple.

She lifts her mother's handbag and takes the mirror from the bag to see Tomalin's comb in her hair. Despite having washed the comb twice she needs the mirror to reassure herself the comb is not a petrified monkey claw. A pestilent gift she was mad not only to have taken but to have put into her hair. She doesn't want Blackshaw to think that's all she wants the compact for, so she also rouges her cheeks. Something her mother does very often when in public. Katerina has never seen why until now. Easy to feel comforted by the little mirror and the brush, to be steadied by a ritual that brings everything back into focus.

"Yes, of course he is damaged. He has suffered great injury but he's not retarded. He can and does read, and not just his lovely monk-bound Bible. Often military histories. Napoleon is a favourite, and Nelson, and Alexander. Knows Roman history better than most scholars—they've published his books on the subject in New York. Gideon tells me he has a number of publications to his name."

"What happened to him to bring him so low?"

"He received the most brutal treatment while in North Africa. Doing research. Wherever Carthage was in the ancient world. Or I should say, wherever Carthage would be today, since the Romans left only rubble after victory." He is beginning to look glassy-eyed. "You may have noticed the man is missing a tongue. Desert nomads dragged him around for a few years and used him as a circus might a performing bear."

Blackshaw lifts his face to the ceiling, eyes half-closed. Is he emotionally moved by the story he might tell of Tomalin's pain—now holding back the tears? Katerina finds that difficult to believe. She glances up at the skylights and back to his face. He could be choked up, waiting to be able to talk again. Katerina puts her make-up away and drops the handbag beside her chair. He tilts his face forward and the cripple in the barber shop has vanished from his mind.

"I find it unnerving when the ship is at a dead stop." Not emotional, the watery eyes indicating only whisky. He turns his glass to watch the level move, as though the glittering amber might tell him something of the ship's movement.

"Even after six years on *Aquitania* I don't think of myself as a seafaring man. For a while I thought I might be and then I realised that there was nothing I liked about the ocean. I remain a small-town doctor, even if it's a town that moves about the world. I don't even enjoy eating fish, to say nothing of seafood. I've never eaten lobster. Aren't they monstrous sea spiders, after all? Ghastly creatures. And what I like about an ocean liner the size of the one we're on is that I rarely have to feel it rocking and pitching. I never noticed it stop mid-ocean in the first few years. Can you feel it?"

Katerina shakes her head. She can't tell and wonders if it is true. How could the ship possibly stop? That seems as impossible as Blackshaw being moved to tears by the past torments of Tomalin. Is there some catastrophe for which the ocean liner would need to stop? A typhoon? An explosion in the engine room? Icebergs? The monster octopus that crushed her mother's mind, rising from the deep? No, Katerina can't conceive of a disaster that might halt an ocean liner. They are famous for pushing through the most ferocious of storms, arriving in port with every window broken and the hull stripped of paint.

The doctor does not rush away from the table to prepare for a dangerous situation. Instead he lights a cigarette. He plucks a piece of tobacco from his lips and enjoys the next inhalation so much he closes his eyes when he exhales. He sighs. Katerina can only take him at his word about *Aquitania* being at a standstill. Perhaps Blackshaw is drunk.

The tone of the conversation in the double-height dining

hall has changed, a lower murmuring and then louder with exclamations as people speak across tables, not just with the people in their immediate company. The red canaries have gone quiet, all of them lined up along their perches rather than climbing the black iron lacework of their cage as they had been doing.

The quail woman and the herniated man both wipe their lips with napkins and carry their wine glasses with them to the windows. Other diners in the restaurant are doing the same. Gazing out the windows for proof that *Aquitania* has come to a stop.

The Atlantic might give them a sign as to whether they really are no longer moving, now only floating. A surprising thought for all of them. The vast sea is nothing but a span of two weeks. At a standstill it easily swallows as much time as anyone could conceive. Katerina stands and intends to go to the windows as well.

"There's nothing to see, believe me. There's a lot of water out there and it looks much the same at twenty knots as it does at zero. You'd have to go all the way to the prow or the stern to see a difference in the water. You'll have to take my word for it." After a few seconds he says, "Sit down, please."

It's not that she needs to go to the windows so much as she needs to move away from her table and Blackshaw. The waitress is bringing out her dessert, so she sits down again. Strawberries and cream. The waitress tells her there will be no more fresh strawberries. These were the last in the ship's storeroom. All their food will be from the ship's freezers from now until they reach Calais.

Blackshaw points to all the jabbering passengers at the

windows and tells Katerina that forward momentum has never before been a question in their minds. There is a sense of destiny for most people who board an ocean liner, a feeling of moment, even if it isn't destiny in the grander sense of the word. Leaving port to cross an ocean the size of the Atlantic is like an arrow or a bullet being fired across a battlefield. Not in terms of speed, of course. It is the feeling that they have been set in motion, and it is a motion that is defined by destination. Now, a target might be missed, the shot falling short or passing over, but perverse is the feeling that destiny, even an ordinary kind of destiny, might be halted midshot. That an arrow could be caught midair or a bullet find itself on a leash the way a child's toy fires a marble attached to a red ribbon.

Katerina eats her strawberries and cream. She asks Blackshaw if he knows why *Aquitania* isn't moving. Blackshaw explains that often ships come to port with missing passengers and missing crew. And no, it's not a mystery. Suicide on a ship such as *Aquitania* is very easy. The ten-metre drop can knock a person unconscious if they land badly. Indeed, it is difficult to land well from that height. Possible depending on the water. If they go over the bow they might find themselves keelhauled before they die. There's a chance of being pulled into the blades of the propellers. More often than not the person goes over the side and there's little anyone can do if there are no witnesses to call it to the captain's attention. Soon Blackshaw might have to leave for the deck but it takes time after *Aquitania* is stopped to drop down a boat and fetch the jumper. The crew is trained in basic mouth-to-mouth resuscitation. Hypothermia is most likely what Blackshaw will have to attend to if the jumper is indeed alive. Almost certain are cracked ribs and broken legs.

As soon as the boat is winched back up to deck, *Aquitania* will be on her way again. Only a question of half an hour's lost time, an hour at the most. The crew gets a lot of practice this time of the year. The period after Christmas is hard on people far from home.

The waitress comes around the table and asks if they want coffee or tea. The doctor tells her he'll have coffee and Katerina requests tea. He asks the waitress to take his glass of scotch away, telling her he doesn't want the rest. He has drunk more than he should have. The waitress says it must be the New Year's atmosphere.

Blackshaw takes a breath and blinks a few times. He looks at Katerina and asks, "That dog bite. Is it any worse? A little better, perhaps."

"I'll show you if you like." She's still wearing her fur. She stands and removes the coat that covers the sleeveless dress beneath. She knows she has long arms and that they will seem naked for a few seconds as they are revealed from beneath the fur. She sees the flash in Blackshaw's eyes. Why else would he want to talk to her? The only interest he might have in her is her flesh. The whims, fancies, desires he mentioned earlier.

"It doesn't hurt at the moment. I'm worried about infection. I do feel feverish at times. I feel strange no matter where I am on this ship." Katerina begins unwrapping her bandage.

"You can come and see me later."

"Yes, you've already said that. It's an unnecessary invitation. What else would I do but seek out a doctor if I was feeling unwell?"

"And yet many women resist." The bandage is marked with blood. She steps around the table to the doctor to show him her arm. He glances at it and then up at the tall girl standing over him, confused by the fierce expression in her eyes.

"Your mother resisted the notion of seeking help until her illness had become debilitating."

The waiter arriving with the coffee and tea takes Katerina's coat away.

She returns to her side of the table, nods and sits down. "I'm by myself now. I worry about being alone in my cabin and overcome with fever." She balls her bandage up and shoves it into the handbag.

"Lovely dress," the doctor says. "Lovely."

"Anne makes her own dresses. She made this one last year." It started as a necessity; a working-class family in Liverpool couldn't afford to buy everything they needed so they made things they could barter. Anne now makes elegant dresses using expensive fabrics, notions and trims. Wherever they travelled in the world she would use tailor's dolls and dummies, and in her room there were as many as ten dresses in various states of completion. She would often dress Katerina as well. Anne demanded that she remain silent and still for long periods of time while she made a dress, which was always far more elaborate than Katerina needed or wanted. A dress that might be worn once, because on the next occasion Anne would insist on a new creation. More stillness and silence as Anne brought out the pins and began to fit her for dresses. And while Anne was often asked to make dresses for others she never did. She was appalled that ambassadorial friends might think of her as a tailor or dressmaker. She would never fix seams come undone. Repair pants for Audrius or Kornél. Darn a pair of socks. Katerina was often asked to do that if it wasn't worth the effort of arranging a tailor. At times the many dummies would appear as an odd congregation of women, all roughly the same age. Anne has never had a friend in Katerina's memory, though they are usually busy with one formal occasion or another, chatting with people from morning to night. Anne dresses the dummies and they have often seemed like friends filling the overly large rooms of houses Anne could only ever feel empty in, to dress her loneliness. They were ghosts to Katerina. As if Anne were filling the spaces with versions of herself that had vanished, and when she made gowns for Katerina and moved her limbs as though they belonged to a life-sized doll she was making a ghost of Katerina as well. The dress would remain on a dummy for weeks after an occasion.

Then there's the uniform that she began making for Kornél, pretending she didn't know that he'd been expelled from Saint-Cyr to keep up the pretence with Katerina. Or Anne needs to sew as some women need to knit to keep their hands busy and their minds occupied. Perhaps for her it is an arrow that cannot be caught in midair; that the target merely needs to be put back in its place. *Klova* stitched onto the chest and gold buttons sewn on to will her vision into reality. Katerina blinks away an image of Anne attempting to catch a bullet between her teeth. Instead it found her eye.

Gerard Cypress is walking through the dining room. Katerina turns to the midshipman, surprised to see him. He noticed her when she was standing, even taller because of her high heels. His smile is broad, as though they are great friends. She can't help but return the grin. Cypress approaches the table and gives Katerina a bow and then stands as if she has summoned him.

"I've a telegraph to deliver," he says and lifts the message in his hand.

"I don't suppose it's for me," she says.

"No, I shouldn't have stopped, but it is so pleasant to see you again."

"More pleasant circumstances, that's certain."

A look of confusion passes his face, so she leans forward, running her hands up and down her arms as though cold. "More pleasant than before. The circumstances now are less lurid." She feels like apologising for the stilted formality, glancing at Blackshaw and then back at the midshipman.

"And less chance of bugs," Cypress says.

Blackshaw's gaze travels from the midshipman to his dining companion and back again. He isn't pleased by their laughter.

"It's not unusual to go a whole crossing without seeing the same passenger twice." When she doesn't say anything, "I suppose many passengers confine themselves to their cabins. I'm glad you're taking in the whole ship."

"You're delivering a message to one of the diners?" the doctor asks.

A curt nod from Cypress. "Uh-huh." He doesn't take his eyes away from Katerina. He doesn't know what he can say to her. If he were older he'd compliment her dress. He'd seen she was pretty; she's much more than that now. And her laughter is so delightful. He doesn't ask her what her plans are later for the celebration. He knows he should get on with his work but all he wants is another opportunity to make her laugh.

"'The crystal bell of a soul ringing for the birth of the world.' Something my father said about laughter. I never understood what he meant until this moment."

"Maybe I can help," the doctor says. "I've already seen a number of these passengers in the infirmary."

"No, I don't believe that's true." The midshipman turns to the doctor. "I don't need your help. I have already seen the couple it is intended for. Can't tell you how many messages already. Celebrated newlyweds over there having a wonderful romance. Telegraphs from friends in Monte Carlo and Naples."

"Scamper off then. If your message isn't for Kitty, why tell us a story? Go on, off you go."

Blackshaw must have heard Anne using "Kitty" while under sedation, since her mother only ever called her Katerina in public. And there was no-one else that called her Kitty, not even Kornél or her father.

Gerard Cypress's mouth twists and sets itself straight again. He nods at the doctor and bows to Katerina. Strides away to the newlyweds without looking back.

She picks up the handbag. Her mother could sign a meal to the room's bill but Katerina didn't think she could do the same. She already checked Anne's purse before leaving the cabin and she has more than enough in cash to get her through two weeks. Blackshaw leans forward and places a palm on the back of her hand.

"I'll look after lunch today. Don't worry about it."

"What did you do with her eye?" Katerina asks before she can stop herself.

"What do you mean?"

"You mentioned sewing fingers back on after they'd been cut off in the kitchen. But it would be impossible, I'm sure, to reattach an eye. I suppose it's something you throw away. There's an incinerator for such things. Yet I imagine it might also be placed in a jar of formaldehyde. Until the patient can make a decision, because an eye isn't something small. It's as large as the globe to the person who needs it. That's the image in my mind, her eye floating in formaldehyde. What will I see if I go down there again? Am I silly to be afraid of such grotesque possibilities? Better to destroy my mother's eye than let it float around like that in a glass jar."

"What kind of … you do have a grotesque turn of mind, my girl. Anne Klova pulled out her eye, that's terrible, but she was restrained and I was able to help the eye back into its socket when she was sufficiently sedated. The optic nerve and extraocular muscles weren't severed. I don't doubt that the eye will function normally, and I can only hope it hasn't been pulled askew. I have the socket bandaged for now. We'll give it time to heal. People may worry about a great many things and in their distress create all manner of damage and disorder, but nature wants to heal—that's built in on the cellular level—and what my profession does is try to help our physiology fulfil its normal function. It's my hope that Anne Klova will not disembark *Aquitania* in restraints; that your mother will be well enough to walk away with you when we get to Calais."

"How is she now?"

"It's hard to monitor the progress of mental disturbance. A broken bone can be complicated. Close observation will reveal predictable results. All kinds of physical conditions are similar in this respect, a set of factors responding in time. The mind has a more volatile sense of time. A trauma suffered in early childhood can erupt thirty years later, after having seemed settled, healed, resolved—in fact, revealing itself as a sucking wound, so to speak, that threatens a person's entire existence. I thought when I was starting out that I would become a psychologist. Much of the field was dominated by hysteria, which for a time seemed to be approaching epidemic proportions. And while much was made of the talking cure, it's the pharmaceutical options that have dealt with the epidemic. Psychologists can't manage the flood of hysteria through talking. Not only because understanding a source of psychological pain doesn't relieve the pain, and can even exacerbate the condition, but it doesn't look at trauma deeply enough. I have a private theory that the real reason for such widespread hysteria, so much emotional suffering, is because trauma is often experienced by us as a species, and it is as a species that our deepest traumas affect us individually. How would a talking cure negotiate such a vast theatre of pain and suffering?"

He blinks and lays his glasses on the table, rubbing his palms against his eyes. Puts his glasses back on and focuses on Katerina.

"Yes, she's doing better. Sleeping with a mild sedative. The straitjacket has reduced her hysteria. Mozart can be soothing so I have the nurse play records. I've promised to let her out of her restraints soon if she can keep herself calm. Leave her to recuperate for the time being."

The red canaries have been making noise. Now they start singing loudly. Perhaps the ship is underway again.

"You're bleeding," Blackshaw says. Nodding at Katerina's face. Katerina hasn't noticed. She leans forward, her stomach touching the edge of the table. There is a drop of blood on the clean white linen of the tablecloth. And then another drop of blood. She is relieved that her dress is clean. She thinks the blood soaking into the linen looks pretty and doesn't move for a moment. Waits for a third drop of blood. They never land in exactly the same spot.

"I get nosebleeds. I'm not sure why. Doctors can't explain them. I've had my blood checked. Different kinds of tests, different doctors over the years. One doctor in Mexico confessed that medicine doesn't have an answer to everything. There are anomalies. I had an art teacher who went blind in one eye for no reason at all. No-one could explain it for her or predict whether she would go blind in the other eye as well. Particularly horrifying for an artist like Mrs Seret."

She speaks as the blood drips down over her lip. She would normally have stopped, pinched the soft part of her nose at the bridge. A waitress halts at the table, aghast. Asks Katerina if she needs medical attention.

"The doctor is right here. But it's OK. Don't worry. It looks worse than it feels." She picks up a white napkin and brings it to her mouth, wipes blood away. The dripping might go on for another few minutes.

Doctor Blackshaw spoons sugar into his cup of coffee. Pours milk from a tiny jug. Stirs. Watches the coffee in his cup swirling around rather than look at Katerina bleeding. It horrifies people when she has one of her nosebleeds. As common as that, yet there is the blood and it can cover her mouth and chin, and it is so sudden and without apparent cause.

"This is mild. It's all right, it'll stop soon. A five-minute bleed, that's all. I've had worse. Fresh blood and clotted blood have dripped down into my stomach. That can be awful. I can get nauseated, even vomit. Dreadful—vomiting because of a nosebleed. The first time it happened I thought there really must be something wrong with me. That was when I was twelve, and as you can see, I'm still here."

Katerina is pleased to see the sickened expression on the doctor's face. She wouldn't have thought it possible. He is leaning forward with an outstretched hand, more of a gesture than an attempt to help, trying to ignore what she is saying, asking her to tilt her head back and put some pressure at the Kiesselbach's plexus.

"Don't worry. It's already stopping." She wipes her mouth again, holds the red-stained cloth to her nose. Sniffs. Takes blood into the back of her throat.

Doctor Blackshaw's arm is still half across the table. "How often does this happen?"

She raises a hand, palm out, waves left and right to indicate time isn't always easy to calculate.

"It occurs to me—when the waitress stopped just then, her concern wasn't for me, was it? A doctor at the table. Her concern was only for the other diners, who might feel nauseated to see blood." Katerina looks around the room but no-one is looking at her now.

"It has indeed stopped. I think you should come see me at the infirmary." When the waitress comes around again Doctor Blackshaw lifts his empty coffee cup and saucer for her to take away, as though she is a nurse he need not thank or acknowledge. "Nasal cauterisation would be the thing to do. Cauterisation sounds unappealing, I know, and there's a platinum needle involved in the burning. I'd give you a local anaesthetic and we'd be done in a few minutes. Nothing to worry about."

Katerina leans forward as if attempting to catch his last words, shakes her head and says, "As long as it's not a knitting needle."

"What?"

"I suppose that's a myth. But you never know. Maybe that's what was used once upon a time. There's better technology. Improved techniques."

"There's no point in worrying about the tools. Whether there's a resemblance to this or that. They're all used to help. That's all you need to keep in mind. And I can help you, if you need any help." Blackshaw's voice is no longer broadcasting. Up to this point everyone at nearby tables would have heard his every word. One or two heads turn to look at him now because they can't hear what he's saying.

"It's my mother that needs your help," Katerina reminds him.

An officer walks through the restaurant and approaches the table. When he arrives he does not acknowledge Katerina. He does not apologise for the interruption, merely bends to the doctor and whispers in his ear. Blackshaw doesn't reply with anything more than a nod and the officer is on his way, striding through the restaurant again.

"There are different problems that need fixing. Many of them are needlessly complicated with a kind of impudent morality. Simple errors that can be fixed in a straightforward manner. Do you understand me?"

"I've already been fixed. Anne managed the whole thing before we left Mexico. Fixed like a cat—isn't that the phrase in English?"

Blackshaw winces at the expression. "OK, yes, but you'll

see me if there are any complications, I trust? I'm not sure about the doctors in Mexico and this procedure is often done by those I wouldn't ask to put a bandaid on for me."

"I'm an ambassador's daughter, Mister Blackshaw." Katerina wants him to stop talking. Blackshaw nods and he might leave it at that. He's done enough. Offered what he could of himself, shown he was perceptive and caring, an admirable man.

"Doctor Peralta only attends patients of a certain rank. It seemed to me it wasn't uncommon for him to leave his hospital when his official duties were all done and take a walk after dinner. To come through at night, when all the servants were asleep and no-one outside on the street would see him come or go. It wasn't complicated. It was as straightforward as you could possibly dream of. There was a sedative and sleep, as though it was all a passing nightmare in a child's mind. I made him laugh when I told him he reminded me of a tooth fairy. What he took wasn't below my pillow and I wasn't trying to be funny. There's no question but that I would have been delighted with Doctor Peralta if it was a burst appendix he was helping me with. I was satisfied with his training and skill. Maybe that's what I thought at the time, only an appendix, which could be fixed that easily, as cleanly as that. It wasn't an appendix. And it wasn't a tooth. I don't care about anything as impudent as morality, but I suppose some problems can be made out to be too complicated and at other times can be made out to be too simple. Afterwards I did feel like a cat that my mother had fixed. And, of course, not really fixed, not permanently fixed."

"Good afternoon, Doctor," says a passing veteran, the kind who wears elements of his uniform years after retirement. Perhaps till death. A British brigadier who is missing an ear, with just an earhole now in the side of his head—the uniform an explanation for that deformity to all those who would never ask. Blackshaw smiles at the brigadier and looks at his watch after wishing the man a good day in his boisterous voice.

All along he's been looking at her with the expression he had when he was kneading her arm, hard thumbs pressing along her veins, pushing out bacteria and blood. And now he stands up, nothing more than the ship's doctor going back to his duties. Gazing out at the rest of the restaurant and then back to Katerina, he pushes his chair back in to the table and picks up his leather bag.

"Come in and we'll see about your nosebleeds, Kitty. And we'll soon know whether there's a likelihood of infection." He puts his glasses back in their case and slides the case into the inside pocket of his jacket. "I'll see you during the evening's celebrations, perhaps, if things don't get too hectic. There will be a wild atmosphere, so take care tonight."

Katerina finishes her tea and waits for Blackshaw to leave the restaurant. The girls at school had talked about knitting needles for the other kind of problem Blackshaw referred to. Katerina knew there was another method but didn't see what Doctor Peralta had in his doctor's bag—she'd seen handbags as big. Blackshaw carried one around twice that size. Katerina had closed her eyes and opened her legs when Doctor Peralta told her to. After he'd left, she dreamed Anne was knitting by her bedside. Katerina drifted in and out of sleep. Was certain her mother was right there beside her, knitting. She could barely open her eyes. It was more like trying to wake from a heavy sedative. As though she'd been anaesthetised and was coming round. Anne was humming a tune, a sailing song from her own childhood in Liverpool. All Katerina could tell was that her mother was sitting by her bed, knitting. She could hear the clack and click of the needles. Unusual for Anne. Katerina's grandmother knitted all the time but Anne had never once knitted, as far as Katerina knew. It looked as if she was knitting a red scarf. Katerina was pleased by the thought that her mother was knitting for her. She tried to rouse herself, to become fully awake, knowing that she was dreaming and then forgetting again. She could feel a great discomfort in her belly. She reached down and found the pain was coming from lower and that she was soaking. Had she wet her bed? That was her thought, her hand dripping blood. When she looked down below the sheet there was more blood. When she lifted her nightdress she found thread leaving her, being pulled out by her mother as she continued to knit. As though Katerina were nothing but an immense ball of yarn. She lay back in her bed and felt more sleepy than ever. She wanted to tell Anne to stop. Couldn't find the strength. All she could do was drift away into sleep. Listening to a hummed song of the sea and the clack and click of her mother's knitting needles.

She stands up. The waitress who attended their table is passing Katerina, rushing to take an order from the brigadier. Katerina reaches out and takes hold of her by the wrist, the way she would a distracted or misbehaving child, yet the diminutive woman might have been fifty years old. Katerina pulls her hand downward until they are side by side. The waitress wriggles. Katerina doesn't release her; surprised by her own anger.

"I need my coat to leave." She is careful not to dig her nails into the woman's flesh but she presses and shakes her, thinking about the way the mother at the next table pressed her son's cheeks into his teeth.

"Yes, of course, I'll get it for you right away, Miss."

Katerina releases her and the waitress hurries to the cloakroom. She returns, waving to the table of men with the brigadier she was about to serve, who are still waiting for her to serve them—a mocking expression on her face, as if to say she needed to attend to the *princess* who would throw a fit if she didn't get her mink back immediately. Katerina can see it was right of Doctor Blackshaw to use his hands with this woman, to settle her and guide her like a beast of burden.

Katerina is passing the aviary and finds that the pianist has returned from his lunchbreak, lingering at the cage before going back to his piano. She stops and tells him she would never normally do this, but if he didn't mind the intrusion she wanted to say she enjoyed his playing, especially the song by Satie, after Chopin and before Gershwin. It was Satie, wasn't it? What else was there for any of them to do but stop and talk, he says, as they crossed the ocean. And, yes, Satie. The *Gnossiennes*. Altogether too melancholy, he's been informed by the maître d'. More than once!

The canaries have become loud with his proximity. Maybe he often feeds the birds and they understand his presence as a source of nourishment.

"They're a pleasant sight," he tells her, "yet canaries rarely sing together. They don't chorus. When canaries were first discovered they were shipped back to Europe and were soon bred by the royal houses of Spain, France and Italy. They were favoured by monasteries. For aristocrats they might have been something rare, vibrantly colourful. Perhaps they assembled them like this, living bouquets of feathers. Canaries do not sound pleasing in groups. Increasingly chaotic and discordant the more of them there are in a space. The same is true for the awful noise of a room full of feeding people. Imagine one bird in a small wooden cage for a whole monastery. When it died a message would be sent and another would soon arrive as a gift from the palace. In the quiet spaces of a monastery, birdsong might float down stone corridors, flittering from one candlelit room to another, mingling with prayers."

The red canaries of the Louis XVI climb the black iron lacework of the aviary, hop around from perch to perch, as though they've never known flight and all they understand is noise.

The brigadier calls for music and his table cries out in good cheer—hear, hear. The pianist bids Katerina farewell with a well-practised inclination from the hips, a bow as much for her as for the disfigured veteran.

❖❖❖❖❖

Katerina unlocks her cabin and steps onto a piece of paper. It tears when she turns on her heel to shut the door behind her. Bends down and sees that it's the page of a book. Thin paper. The kind used for Bibles. Roughly torn down one side, a page from the Book of Job.

Sweating beneath the mink; the silk lining sticks to her with a suffocating adhesion. She locks the door and screws up the page. Flushed after getting through crowded corridors and down bustling stairways. Feverish from the bite on her wrist. Weeping from the wound. Or it could be sweat.

She throws the screwed-up page in the direction of the rubbish bin, decides the very next thing she has to do is find the swimming pool. She'd seen there was an onboard bathing area when reading about *Aquitania* while embarking at Veracruz. A swim would be lovely. It'd hardly be a lap pool so she can't expect to do anything more than paddle. The thought of sinking below water is inordinately appealing. Anything deep enough for full immersion, to close her eyes and release herself from the need to decide what to do—a choice that nullifies all other choices. For a few minutes at least.

Not too many other passengers by the pool, with any luck. But it will be fine. Everything will turn out just fine. Soon Anne might even be released from the infirmary.

Before she can take her coat off she knows her first assumption was wrong. No, it wasn't one of the many proselytising Christian groups bound to be on *Aquitania*. They weren't likely to rip ragged pages out of a Bible and randomly pass them under cabin doors.

Katerina peels the coat off, turning it inside out, and throws it; lets the fur stay on the dusty floor when it silk-slides off the foot of the bed. She checks the dress again for drops of blood. Can't see very well in the dim light. So much of her time aboard *Aquitania* she has been straining to see or make something out. Lighting is required through the hundreds of cabins and the many lounge and smoking rooms, reading and writing rooms, hallways and stairways, with demands made by elevators and other machinery as well, so perhaps there is never enough electricity for full illumination everywhere at once on an ocean liner. And maybe most passengers do not insist on brighter illumination because they find comfort in the soft haze of a sea voyage. Even after searching she isn't sure her mother's dress is clean.

Easy to miss a little drop of blood. Anne will, of course, spot it immediately. The expression "she had an eye for detail" passes through Katerina's mind before she can stop herself.

Her fingertips push at the bone above her nose and then press at the thin flesh of her forehead. Vague pain somewhere inside her skull. A nosebleed could bring on a migraine. If that happens she'll be in bed for days and painkillers will be practically useless. She recalls the opium she bought from the shoeshine boy and thinks it might help if she needs it for that kind of pain.

Katerina picks up the crumpled page and carefully unfolds it, walking over to the jadeite lamp. Lays the paper there in the light. Smooths it out with the palms of her hands. Brings together the paper at the rip. Reads what has been circled in a thick line of graphite—the marks of a blunt pencil.

> *Canst thou draw out leviathan with an hook? or his tongue with a cord which thou lettest down?*
> *Canst thou put an hook into his nose? or bore his jaw through with a thorn?*
> *Will he make many supplications unto thee? will he speak soft words unto thee?*
> *Will he make a covenant with thee? wilt thou take him for a servant for ever?*
> *Wilt thou play with him as with a bird? or wilt thou bind him for thy maidens?*

All these questions had recently been bound in human skin. The word of God made flesh by the devotion of a monk. Her hand reaches for the comb Tomalin gave her. Her first impulse is to throw it away but she's been wrong about a number of different things since coming aboard this ship. Her sense of judgement is off, or perhaps it's the strange environment, and the New Year's mood is affecting everyone.

Think about it for a moment. Think it through, she tells herself. It might be enough to go to Alder Gideon and ask him to put a leash on his dog. It is either that or cower in her cabin at the prospect of Tomalin coming in the night when she is sleeping.

She has no doubt that Tomalin doesn't merely find objects like moa necklaces and Knights of Malta medals. Tomalin is a thief. Doctor Blackshaw said so, if not in so many words. And if Tomalin is breaking and entering, it is easy to imagine him moving in the darkness of a cabin, his face contorting in the various expressions that cross his face, each one more awful than the last.

No chain on the door. There's only a lock to which Tomalin might have the key. She could push full suitcases against the door or use a chair to barricade herself in, but the thought of going to such lengths is frightening in itself. Where might such a notion lead? It couldn't stop at an invasion of her room. A pleasant chat and then he leaves? She blinks when she sees the shredded base of his tongue again at the back of his mouth. No, there would be no conversation with that maimed lackey. The kiss of mutilation, that's what he'd give Katerina.

She folds the page of Job and puts it into the handbag

before she leaves her cabin. Alder Gideon is a decent man. If they were in a village or town, an upright man such as he would serve as justice of the peace.

She opens the door and stops. Looks down at her feet. Still wearing high heels. She should change them before rushing around again. Will Gideon believe her anyway? She only has the ripped page of a Bible. That, and a lovely comb, a pleasing gift which she would present as proof of sinister intentions. How would she explain herself through the anecdotal suggestions a doctor had shared while drinking too much over lunch? If asked, Blackshaw might say she read all kinds of ominous implications into playful dinner-table chitchat.

The cabin door directly opposite hers opens.

All Gideon knows of Katerina is that her mother has gone insane. "Runs in the family," he might mutter as he frowned at a pitiful girl. "The apple doesn't fall far from a burning tree." Does she even have cause to be worried? A lonely man hoping for affection, seeing himself not as a leviathan but a servant. "Play with him as with a bird." Perhaps her mother's hysteria really has affected her own mind.

One woman is standing in the doorway opposite, talking to a lady within the cabin, both about to emerge into the corridor. The two sisters stop talking, surprised by Katerina. The coincidence of two doors opening at the same moment. They introduced themselves on the first day on *Aquitania* as Querida and Allegralita. Anne made a point to ignore these Argentines. Every attempted conversation was repulsed. Despite which, the Argentines knocked on the door asking to form teams to play card games. Then the sisters went on a whist drive and came back yesterday to tell Anne and Katerina their social event had been a great success and perhaps they'd be interested in another such evening of whist.

"Stay clear of the corridor, ladies, please. We beg your pardon, but do not promenade for the next few minutes."

It's the voice of a crewman. It is not stern, merely loud. The sound of chattering boys, thumping and yelling, heckling.

"We have a grand event on the horizon. We are on the verge of one of the great moments in history, are we not, gentlemen? Yes, we are indeed. We hope you will enjoy the astonishing spectacle, ladies. Please be prepared. Have your smelling salts at the ready. All right, gentleman, all is set. Let's begin, good fellows, let's go. Everyone awaits the magnificent spectacle."

Lost in a welter of thought, Katerina barely noticed the commotion outside her cabin. The sisters have come to their door with bewildered expressions. They stare at Katerina for an explanation. She can only shake her head at them. Querida is the one with her hand on the door and Allegralita is holding a violin in one hand and a bow in the other.

Querida and Katerina lean out of their cabins as they might the doors of moving trains leaving a station. Other passengers further along the corridor are also leaning out of their cabins. Katerina notices the tow-headed shoeshine boy who plays the ukulele. He's taking bets from passengers who have stopped to watch.

At the far end of the corridor, boys from other decks stand at a silk ribbon stretched along the floor, from one wall to the other—a marigold ribbon which might be otherwise used to tie a hair bow, probably stolen from one of their mothers.

Six of the Norwich boys are on their haunches, shoulder to shoulder, with tin cups facedown on the floorboards.

"Are we prepared, gentleman?"

The crewman is an engineering officer with grease on his overalls, so his authority in this part of the ship is doubtful. He has a dirty rag in his hand which he uses to wipe at the oily creases of his palms and fingers, and a pristine white peaked cap cocked to the side on his head, which he evidently touches only at the start and end of each shift. He has stoked the excitement of these children as he might the engines below decks.

"Are our racers at the ready?" the crewman asks, rolling every *R* extravagantly.

The Norwich boys are beating their metal cups with spoons, making an escalating racket.

"Gentleman, get set for the count. When next I say go, you will release your ink-black beasties."

He counts down from three, a closed fist beating lightly on his chest for each number. On the final count the crewman opens his fist, bending down as though he were letting dice fly across the boards. As if he were encouraging the young lads around him to find something from their own chests to throw out into this race.

While the engineer made his count the boys hammered tin with their spoons all the more frantically, and now on the call, raise their cups. The cockroaches do not scurry as intended. The beating of the cups has not made them frantic with fear. It has only stunned. Shell-shocked. The boys begin stomping their feet behind the cockroaches to encourage them forward, towards the marigold finish line stretched across the corridor five metres away. There's a tinfoil trophy set on an empty honey jar. The boys roar as one of the cockroaches gets accidentally crushed by a thumping boot, laughing as they elbow each other in chests, arms and stomachs.

A man in pyjamas stands barefoot in the doorway of his cabin. A woman in a loosely tied dressing gown stands behind him, in her slippers, yawning on his shoulder. He speaks to her without turning. Inclines his head to the side, towards her face. She leaves, returning a few moments later with one boot. She hands it to him and he holds the boot as they watch the cockroaches begin to scuttle around the corridor. He has a long beard, down to his solar plexus, but his hair is short, cut very neat. He notices Katerina and raises a palm. Katerina would have thought him a man of God, a preacher with a small church somewhere waiting for him to return across the seas, except that kind of man usually doesn't sleep in until after lunch and appear barefoot and in pyjamas.

An older boy with a cigarette kneels down behind his cockroach, π painted on the insect's back in puce. It's apparent to Katerina he intends to use the cigarette's ember on the hind legs to encourage forward movement but confused voices rise around him in a commotion, calling, "No touching," "No interference with the racer," "Don't push it along."

"Keep ya fucking tongues in yer heads like good tight cunts," he bawls. "I won't be touching. Interfering none. Won't be fucking pushing the bug. What the fuck kind of shite-for-brains am I ta fucken push it. I got an idea for encouragement just as fucking reasonable as making the boards jump and shake like it's a dancing competition rather than a race."

Querida reaches her arm across the corridor, offering her hand. Katerina can't speak over the din. All she can do is take the woman's hand and allow herself to be walked across the track as though being escorted through the confusion of a street brawl. Caterwauling from the boys, as if another of their cockroaches might be crushed before having a chance at glory. Numbers and symbols have been painted in the bright colours of nail polish. Each cockroach moves in the direction of the wall with hope only to escape what for this kind of insect must be an apocalypse of attention.

Katerina is surprised by the light in the room. A smaller cabin and there are no portholes at all, but it's not dark. They have a number of electric lamps and there are coloured candles flickering in saucers covered in melted wax. A pleasant if close feeling in the cabin. Silk scarves have been hung on the walls, making the room feel like the inside of a tent; a more expansive mood than the press of bare walls in the Klovas' larger cabin.

The door is shut and locked. Querida kicks a draught stopper to the bottom of the door. Jams it into the space with her toes. She's wearing thick woollen socks. No slippers. It makes Katerina feel even more uncomfortable in her high heels. Socks are so practical yet she has brought none for the voyage, only light stockings. Querida is wearing trousers that remind Katerina of Marlene Dietrich.

Have you seen a man lingering in the hall outside? Katerina wonders how to put the question. There are so many outside in the corridor right now. Might as well ask whether there has been anyone loitering about at Grand Central Station. What does a man lingering in a corridor look like on a ship as frenetic with movement as this one? And the page of the Bible might have no significance behind it at all. Surely it is a coincidence that Blackshaw talked about one over lunch. Bibles are all over the place, every room has one. Who knows why someone would rip out a page? Or how it might end up on the floor. It might waft under a door. There need be no intentionality whatsoever. Anne has bred a paranoia in Katerina's mind, seeing meaning in unravelling layers, never to rest on a final, definite reason.

"Warm stay on the inside," Querida says. "Noise stay on the outside." It takes Katerina a moment to understand she's talking about the draught stopper, woven to look like a particoloured snake—wings painted on its side to resemble Quetzalcoatl. They must have brought it with them for the journey to Europe. Useful not only for warmth at the moment, also good for keeping out frantic cockroaches. The barefoot preacher with his boot in his hands wasn't standing in his doorway to enjoy the spectacle.

"We don't need to speak English. I'm more comfortable in Spanish," says Katerina. She's about to explain that she can't stay when the Argentine comes forward and shakes her hand as though they are meeting for business.

"Good morning," Querida says, holding Katerina's fist in both palms.

"Good morning?" asked Katerina. "What time is it?" She glances at the locked door.

"I should say 'good afternoon', shouldn't I?" She is looking at her sister when she asks the question. Allegralita has a watch on the end of a chain, which she tugs out of the pocket of her waistcoat. She doesn't look at Katerina, doesn't say hello, and doesn't give the time.

"This ship is like a whale to us," Querida says. "Pinocchio in the whale with his little candle. How many days have passed? What would it matter if it was morning or night beyond the walls of a whale's flesh?"

Querida steps closer and then brings out her handkerchief,

pointing to her own chin as one would to mirror an unseen mark on a friend's face. Querida has assumed it's food left from lunch on her new guest's face. Katerina takes the handkerchief and wipes where the woman indicates and checks for the nod that says it is gone. As she rubs, Katerina notices there's a drip mark from that point on her chin to the collar of her dress and another drop of blood on her breast. The lights in this room are for seeing properly. The two women of this cabin don't enjoy the haze of an ocean journey.

"A whale cannot devour a man." Allegralita has been talking while Querida helped their young guest to clean herself. "It's been proven to be impossible, physiologically, for a whale to swallow a human being—despite the testimonies of Jonah or whoever. Perhaps the mouth is large enough but if there are no teeth to chew us up, that'd be about as far as it went. I think the scientists found the throat was nowhere near wide enough to accommodate the torso of a full-grown person."

Querida leans forward and speaks to Katerina in a half-whisper. "I'm sure a little wooden puppet could get down into that big belly."

There's a knocking at the cabin door. It is followed by another *rata-tat-tat* on the wood a second later.

"Yes, yes," shouting and continuing in a loud voice as Allegralita walks to answer the knocking, "I can't grant you access instantaneously. Am I standing by the door, waiting for the knock to come? Premonition and alacrity sublimely coordinated. Divine will animated." She opens the door as she speaks, a boy rushing in with a violin case under his arm not hearing a word she's saying.

"I'm sorry I'm late. There was no getting through that crowd outside. Almost got robbed." The boy was small, perhaps as old as sixteen. He takes off a bowler and places it on the hat rack by the door. He places his violin case on the bed and rolls up his sleeves and opens the case and is ready to play only ten seconds after entering the room. "But I wasn't robbed. I can still pay for my lesson, Señora."

"Maybe you'd enjoy a glass of water," she says.

"Might I have the hot water with honey, like from yesterday? I enjoyed that."

"That's fine, Joseph. Bring the pulse down," Allegralita says. "We can play at any tempo if the heart is at rest. If the heart is racing, there is no tempo. We chase the notes along. Pure calm is the only place from which to create music."

Joseph notices Katerina, moves a hand to lift his hat, and discovers he's already removed it. His hand turns the movement into a fluttering gesture of ruffling fingers, as though he's released a bird from his ear. He takes the hot cup of honey water with an eager nod, and says thank you, regaining his breath.

He sits down on the bed, bows his head, violin on his lap. He uses a tutored Spanish with the two Argentine women yet he forgot himself and started telling the cabin he'd nearly been robbed in Caribbean-accented English—then reassured everyone he could pay, in Spanish. His hair and complexion make Katerina think he might be subcontinental Indian from the West Indies. He lifts his head a moment later, fizzing with energy.

"One of the boys has seen a Brazilian wandering spider out in the corridors, as big as a bread plate, walking along the ground. That's why they're called 'wandering'. Maybe they're so heavy they can't climb the walls like lighter, regular spiders. The boys say that the hold is full of rare insects and reptiles and animals from South America, bound for a zoo in Europe. The boys went down to see the animals and one of them released the latch on a box of spiders. They were laughing and maybe they were joking. They were saying that some of the spiders are even bigger than the Brazilian wandering spider. The boys say it's the deadliest spider in the world. It's frightening. Those boys want to catch the spider. The cockroaches would get a move on then. And another one of the boys said he could see another kind of race that would make some ladies scramble. I'm telling you because those boys might have a prank in store for you. None of them said they'd actually caught any spiders and maybe it's all just so much chatter. They talk so much nonsense. But I did almost get robbed. I could feel their fingers trying to get into my pockets. So that's why you heard me knocking so frantically, I'm sorry."

"Drink the water. Calm down. I'm not afraid of spiders," Allegralita tells him.

Katerina pulls the handbag to her and looks inside to make sure she hasn't been robbed. She shakes out a cigarette from the packet, embarrassed that Joseph's story has made her check her money. She lights up and must suppress a cough. Querida reaches above and turns a dial on the ceiling ventilation without needing to stand on a chair to reach it. Katerina's cabin doesn't have one because of the windows. The windows are useless, though, unless the wind is blowing towards the cabin; the air coming from the pipes feels fresh from the ocean, and sucks away the smoke. Katerina has spent much of her time in the cabin over the last three days choking on Anne's tobacco smoke. A superior room, according to the brochures in Veracruz, because it has a view, yet ventilation makes two tiny porthole windows trivial compared to a couple of weeks in a room with good clean air. On previous ocean crossings they've never had to worry about weighing up such compromises.

Katerina shivers with cold. The room is warm enough but the fur coat now lying on the floor of her own cabin made her sweat and the sleeveless dress she wore for lunch is still damp. The vent above their heads has stirred the air in the room. She says no when Querida asks her if she wants a blanket and says no again when asked if she would like a coat. She doesn't want to stay in this room. As soon as the cockroaches outside are gone she'll be able to leave.

Allegralita tells Joseph he needs to stretch his fingers, roll his shoulders, settle himself. She doesn't have any more students because of the New Year's celebrations, so there is no time limit today as there was yesterday. He does not need to worry about robbers or spiders. *Aquitania* is a world-class ocean liner. There are over a thousand crew and they can deal with pickpockets and nasty insects.

Katerina thinks about Doctor Blackshaw telling Anne this morning not to take her own fears seriously. And then of the first few hours aboard *Aquitania*, when Anne asked Katerina to consider what kind of person takes a job on an ocean liner. A porter with hat askew and shirttail falling out the back of his pants was bringing their luggage into the cabin but Anne wasn't concerned he might be able to speak French. Far from home for months or years at a time, confined spaces, severely limited freedoms, poor wages. The crew is made up of navy washouts, social degenerates and outcasts, ex-convicts fresh out of prison. *Merci, Madame*, said the porter. Fixed his hat and tucked in his shirttail, winced at the effort to straighten his spine and hobbled out of the cabin.

Querida asks Katerina if she wants a cup of honeyed water or tea and Katerina says she'd be grateful for a cup of sweet tea with no milk. Querida tells her to sit at the table, where there is an ashtray. The ashtray has a picture of a grand Florentine building and the words *Hotel Savoy Firenze*.

Allegralita pours herself a glass of bourbon and hovers the Four Roses bottle over Querida's empty glass. Querida looks up at her before she nods. Allegralita takes a big mouthful of the spirit before turning to her student and beginning the lesson. Querida picks up her glass and takes a smaller sip. There isn't much left in the bottle but even so it doesn't cross their minds to offer Katerina a glass of bourbon. The whisky she drank at lunch is still in her system, dull and burning low like an ache in the blood. Another drink might relieve her, though she doesn't want to get drunk again. These sisters won't give her a drink. The lights in this room are bright enough for them to see how young she is.

Katerina notices a moth on the wall. Larger than a normal moth, this one is as big as her hand. She wouldn't have thought much about it, but since they've been talking about the jungle animals down below being transported to a zoo in Europe, she wonders whether this is a moth that managed to get out of its box. Perhaps it is food for one of the exotic animals. A particular spider or snake that feeds on this kind of moth. She doesn't mention it to the two women in the cabin. No doubt it has nothing to do with anything down in the hold. Joseph has brought the idea into the room with him.

Allegralita instructs the boy to play an F-major scale and arpeggio, takes a step back to the table, lifts the lid on a brass globe cigarette dispenser, places two cigarettes between her lips, lights up, and when Querida brings over a tray with a pot of tea and cups, she places one of the cigarettes in Querida's mouth. So coordinated a movement within the small cabin (made all the more intimate because of four people) that Katerina thinks perhaps the sisters have made many ocean crossings.

Querida winces on an out-of-tune note. Katerina asks whether she is a music teacher as well. Querida tells her she is a dramaturge with a spell of work beginning in the new year with the Arriaga Theatre in Bilbao, though she often teaches acting, singing and dancing, elocution and etiquette, whatever pays the bills. Her occupation has always been, and ever will be, a precarious existence, she tells Katerina.

"As you can see," Querida says, waving a finger at the shambolic room as though tracing the crazed course of a fly in the air. "And what about you? How do you plan on spending the rest of your life?"

Katerina raises and drops her shoulders. "I was Christian de Neuvillette in *Cyrano de Bergerac*." She thinks the image might please the mannishly dressed Querida. "A school production, but we performed in a theatre, and our costumes were remarkable." Anne did not attend a performance. She would have found all the brocade and feathers gaudy.

"We had to play all the parts because it was an all-girls school. My father told me he enjoyed my Baron de Neuvillette. Encouraged me to take acting seriously." But it was all in fun. The thought of acting for the rest of her life, taking it *seriously*, is nauseating. She already feels sickened by the play-acting in everyday life.

"'I ... I am going to be a storm—a flame ... '" Katerina says after Querida asks her for a passage from the play. "I don't remember my lines. It's all Cyrano. Anything good in the play goes to him. I did enjoy mocking the grotesque nose. That's the best it ever gets for de Neuvillette. I thought it was interesting that Cyrano thinks it is impossible for him to be loved because of a disfigurement so he must use the baron to communicate his beauty to Roxanne—really to the audience, to the world. Yet he wants to be loved precisely in the ways the world has mutilated him."

There are two seats by the table. Allegralita drags over a large square suitcase to use as a third seat. There are a couple of heavy tomes on the table: volumes 20 and 21, ODE–PAY and PAY–POL of *Encyclopaedia Britannica*.

"Ode to pay," Katerina mouths the words. The accidental meaning makes her think of the page of the Bible slipped under her door—an ode to what still needs to be paid.

"They're samples," says Allegralita as she pushes them away. "They don't belong to us." Allegralita reconsiders the two volumes, picks them up, and dumps them on the floor by the rubbish bin.

"The man next door is a salesman. He's an insistent fellow to say the least. Have you talked with him yet?" Querida asks.

"I saw him standing in his doorway," says Katerina. "Made me think of a Sumerian bas-relief. He's a man with a remarkable beard. No, we haven't spoken to him." The cigarette is making her eyes burn so she tries to stub it out but the white cylinder of the cigarette crumples without putting out the ember. "I thought neither of you spoke English well enough to read these."

"I'm American," says Allegralita, switching from her flawless Spanish. "I should have pretended I didn't speak English. Who knew he would be so fucking pushy."

Katerina watches Allegralita for a few moments. The woman lays emphasis on that particular tactic of pretending not to understand English. And she is also making it clear that it was not her idea to have Katerina in the room. The sooner she leaves the better—yet Querida brings out a valise, an expression of anticipation on her face.

"You're not likely to bring out the cards, are you?"

"Sorry?" Querida asks.

"For whist?"

"No, why?"

"We took you for card enthusiasts when you came around on your whist drive. And I thought perhaps you were two lonely women looking for company. I was wrong, though, wasn't I? You were looking to drum up some business. To find music and acting students."

Querida asks Katerina if she wants another cup of tea. Katerina isn't sure whether she has insulted the woman but suspects she has. "I'm glad you're not lonely women looking for company. That you're practical people, making money wherever, however you can. Maybe you could sell me some socks," Katerina says and laughs as though it was a hilarious thing to say.

"I have a salve from Napo." Querida draws out a tin from the valise. "I've found it wonderfully useful for myself and friends."

"Salve from Napo?" Katerina has no idea why the Argentine wants her to see the tin of salve. She has the uncomfortable notion that Querida is going to ask her to help sell the salve to passengers aboard *Aquitania*—door-to-door like the encyclopaedia salesman.

"The Napo River in the rainforests of Ecuador."

"Excuse me, I'm not sure what you want," Katerina says.

"Your arm." Querida takes hold of her hand to have a look at the bite. The gentle touch of her fingers alone feels curative. Katerina has to resist the temptation to sigh and fall into the lovely caresses of the short-haired woman.

Querida notices not only the toothmarks of the dog but with even more revulsion the bruises forming along Katerina's arm from Blackshaw pushing out the bacteria.

"These are not the hands of a doctor," Querida says.

"I bruise easily. I get that from my mother. Kornél practically never bruises. He's proud of it but I was told by a doctor there's no significance."

"Just hope you do not need to see this doctor again for anything."

"I can't help feeling there's more benefit from his treatment than the Napo salve. Pain seems a part of everything. Painless solutions don't really work."

"Depends on the problems you're looking to resolve," says Querida, and then asks, "don't you think?"

"I'm not sure what we're talking about now. I'll need the doctor again for penicillin. I'm feeling cold, and then I'm feeling hot, maybe a little feverish. I'm not sure even about that. It's been such an awful morning, but it's been awful for days, and it's been awful for weeks."

"Over whist the other night—such a shame you and your mother couldn't attend—someone told me you're an ambassadorial family. Is that the way it's phrased? Strange occupation, when you think of it, involving as it does everyone in the family. All of you must be moved from one part of the world to another and so much of the work is done through social engagements. You must be sick of such things—why would you want to play whist?"

"What in the world?" Katerina says. "Who told you this?"

It isn't something they talk about and she finds it hard to believe it would come up in a conversation at the card table. And yet she mentioned it to the doctor over lunch. She tells herself that it was the stress and the alcohol producing a very unusual circumstance. And the confidentiality of a doctor surely applies even if they did not speak in Blackshaw's office. She burns with the thought that she said something she hadn't wanted to speak about. Before this morning they barely talked to anyone on the ship. "Can't imagine anyone telling you anything like that over whist."

"Maybe someone on the crew saw something in your papers. It's noteworthy, especially when the style of travel is hardly ambassadorial. I'm sorry. You must know how people enjoy talking about such things, and there's so little to do on an ocean voyage but talk about the people you're travelling with. And I must say, having talked with you, it doesn't seem far-fetched at all. A person's bearing can tell you much more than their words ever will." Katerina feels the compliment. Can also sense the way it seeks to bend her forward to the woman. To ask for more lovely words, to be patted on her head—a well-behaved dog.

"Gossiping women. That's what that sounds like to me. The far-fetched stories told over a card table do not appeal to me." Katerina's ready to stand and yet does not want to yank her arm away from Querida.

Querida smiles as though she can't possibly credit Katerina with saying anything rude. "It seems that it certainly wouldn't have been a sanctioned move. Is that the word? I thought perhaps here were two women in desperate circumstances, fleeing from one situation to another. And I wanted you to know that there's help close at hand." She has Katerina's arm and strokes the back of her wrist. "There's no need for you to be alone in your troubles. There are often painless solutions." Querida's fingers and the salve feel so pleasant Katerina wants to close her eyes and accept it all at face value.

"There's a line that comes to me from the play," says Katerina. "Another great one that went to Cyrano but I always wanted to say it myself. 'Tonight, when I cross the blue threshold of paradise, I shall wave one thing in salutation. Since there's one thing I have left, unmarred and without stain, which I take with me despite you … my white plume.'"

Joseph is playing a song by Brahms, making mistakes. Neither Allegralita nor Querida seems to notice now. He stops and apologises for the errors and Allegralita tells him to continue to the end.

"No point in getting stuck with a piece of music. Always push towards the end whenever it is in reach," she tells the boy.

"You've done enough. Please release my arm," says Katerina. "Thank you. It's much appreciated."

"Would you like to take the salve with you?"

Katerina shakes her head and stands. Feels unsteady on her feet, the high heels making it all the worse, in a room with too low a ceiling and too many people.

"No, I'm sure I'll manage without the Napo paste. Smells like a food spread to me. And I shan't trouble you both any longer. No-one needs any more trouble than is already theirs to own." Katerina stands up. "I'm going to go. I was on my way somewhere but then there were those boys outside and their commotion. Hard to believe your eyes. Insects scuttling across the decks. And if not, they're climbing up from under the beds. They call those ones kissing bugs. It's all just so revolting. Everywhere you look. Hard to know how to stay clear of it all. Jumping over cockroaches! Don't know what my mother would have made of that particular spectacle."

Allegralita, already standing, has walked over to move the Quetzalcoatl draught stopper, unlocks the door. It's the first time she's looked at Katerina directly.

"Yes, I was surprised to see you alone." Responding in English for a second time. A southern American accent and speaking quickly—the door already open. "Any time you've been allowed to wander before, it was on a leash in the hand of the *grande dame*." They have all walked out into the hallway, Querida looking as if she'd rather keep walking away from Joseph and his attempt to play Paganini's "Caprice 24". Allegralita doesn't feel obliged to say goodbye—re-enters her cabin and finishes the Four Roses directly from the bottle.

"She's known better times, your mother has, no doubt, but she looks to keep your mind in the orbit of her needs and wishes," Querida says. "My mother was that way. Perhaps *yours* isn't like that. We see mostly ourselves in the world, don't we? Because we see with what we understand. Everything else falls into the great blur at our edges." She offered Katerina a handshake when they met today. Now she lifts a palm the way Indians do in cowboy movies. "Thanks for paying us a visit, Catalina. Fare thee well."

❖❖❖❖❖

The doors of the elevator open. Katerina has to push to get out. She asks politely to pass in English, and then swears in Russian for people to move the fuck out of the way. More of the ship's passengers are trying to force their bodies into the already full elevator. She uses her shoulders and elbows with an aggression that makes a portly gentleman exclaim. The doors close on her and buck open again before she manages to exit.

Enthused faces despite the press. Glimpses through the vines and flowers of the fine wrought iron and glass of the elevator doors. The crowding in together part of the fun of a special occasion. Up they go. Rising to the uppermost deck. Black and grey and white pant legs, patterned stockings and high heels and dangling furs. And then the oiled serpentine cables moving through the void.

...high communion find;
His service is the golden cord
Close-binding humankind

With a railing behind them, three nuns stand on the

landing, two of them with guitars and the third with a tambourine. They have been singing "In Christ There is No East or West" for passing fellow passengers. A stairway winds down to the level below. Booming acoustics despite the noise of people ascending and descending.

The nuns harmonise but do not try to be too sweet. Katerina notices they can play well enough that their instruments aren't purely tools to promote Christianity. She wonders whether perhaps one of them carried her musical interest with her into the convent from the outside world. They were all clean and exuberant with their fresh devotion. Only a few years ago they would have been young girls. They might have sung of romance; their love now has a new focus. It doesn't seem to matter if it's one man, all men, or the divine man. *The same silly sentiment*, thinks Katerina. *A song for a heartthrob.*

When she left the Argentines she stopped a porter for directions to the swimming pool and was told that it was being used by men. It didn't make sense to Katerina. Of course it was being used by men—could it ever be open to animals?

The porter explained to her, as to a cretin, that the area was open to women in the mornings, male passengers at other times. She nodded, feeling the heat of embarrassment rising through her body, up to her face; all the worse when her face reddened.

With an unusual brusqueness, she told him to bring her a tub and hot water for a bath. He shrugged, said he might be able to help her in the afternoon sometime. Hectic day for all the crew today, as surely she could imagine.

"And is that all you want, girl?" Distaste and hunger mingling in his ugly eyes. She had seen the metal glint of a wristwatch at the cuff of his sleeve. And then (shakes her head at the memory now) she took hold of his wrist and pulled back the cuff to look at the time. He jerked back his hand and told her he would've told her the time if she'd simply asked—lifted his arm as if to dismiss her. She lowered her head, and with the heels of both hands, thumped him in the chest. Unbalancing him. Not leaving it at that, she stepped forward and pushed him aside with her shoulder. He'd reeled back into the wall. Falling on his arse. Banging the back of his skull against the wooden panelling with a percussive effect. Passengers stopped, stunned by the violence, curious as to how and why.

The porter apologised and said he would bring her the bath as soon as possible. Picking himself up quickly, as if he'd stumbled. Speaking as though being battered and pushed to the ground by a passenger wasn't uncommon. Embarrassed that he'd been sent sprawling in circumstances that could not appear favourable for him in any light.

She chuckles at the thought as she walks to the Palladian Lounge, also recalls with pleasure digging her elbow into the paunch in the elevator.

In the doorway there is a sandwich board with a Red Cross image of a nurse, asking passengers to give blood. Printed by hand on the poster are details about the deck and room to which one should go to donate. The sign emphasises that the willing should give their blood *before* the festivities. Katerina wonders if you can get drunk through a post-revelry infusion and whether the nuns have been so effective in their singing that they've cleared the near-empty lounge. She imagines the glassy-eyed doctor, not yet sober from lunch, searching for elusive veins, a needle in his rough fingers.

A few stragglers are finishing up, draining their wine glasses and cups of coffee. She doesn't sit and wait for service. Instead she buttonholes a waiter about to fluff cushions and asks him to bring her a pot of tea and some ginger biscuits. "And please make sure the tea is very hot," she adds as the waiter leaves to get her order.

Apart from one group of men clustered near the fireplace, Katerina is alone in the enormous rooms. She sits on a sofa and feels the body heat of a person still in the cushions—a ghost of presence. A cigarette in an ashtray continues to burn, waiting for the next inhalation. An Agatha Christie is bookmarked and set on a coffee table, the next twist set for a gasp. The whole Palladian Lounge evaporating spectres, quieter and warmer for the gradual absence. The tide of life easing away for nothing more remarkable than an ocean twilight.

The last two afternoons Katerina has followed Anne out onto the crowded decks for sunset. All she wants today is hot tea. And the hard biscuits, which taste nice but she looks forward to the texture most of all. Crushing something in her teeth is appealing. And tea often comes lukewarm, cold by the time she gets to the last sip.

The passengers by the fireplace murmur. Subdued and excited at the same time. Strange how silent they are otherwise. About thirty men in light, pale leisure suits. Many of them holding white hats behind their backs. Most would soon return to their cabins and put on their more sombre evening clothes. They are bound to unpack their best clothes for the New Year's celebrations. Katerina read in Veracruz that there will be circus costumes for those who want them. It is a New Year's tradition and many will have come prepared with their own creations. Hard to imagine any of these grave men dressing as trapeze artists or lion tamers. She can't see their faces clearly but their bodies are still, with the intent of visitors to an art gallery, yet clustered more like medical students over an intricate surgery.

"Shall I pour you a cup, Miss?" The waiter has wheeled a trolley to her couch.

"Leave me the pot, please." The waiter puts the tea down on the oval table before Katerina. "Is it hot?" She feels petulant asking but she wants the warmth as much as she wants the taste of tea.

"Yes, I made sure of it, Miss. It will burn your tongue if you're not careful." He places the pot, the cup and saucer, the milk and sugar on the table.

"Lovely to have so much unexpected space," she says. All the many couches and armchairs arrayed about an emperor's salon.

"Sunset on the ocean can be a sight to see. Always a unique perspective of the wide world beyond. And twilight on the upper decks is ever lovely. The first few days of a crossing have passengers enthralled." The crew talk about it so often and with such sincere intent they get everyone moving out to the decks every day. They are incessant about the need to go out and get air. They might be relieved of the press of passengers for an hour.

"The marvellous way water reflects colours, and what a vast panorama the Atlantic presents to the open-eyed traveller!"

"Why are those men over there so silent? How are they so absorbed?" she asks.

"A world chess champion is aboard, Miss. It's fifty against one and those men think there is a possibility of beating him. Mr Euwe is no longer the champion of the world. No, he lost his title last year." The waiter places a fingerbowl on the coffee table. "They have paid a great deal of money for the privilege of being destroyed, all fifty of them at the same time. They think perhaps there is some chance." He puts down the bill for Katerina. "Of course, they don't. There is no chance at all."

A diving suit, one with a copper helmet, stands beside the fireplace. It might have been a suit of armour in a different setting. The faceplate reflects the lights of the ceiling and it catches Katerina's eye. The waiter brings out her ginger biscuits and places them before her. He pours her the tea and encourages her to drink. Hot, but not scalding now. He straightens up as though he has a pain in his hips. Stands there with both hands behind him pressed into the small of his back.

"You wouldn't mind if I sat a moment, would you?" he asks as he perches on the arm of the sofa. "It's a rare moment when there are few customers, and the ones that are present all involved with a game."

"Fine by me." He's a fellow too fat to be running plates around a busy reception area and she doesn't mind him having a rest, but he's pathetic. She lifts the plate of biscuits and insists he take one. She drinks her cup of tea in four gulps and pours herself another cup.

Mr Euwe walks away. The waiter tells her Mr Euwe will give the men half an hour to consider their next move. Before leaving the room he orders a bottle of Armagnac for his opponents from a passing waitress. They become animated in his absence, openly discussing all the potential ramifications none of them could fully understand. They might have thought they did after the first couple of games but they have realised that there is a dimension of playing chess they have no access to, a level of comprehension that only Mr Euwe and few others in the world can achieve. Their conversations are therefore full of doubts and questions of how many moves they would be safe for, at a minimum, none of them suggesting victory is a possibility.

The waiter notices that Katerina loses interest in the chess enthusiasts, that her attention is shifting to the diving suit with the shiny copper helmet.

"Only a few years ago a group of drunken fellows decided to take that diving suit and put it on. One of them would wear the suit and they would fetch the man's beloved, ask her to come help look for him, telling her that he was missing. Might a rogue wave have swept him overboard? And then they would ask her to wait for them by the fire as they brought him from the infirmary, new information arising that he'd been hurt, a minor slip on the deck. While she waited, the diving suit would begin to move. The suitor would frighten her. He would then remove his helmet. Reveal himself. Open the treasure chest. And voila! A wedding ring with a diamond the size of a cherry. It's a real diving suit, so it's extremely heavy. As it turned out, the man in the suit had to wait a good while. The count for New Year's Eve was ideal for the surprise. The beloved became anxious indeed about her lost suitor. In her hysteria she ran about the ship. Two of the friends involved with the surprise proposal searched for her in the mayhem of celebrations. Found her after the clock had struck twelve. The appointed time gone, her anxiety so extreme the friends of the suitor decided they must tell her the truth. She calmed down and then laughed. What a story to tell the children one day! And then she felt awful for making her suitor wait such a long time. He will have suffered in the suit for no reason. And he'd be awfully embarrassed, wouldn't he? Perhaps he wouldn't offer her the ring after all. They all returned to the diving suit. She stood with a glass of champagne before him, as though merely awaiting his return, prepared to scream when the suit began to move. The many friends of the suitor gathered and they all did count from ten to one, louder and louder, sure that their patient companion within the diving suit would hear them. At the appropriate time, the diving suit did not move. The suitor continued to stand, motionless, a phantom within a suit of armour. Had he fallen asleep in a drunken stupor? When she looked in through the glass of the brass helmet, she saw her dear man had closed his eyes. She removed his glove and placed a kiss on his hand, near the finger that would bear a wedding ring. Alas, the hand was pale and cold. He did not awake when she tapped on the faceplate of the helmet. He had suffocated ever so gradually within the heavy suit. He'd been drinking, so perhaps he'd fallen asleep. His air tube had been crushed beneath his heel. The helmet is very shiny but these days the hose is not connected at the back of it. It can't be made airtight now. Even so, every New Year's Eve, when the count begins, the suit jerks into motion. At nine it moves. At eight it searches. At seven it finds a woman resembling the beloved. At six it draws close. At five it embraces her. At four it finds that the woman is not the beloved. At three, remembers death. At two, feels the hatred of all hell for the living. At one, the poor girl is crushed in the diving suit's embrace."

Katerina has been eating the biscuits as she might have popcorn in a movie theatre.

"That's a good one. I do enjoy ghost stories," she says. "And I'd love to wear that suit. Make it move around at midnight to hear one of those nuns outside scream."

"For my part, I think it would be a little too snug about the belly."

"Might you get into trouble with the maître d', sitting and talking for such a long time?"

"The boss is far too busy in the kitchen with preparations for tonight to wander through the lounge during the twilight hour."

Katerina reaches into her handbag and places coins on the bill as a tip and signs the tea and biscuits to her cabin. She pauses before closing the handbag—brings out her two balls of opium in the palm of her hand.

"I forgot I'd need a pipe when I bought these earlier today. A pipe wasn't something I remembered to pack in my luggage."

"Miss, I think … I can help you with that." He stands adroitly, the pain in his hips forgotten. "I'll need to go to my cabin but I shan't be long."

Katerina sets herself to write a letter to Kornél. She's not sure how to approach the awful collapse of their mother. She won't tell him about Anne plucking her own eye out of its socket. And she can't write to Kornél about needles of tranquillisers, the straitjacket. She might write, *Mother is unwell*—and then what? A milder version of events would require outright lies, so her pen is suspended over the paper for minutes.

She begins with a quotation by Melville:

But even so, amid the tornadoed Atlantic of my being, do I myself still for ever centrally disport in mute calm; and while ponderous planets of unwaning woe revolve round me, deep down and deep inland there I still bathe me in eternal mildness of joy.

Katerina has never been able to make much progress with *Moby-Dick*, though she's quite enjoyed shorter pieces by Melville. The words she puts to paper for her brother have separated themselves from any context and become a poem that she often comes back to in her mind.

Inevitable that it would return to her now that she's crossing the Atlantic again, remembering only after writing the words that she first came across the quotation in a letter Anne wrote to Audrius in the days following his departure from the embassy in Mexico. Katerina had seen the letter on the desk in the abandoned study. "Abandoned" wasn't a word she would use until a year had passed. Her mother would never use that word. Abandonment was one thing for Katerina; for Anne, another. Katerina never questioned the love of her father—within months he'd sent a magnificent chestnut Andalusian over the ocean, and there was a steady flow of jewellery and dresses, letters and books, which only stopped in January because of a difficult diplomatic assignment.

Anne had begun her letter to Audrius and left it on the bare rosewood desk. It was there for days. Katerina wandered through the study often after he left for Europe. She assumed that eventually her mother finished the letter and posted it to Audrius.

She finishes her second cup of tea and balls up the piece of paper. Writes a few more words to Kornél and screws that up as well. She finds another letter from her brother addressed to her. It's dated two weeks after the one she keeps in the Antal Szerb novel. Correspondence from Kornél was previously rare so his expulsion from Saint-Cyr must have generated this flurry of letters gathered up in her mother's handbag.

Katerina hears the ripping of paper. Puts down Kornél's letters. The sound is repeated again and again. She thinks of the page she found in her cabin. Torn from the Book of Job. She looks up and finds a man tearing a piece of newspaper to shreds. He seems angry, though the anger doesn't reach his eyes. He looks up at Katerina and tells her he didn't mean to bother her.

"Why would you bother me?" When she returns her eyes to Kornél's letter the ripping continues.

"Can't believe everything you read, can you?" he asks.

She furrows her brow because he seems to be referring to the letter she's reading.

"You can't always believe your eyes, either," he says.

"Maybe you *are* bothering me," she tells him.

"Really?" he asks. "Really!" He's a young man wearing a top hat and a tuxedo with a crimson satin vest. When she drops her eyes he talks again to get her attention back. "All the news that's fit to rent." He crushes the ripped-up pieces of paper in his hands, moving the bundle from one hand to the other, squeezing the paper as though he might destroy the newspaper all the more in the press of his grip. He hits himself in the forehead with the small bundle of paper.

"So hasty of me. Not the fault of the paper that the news of the world can be so awful." His right hand begins to pluck at the paper in his left hand, bringing it out, bit by bit, and then pulling it free, revealing a piece of newspaper that is very crumpled up yet not at all torn. He leans over and hands it to Katerina.

"Read for yourself. I think you'll find it quite interesting." She takes the paper and can't help smiling at the magic trick. She opens her mouth to ask him how he did it but that's the expected response, so she smiles and nods that it was done well. Already dressed in his costume for the evening.

Flora is standing there, watching Katerina and the young gentleman.

"I'd come with an idea I should apologise but I don't see why I would now. You're having a lovely time with this magician," said Flora.

"An apology isn't necessary," Katerina says. And because Flora doesn't move or say anything, "You can go. You needn't stand there forming a judgement."

"True enough. I might drift away, not a bothersome thought in my mind, but I've been looking high and low for you, Miss Klova. Sorry if I was callous, yet I've lived all my life with my failings, and you wouldn't keep me up for more than a few minutes. I've spent over an hour searching, going to your cabin multiple times and ranging across the decks. I even visited the chapel because those that have your troubles are prone to prayer."

"Your purpose is not your own, I understand. I'm appropriately grateful for your trouble, only up to the point you become a nuisance. Why are you here?"

"Happens that I've also got a note from your mother." Flora tosses a letter onto the coffee table between them. She turns to leave.

"Is she well enough to write?" asks Katerina. "Can she see to put words down? Blackshaw ... Doctor Blackshaw, told me she was bandaged. Has there been a recovery?"

"I wouldn't say that's true. She was lucid for a spell after sleeping, had a little pea and potato mash with orange juice and is asleep again now. Doctor says it's a good sign. Matron says it's rare for a descent to be straight down. A soul grapples if it's still got some grip. Matron's a bitter bitch, though." Flora crosses her eyes and shrugs. "Mrs Klova wasn't saying much. She wanted me to find you. Very clear and decided upon that course of action. Had me put down words from a song you were fond of, in better days. Mind still in a muddle, for mine, but at least she's not talking octopuses."

"My thanks for the message." Katerina opens it. Reads words they first heard sung in a Portuguese folk song, a couplet from a fado she and her mother both enjoyed one evening at a restaurant on Rua de Santa Catarina in Porto. That night, Anne had laughed at the overwrought lyrics. And then, after she began to get drunk on wine, said more than once that the singer had a remarkable voice.

Oh, but I have seen the way love ends
and I have seen the way the world dissolves.

We will drink our oblivion from cut crystal
and our babies will make milk from our blood.

Anne wasn't talking about a song in her note. She was using the lyrics to tell her daughter not to destroy the cache of letters kept in a cherry-wood cigar box. The only word that matters in her message is "love". The signal in a go/stop code to Katerina that the letters are to be saved for the time being. If Anne had used the word "hate" (none of the sentences would matter but it would have been a pleasant, sentimental message to confuse an interloper) that word would have been a signal to destroy the letters. Katerina hadn't waited for "hate" to throw Audrius

Klova's cigar box into the Atlantic. She is appalled to see the word is "love".

She shows Flora a one-pound note, explains that it is a tip for the message being brought to her, and for a reply she will take back to Anne. Flora is distrustful until the money is in her hand and then she says, "Of course, Miss Klova." As though there is no question and she's never been any trouble to Katerina.

Madame Klova,

My dearest Mother, your health is the only thing that matters to me. I would hate, really hate, for you to rush back into the world, on any account. Especially tonight. Such a wild evening ahead of us. We both need rest. Please, dear, rest. And forgive me. I should have come back to you sooner. Trust that I will not leave your side again.

Yours,

Kitty.

❖❖❖❖❖

Smoke trickles from her nose—an exhalation that rises to swirl around the light above their heads. The bare light bulb sways with the ship's movement. Growing brighter. And then going dim without cutting out. A flicker in the electrical current. She doesn't feel *Aquitania* rocking. Closes her eyes. She's swaying when she sits back down on the bar stool. It might be the ship and it might be her own breathing. It might be the light bulb moving her to its metronomic push and pull. Or the blood shifting through her body. Her heart feels big and thumps at her ribs. She places her hand on her chest and pats it as if settling her favourite pet to sleep. *Thump, thump*. A cat's tail, flicking back and forth. Back and forth. *Thump, thump*.

The waiter says he's thirsty. Should have thought of water earlier. Always gets thirsty when he smokes. He'll be back shortly with two glasses. When he comes back, he says, they'll smoke the second ball of opium. He must redo his tie. Blinks his eyes, looking for focus in the dim storage room. Adjusts his glasses. Pulls down the tight vest over the mound of his belly. Takes a deep breath before stepping through the door back into the Palladian Lounge.

"It's a sound idea," she says. Leans forward when attempting to nod.

He's already left the storage room before she speaks. She contemplates lying down on the ground but the floorboards below her bare feet are worse than dusty. She can see rat or mouse droppings. It's too cold to lie on wood. Her fur is still on the floor of her cabin. Not much space for her among stacked armchairs, tables, a leaning tower of empty ice buckets and an industrial vacuum cleaner with the longest hose attachment she's ever seen, snaking about the floor.

The smoke is settling around her. Keeping her eyes open is not easy. She doubts there are any vents in the storage room. Blinking makes her eyes sting.

The waiter doesn't return. Clarence or Clifford. They told each other their names but she can't recall. It was awkward. There was a friendliness that could not result in friendship. Expedience over companionship. Kenneth? She can't be sure how long the waiter has been gone. Might be a few minutes, possibly an hour. She believed him when he said he would be back with glasses of water. Now she thinks it unlikely.

She shrugs. "Not enough air in here for both of us anyway."

The waiter found two bar stools for them to sit on but there wasn't space to bring down the large armchairs used in the Palladian. They both stood and leaned across a stack of rolled Persian rugs to use the pipe. After he'd had his smoke, he lay there, the upper half of his body on the carpets, until his legs buckled and then he was in pain despite the opium. The bar stool wasn't much relief. Easier to say he would go and get water than to tell her he was going somewhere with more room and air. A place to lie down. Or he was muddled in his mind because Katerina was sure he was intent on sharing the second ball with her. She didn't know whether he had taken his Chinese pipe and opium lamp with him because she couldn't open her eyes for the moment. They would be clues to his intentions of leaving or returning, though his intentions might not matter. There are passengers out there gathering for the evening and his boss will have found him and pressed him back into service.

"And yet intentions do matter. He was a lovely old fellow and I'd rather not have been duped, abandoned in this room like a cat no-one wants anymore. At least there are mice. Or rats. Hard to tell from the evidence left behind." She can have the second by herself if she still has his accoutrements. It occurs to her that perhaps he took his things *and* her ball of opium.

The light bulb grows brighter. She can feel its heat and leans away. She has kicked off the heels so her feet can feel the cool wood. A sleeveless dress wouldn't be comfortable even if she could clear away the rat shit. She wants to stand. Doesn't do more than raise her palm from her chest.

The light bulb dims. Doesn't quite switch off. She opens her eyes a moment. Blinks. Keeps them open. The frame of the door is an illuminated rectangle and she can hear the passengers outside in the Palladian Lounge getting loud. New Year's Eve will make them louder. And louder. This is not the place to get thoroughly deranged on opium. She tells herself to get up but her palm settles against her chest.

"A little air in here, please." A smile lifts her lips at the corners. "Said the man in the diving suit to his beloved." The murmured sound of a sleeper on the verge of waking.

Her eyes are closed again. Her mind feels itself enfolded in sleep but Katerina is not dreaming. She can hear the banging of a crow against a glass wall. Before the crow, a twelve-piece ensemble had tuned up in the ballroom and were now having their meals in preparation for a long night of music. She's always loved the sound of an orchestra tuning their instruments, often more than the performance itself. The swell of sound, lusciously discordant, a chaos of preparation and possibility. And then their voices in the kitchen showed them to be ordinary peasants filling their stomachs with meat and wine. Ignoring her as she drifted around. Eating with their mouths open. Laughing when one of them farted. Her mother had told her that morning that these were the finest musicians in Portugal.

The immense oak table was all set in the long dining room, every empty glass sparkling in the lazy movement of light through the room, the silverware glinting in the warm afternoon sunshine. Anne had designed a dress for herself that had made Katerina gasp when she first saw it and Audrius fell to a knee as though struck down. He'd chased her around the bedroom telling her he wanted to kiss her feet and managed to trip her and stumble after her until they were both a giggling mess on the carpet. Anne called out for her daughter or son to come and save her from the Russian bear. Even at the ages of eight and twelve they understood that neither she nor Kornél was meant to go to her rescue. Quite the opposite. Whatever her mother's words told them ("I'm being eaten alive") the tone of her voice said this was delightful ("I'm being ravished by a bear"). She would have to iron her dress again.

They'd recently moved to Lisbon, a good post which delighted Anne with its promise of continuing ascendancy. They had moved in to a restored villa built by a Roman consul which made them feel as though they'd previously only ever lived in concrete boxes of varying sizes. They were so new to the city they had yet to fully arrange the household staff.

There was a woman in the kitchen who had worked for the previous ambassador. She'd put in a resignation soon after Anne arrived. There had been an altercation. Audrius didn't know or care what had happened. He wasn't the kind of diplomat to fret over a dinner engagement being deemed a success or a failure. A success could be boring and a failure gave everyone a laugh. He made the men he dealt with feel as though they were all above any real investment in what he called the merriments and entertainments. Hire whoever you want, he told Anne. Or why don't we book the best hotel in the city instead?

Anne waved him away. Told him to go and organise the spirits. She hadn't thought the night would need the hard stuff, as she called it. He would return late for the dinner with boxes of chalices and goblets, specialty glasses to drink the crates of potent Trappist beer he'd bought.

There was a general servant who would help around the house—Anne kept him moving from one part of the city to another, getting the right kind of champagne, and the perfect type of cheese, particular flowers that needed to be absolutely ideal to an occasion and the moment, and she'd send him out again as soon as he returned.

The fish he'd brought in the morning wasn't fresh enough. So off he went again in a desperate search, midmorning, for something he hadn't been able to acquire when the market had just opened. It didn't bother him. He wasn't rushing around Lisbon, no matter the kind of haste Anne wanted him to feel. When Anne left to put on her make-up, Katerina saw him light a cigarette and walk about the villa as though he might have a coffee, perhaps a snack, before attending to Anne's request. He'd leave their employment without notice the next day.

The crow flew in through an open door. Not a small, pretty bird. It was injured, grotesque and black. Katerina wasn't sure that it was a crow. Maybe it was a Portuguese raven. It may have flown into the villa as a sanctuary from the world outside. Drops of blood fell from the bird. It flew around the dining room and Anne rushed back from putting on her make-up, horrified at the thought that the injured crow would drizzle blood across all her freshly laundered linens, the crystal glasses on the immense table in the middle of the room. And there would be spatters of blood across the perfect arrangements of flowers. Anne ran after the bird as though she might catch the droplets of blood, calling out, "My flowers, my flowers, my flowers!" in three different languages.

Katerina was eight years old and as horrified by her mother's hysteria as she was by the awful black bird crashing around the room. Kornél was twelve, old enough to tell Mother that no drops of blood had fallen on the flowers. No drops of blood on the glasses, plates or cutlery. Everything was clean and ready for the guests. He looked again over the table, rushing from chair to chair, telling Mother again that there was no blood as she rushed about the dining room with a fire iron in her hand. She was bumping over empty wine glasses. They exploded into the finest fragments of glass and Anne wasn't yet wearing her shoes for the night.

Katerina looked out from beneath the table and saw that the crow was huge. Each beat of his wings could be heard as a *wump-wump-wump.* The noise it made, especially when it crashed into a glass wall, was so awful that Katerina put her palms to her ears and closed her eyes. She would open them again a few seconds later. She scurried under the big table in the dining room to get out of the way and saw her mother's feet rushing about the room, leaving bloody footprints behind her.

There had been an earthquake a few years before. The walls of the huge dining room had cracked, and when they were repaired, the west-facing wall was replaced with expansive windows that would catch the afternoon sunlight. The crow was crashing into those thick windows. They could not crack but they were smeared after every impact. The sun was streaming into the room and the glass was very clear so the bird didn't see the wall of glass as it tried to escape. It grew more panicked as it crashed headfirst into the glass. Anne struck glancing blows with the fire iron. Landed a strike that took flight away from it and then all it could do was hop about with one wing extended, causing even more havoc on the table.

Anne was shouting louder than Katerina had ever heard. It was in an accent of English unusual to her children, who'd only heard received pronunciation. "Everything will be spoiled. Everything will be spoiled." So vehement was she, so many repetitions, Katerina started saying the words as well, as though they were a chant. "Everything will be spoiled." Maybe that's why both Katerina and Kornél were huddled and crying beneath the dining room table after a few minutes. Kornél was whispering his own chant: "There is no blood. There is no bird. There is no blood."

As Anne moved closer to the crow, the bird took to the air with one good wing and one injured, spastically flying about Anne's head. She became panicked that now she would be attacked. What would guests think if there were not only drops of blood on the flowers or in their glasses, but she was bleeding from her face? Her make-up had already created a grotesque mask from her sweat and tears.

Katerina was petrified at the shrieking of the bird and her mother's own far more guttural noises which sounded to her like those a man might make, not the refined lady her mother always was otherwise. The room had been prepared for important guests arriving soon. The crow would not stop screeching and it went on and on. They couldn't leave the bird and let it work its own way out of the room, or to die as it eventually would, yet the longer Anne stayed in the room waving around her fire iron, the more frightened the crow became, swooping about on its maimed flight paths, crashing again into the windows. The sound of the bird colliding with the glass was distinct to Katerina. She can hear it as clearly as she could that day in Lisbon.

Anne managed to make solid contact when the bird flew into the air again, and it went to the ground, unable to fly at all now, but it was not dead. It hopped about as though it wanted to take flight once more. Flapping a large black wing, the other hanging limp. The noise it made was the sound of pure pain and terror. Anne left the dining room and came back with a blanket. She threw it at the crow. It didn't cover the bird. Anne had been too afraid to get close enough. The crow scrambled under the table and was close enough to Katerina that she could kick at it, forcing it back out into the dining room. Anne picked up the blanket and threw it over the crow. In the last glimpse Katerina had of the bird she saw it settle and submit to its fate. Not struggling at all as Anne wrapped it up in the blanket. A thick woollen throw Grandmother had bought Katerina.

Anne squeezed the bird tight in the blanket. There was no sound from the bird. The villa was silent. The musicians had left and did not return for the performance. Anne was whimpering as she squeezed the bundle in her hands. She walked outside and Katerina watched her stumble into the back garden. Anne unrolled the blanket in a quick movement, turned and fled so that she wouldn't have to see the crow again, not even to know whether it was alive or dead. There was an expression on her face Katerina could not understand. Guests would soon be arriving and the room was destroyed. Blood all over the floor. Glass and crockery everywhere. Make-up streaked down Anne's gruesome face. She wouldn't be able to wear shoes again for months. Hair dishevelled and soaked in sweat, crimson spattered around the torn hem of the loveliest dress she would ever make.

Katerina and Kornél sobbed below the table. And he was still saying the same thing. There was blood all over the floor so it had never made sense until Anne began talking of an octopus this morning. "There was no blood," he said. "There was no bird."

❖❖❖❖❖

The evening brings a few drifting snowflakes. It's not snowfall and it doesn't rain, yet both feel imminent. Passengers stroll the boat deck, the women dressed in wool, the men content to amble in scarves and gloves, fingertips on the brims of their hats.

Katerina is wearing her mother's long sable coat, her own leather gloves, an ushanka and valenki. She is over a foot taller than her mother but the sable covers enough of her body, more than her own coat. Her mother's perfumes are trapped in the fur and Katerina prefers that to the sweat and dust in her own coat. Snowflakes get caught in the sable. They melt and the droplets of water look as if they are spinning in the bright lights illuminating the boat deck.

A formation of men march up the deck. They are shouting and gesticulating. They're not using words and their gestures are chaotic. Seven of them in total, all in uniform.

One of them points at a grand lady and all of them march at great speed, collide with her. They step back, each of them raising his pistol and firing. She is wearing an embroidered floral tulle gown. Dripping red after a few moments. She doesn't scream.

The grand lady can't say a word. On the verge of tears. The men are all shouting in overblown outrage and now their words aren't gibberish. They shake their police batons at her and tell her she has broken the law of the evening.

This is no costume she is wearing! What a blatant infraction! And *parading* it before everyone else aboard the ship! *Flaunting* her disregard! The corruption of *innocents* is what she should be charged with! Good passengers would think there is *no rule of law* but there most certainly is! "The rule of law," they all chorus in chaos. These outrageous folk, flouting the *spirit* of the evening, they won't be tolerated! The men in uniform shout these words at each other as much as the passengers on the boat deck, or indeed the grand lady.

They are right. She is not in a costume. The grand lady has dressed in her best outfit for New Year's. She is elegant, the most enchanting woman on the boat deck. Some passengers haven't changed but they are not shot because there is still time to get dressed for the celebration. Everyone has until nine o'clock, and then there will be no more leniency for those that do not respect the law of the night. Another chorus of "The rule of law, the rule of law," as they march across the deck, waving their water pistols and plastic batons at the other passengers.

There are seven of them, none out of their twenties, dressed for the evening as Keystone Cops. Beneath their ridiculous uniforms they all look similarly lean and strong, as though they were all part of an Olympic rowing team. They've filled their pistols with red wine and begin firing into their own mouths.

After a few gulps they fall to the ground, all spontaneously committing suicide. They lie on the deck, unmoving for far longer than the joke requires.

Katerina begins to walk through the tableau and they spring back to life with their pistols raised. "I do have a costume," she assures them. "I'm on my way to get it. Please, let me pass. I respect the rule of law, I truly do. The rule of law is all that matters to me."

The opium has distorted her senses: when she first saw them she didn't understand this was all in jest, and at this moment she feels much of it is in earnest. They might be playing but they have ruined the grand lady's expensive dress with red wine and do clearly enjoy dishing out disgrace.

They circle her, and inspect her. One of the Cops lifts the hem of her sable coat to confirm the lining is excellent. None of them are using words now. They all make harrumphing sounds. One of the Cops holds her from behind while the Police Chief comes close. He opens the lids of her left eye, with thumb and forefinger, gazing as if through a keyhole into her soul—to ascertain the truth. When she starts laughing, they say they will allow her to go on her way with a warning.

They march in single file again. One stops to tie his shoelaces and three fall over the top of him. They dust themselves off, indignant, bumping into each other and passengers. One of the Cops makes as if to go over the rail and fall into the Atlantic, saves himself at the last moment, balancing on his lower back. It's stunningly brave, or stupid, for a gag. Or maybe a near accident, though the Keystone Cop doesn't break character.

They all raise their pistols when they see a little boy who might, or might not, be overdressed—certainly not in costume.

Seven pistols are levelled at the child, ready to turn him red. He grins at the Cops and opens his mouth wide.

Low clouds are scudding south. Heavy black masses moving across the ship as she makes superb eastward progress. It has been uneventful weather until now. Katerina is told by a chatty man, idling by her on a wooden chaise longue, that very bad weather was forecast but *Aquitania* might pass it by. That they could outrun the storm.

Katerina looks out across the Atlantic. Vast dark curtains before a disappearing horizon—all different degrees of descending black. Wonders if she will feel even a spray of seawater. Perhaps on one of the lower decks. A wave surge of that scale would come with ship-sinking weather for that to happen up here.

Katerina has stopped to open the handbag hanging on her shoulder. When she looks inside she's already forgotten what she wanted. She closes her eyes and opens them again, in that brief moment, feeling the shift and sway of the entire ocean below her. A rat hurries across the deck, bolting from a mass of coiled ropes to the shadows beneath one of the many lifeboats that line the railing. She opens and closes the compact mirror without looking at her reflection.

The chatty fellow is struggling with a newspaper, holding it open with difficulty as gusts of wind cross this most exposed of decks. The newspaper would be days old at least. And difficult to read despite the light fixture above him. The paper is a prop for the type of man who can never be seen to have idle hands. His forecast information might have come from *Aquitania*'s officers, or perhaps he has crossed so many times he knows the Atlantic's weather.

They are near the second of *Aquitania*'s four funnels, and

at the height of the boat deck the funnels don't tower above them, as they do from the docks when there's a monolithic impression the ship gives all its boarding passengers. A Harlem Globetrotter could close his eyes and toss a basketball back over his shoulder into a funnel. She looks up again. Well, maybe not over his shoulder.

The plumes of hot steam are swept to starboard despite their speed. She is gazing upwards for minutes, fascinated by the way the smoke, made stunningly bright by *Aquitania*'s array of lights, roils and tumbles and sweeps into delicate streamers disappearing into the dark of the falling evening.

Katerina doesn't respond to the talkative chap with even a nod. She is intent on breathing the restorative breaths advised so avidly by the crew. She didn't smoke a second pipe; enough in the first for the opium to swell and to give her stretches of dilated time in which she is overcome by a delicious daze.

"There are ocean liners that have a fake funnel." The chatty fellow sees her gazing at the funnels and perhaps he's also the kind of man who can only be of any worth because of the knowledge he might impart. He closes his newspaper and leans forward, feet on the deck. Ready to stand yet he is also poised to invite her to take the empty chaise longue beside him. He has a pot of coffee and two cups.

"A fake funnel!" he says, tilting his head back with a smile. He continues as he gazes upward. "How might you keep such a thing a secret?" He folds up his newspaper so that it is small enough to fit into the large pocket of his pea coat. He blows on his hands, teeth a tobacco yellow, long, thin, sallow fingers, a wedding band on his left hand, and an oval garnet ring on his right, rubbing his palms together and blowing warm air onto them again. "The *Titanic* was one of those ships with a fake funnel."

The notion of a fake funnel makes Katerina think of the chaps who stroll around the ship with unlit pipes in their mouths. They must have become accustomed to the sensation of having a smooth piece of wood between their teeth. A horse gets used to the bit of a bridle. Gets used to being controlled in that way, turning its head left or right at the slightest twitch from the rider. The smoking rooms on *Aquitania* are rarely empty, always many chaps in them playing chess, cards or backgammon, each of these men turning his head left or right with every switch of the riderless conversation.

"An ocean liner's engines produce a great deal of steam. The *Aquitania*, as you can see, has four working engines and no fake funnels," he says. He might be American, the kind that speaks as though he wishes he were English. Or perhaps it is the other way around, an Englishman who is a de facto American. He lights a cigarette after offering Katerina one. He smokes quickly, taking the tobacco deep into his lungs, drawing back soon after exhalation.

There's a practised quality of agreeability, a force underlying the charmingly quizzical tone compelling her to smile and go along with him. Katerina takes a couple of steps away, as if the man hasn't said a word to her. He'll have to assume she doesn't speak English. Katerina and Anne play the game in French or Spanish, sometimes Portuguese; never in Russian.

"Fake smoke," she says and turns around, still within conversational distance of the man on the chaise longue. He looks at her in complete bafflement. "Fake smoke for the fake funnel," she says in Russian, enjoying the Slavic flavour of the sounds in her mouth. "That's how you might keep it disguised."

Anne Iverson had arrived in Russia from England with rudimentary Russian. An ardent communist who sought to be of use to the revolution, hopeful of being important in international negotiations, or as a translator of political essays and articles, even poetry or novels if that was deemed socially useful. She was given the less noble role of tutor, teaching languages to the children of important Leningrad families.

Anne had found that however much she believed in her political ideals, she had a distaste for all things Slavic. She might have intended to master Russian on arrival yet her understanding of the language remained shallow. When she was with Audrius Klova, that distaste was playful and mischievous. Katerina knows it comes from a much deeper, bitter place.

Audrius isn't a volatile man. He can be violent, but he isn't disfigured by violence. His mind doesn't get hot with anger, it goes cold. Katerina can feel the same tendency in herself. Even when Audrius drinks, he becomes sweeter, more prone to merriment. Anne grows quarrelsome, enjoys goading him in needless arguments; she'd run from the room as though he were in pursuit, on a monstrous rampage, when she did manage to get him riled up enough to shout an obscenity in Russian.

After one such argument Audrius told Anne that the English had never in their history been loyal to an ideal. The argument raged for hours and it was close to dawn. Kornél slept right through it, while Katerina wasn't able to ignore what to her sounded apocalyptic. She was a child and her parents still seemed colossal.

She crawled from her room and lay on the carpet by the stairs, head over the top step, listening and dozing as the fight below boiled and cooled, and boiled again. The argument subsided and they were reconciled, perhaps they were about to kiss.

Before they did, Audrius told Anne what he thought of the English. He continued, sedately, almost lovingly, that the English had never been loyal to a greater principle of civilisation, they had only ever been able to be loyal to themselves, to their own interests. "The English are defined by their petty vanity and an unrivalled purity of hypocrisy." Maybe Anne was sleepy. Katerina couldn't see her parents but felt disturbed by her mother's silence. She'd been so vocal and volatile for hours. There had been so much shouting, so much abuse beforehand. And now the worst was delivered in a whisper. They'd rarely argued for longer than ten minutes before. She imagined her father's hands on her mother's throat even though Audrius had never before struck Anne.

Katerina could only hear her father's voice, Audrius continuing in his drawling French after the long silence. His people kicked down the pedestals of the elites, ended their royal history with a volley of bullets, and carried the flag of world revolution out to the streets, battling from door to door, city to city—and if her ideals had lost something in the translation from her immaculate conception, the process of the word being made flesh always resulted in elements of corruption, "yet that, my darling, is in the nature of the flesh. Not in the soul of my revolution."

A musician is sitting on a thin cushion placed on the boards of the deck, playing a harmonium. The instrument is collapsible and the bottom half resembles an open suitcase, with the handle below the raised keyboard. His left hand pumps the bellows behind the harmonium and his right hand plays the miniature piano keys. The top half of the case, lovely blue felt inside, has been removed, and if he were busking it could be used to collect coins. Marbles roll across the deck but they don't bother him, even when two of them bounce off his instrument.

Passers-by aren't sure whether they should stop to enjoy a legitimate performance. The music is pleasant—it is also odd and the instrument unusual. His white beard is long enough to touch the deck from his cross-legged position. A general dishevelment. An embroidered white kufi cap. He doesn't look like he comes from Africa or the Middle East. The Keystone Cops didn't feel the need to even pause before the harmonium player.

Katerina still can't trust her senses. Is he dressed up for the night? An improvised costume, and an instrument that might be found outside a circus tent. The unusually long beard is real and the music is complex. No clowning in the song he's playing. Virtuosic in the simplest terms. Unbearably sweet, intricate and delicate. Threatened at every moment to be drowned out by the noise of the water and the wind, passengers walking and talking. The endless chatter butting hard against the gentle lifting notes—sustained by the bellows of the harmonium.

The other passengers strolling along the boat deck disregard it as not more than pretty noise adding a touch of the exotic to their evening on the Atlantic.

Katerina sits on a bench near the harmonium player and wants to tell him she's enjoying his music. Waiting for him to stop. If he's a busker she will give him notes, not just coins. And then she will ask him to keep playing and she will shut her eyes and not think about Audrius's letters, already beginning to disintegrate in the sea.

The Norwich boys come running across the deck. One of them has dropped his bag of marbles and they are all scrambling around to pick them up before the marbles roll off the boat deck. If the marbles are lost to the ocean, no-one will be winning them back from the boy and there will be no more games. The rolling marbles are a hazard to the passengers and crew walking across the deck, but almost everyone smiles at the rowdy boys scrambling around calling after a catseye, an oxblood, an onionskin, a clambroth, a sulphide, a tiger and a devil's eye.

The musician isn't disturbed by the boys running around him. They don't seem to be aware of the harmonium player and his instrument as anything but a living statue to step around.

They notice Katerina and doff their hats. Gather about her as though they are supplicants before a saint. She looks at them, worried, smiling to show them she isn't afraid of the next thing they might say or do to her.

"Hello, Mademoiselle," each of them says.

"Nice to see you out and about, Mademoiselle."

"You look like the loveliest bear in the world."

"You do, Mademoiselle."

"Lovely furs you have, Mademoiselle."

They are mocking, overusing the word, pronouncing it *Mam-zel*.

"Can we touch you, Mademoiselle?"

"Stroke your fur, Mademoiselle?"

One of the boys comes near and caresses her arm when she nods. He then places a kiss on her cheek.

They run away as a rampaging herd but it was the kiss of a child. She hasn't thought of any of them as innocents before. Well, if not innocents then children, exploring the world and the ways it might allow narrow, brief, moving spaces for them, for their hopes and desires. "I kissed Mam-zel," the boy said as he ran through the strolling passengers. "I kissed Mam-zel. Suck it, tossers. I kissed Mam-zel." Katerina smiles after them. And then closes her eyes. The agreeable sensation of opium in her blood might last for another few hours. The harmonium player begins a song with an Indian air.

She feels her wrist throbbing from the dog bite. There's a pleasant warmth at that pulse point. Blackshaw's lather-scented words, "dog bite at pulse point", in her mind as though her own. Ideas and words from another person flow—blood merges—the puncture marks disappear. A mind becomes like the drain at an abattoir, gurgling with the blood of a variety of beasts. She shakes her head. The beasts aren't always crude, or awful.

A couple have been sitting beside her on the bench, also listening to the harmonium player. "Sophie, please," he says. "Sophie, please don't be difficult." Katerina listens to their squabble, over before a show of teeth. Sophie doesn't use her lover's name before they leave. *Hadrian?* Katerina wonders. It might be the Hadrian carved into the wood of the backrest on the third-class promenade on Deck D.

She has a vivid memory of stifling air, heavy with sun and exhaust, shifting around her, mingling with cooler air, and a body, fresh from a shower, wearing no cologne, close enough in moments to smell the soap that washed his skin clean.

The quarrelsome traffic outside on the roads, coming through with heat and noise every time the doors of the tram open to let a passenger enter or exit. Only a vague destination in her mind as her bones rattle on the wooden bench. On Avenida de los Insurgentes. Riding through the city. She had no idea how she was meant to spend her days. Not at school anymore. Her friends were in their regular classes. And not really friends now. Katerina had thrown her uniform, from hat to dresses to gloves and shoes, into the incinerator. She was wearing an off-the-shoulder feather-print dress she'd bought in a store that morning, leaving her street clothes in the change room.

She'd watched a matinee screening of *Allá en el Rancho Grande* and stepped out of the dark theatre into the blazing crash of the city. All she saw and heard felt cinematic and she wanted that feeling to last. It'd soon evaporate and the world would become ordinary again. She thought she might go and see the same movie tomorrow. She could think of nothing else to do. She rode the trams for hours yesterday, watching the city go about its business, everyone knowing where they were supposed to be. Even those loafing, swaying with the exhalations and inhalations of the great city they were all a part of—that she was soon to leave, expelled with as little significance as a cough from an old woman's lungs.

Anne was off at Cancún—a health retreat positioned between the Yucatán jungle and the Caribbean Sea, snorkelling lagoons when she wasn't soaking in a natural spa. Before Anne departed, she'd told Katerina that they might be leaving Mexico. They had talked about it for a while. Anne had firmed on the decision. Sent her a telegraph stating that they would definitely be going back to Europe for Kornél's graduation. Anne had stopped using Audrius's name in any but the vaguest terms. He was in Europe. It wasn't clear where, or when, they could be reunited. Katerina had been sure it would be at Saint-Cyr. Has realised on *Aquitania* how naive it was to make any assumption.

Katerina had recently started the new school year and found no point in continuing for another few months before leaving. As soon as Anne went to Cancún, Katerina decided she was finished with school for good.

A very old woman had crossed the road the previous day, emerging from between two cars. Cut to pieces when she was run over by a tram. Katerina had already heard from the cook but people were talking about it on the tram, some of them with amusement. They came up with sensational details about how the crone had been eating fruit as she crossed, and when they found them after the accident, her dentures were deep in the flesh of a rolling red apple.

A man was standing before Katerina, gripping one of the straps above, despite there being many seats he could use. He was wearing a blue shirt with white collar and cuffs. Cream-coloured pants with a sharp crease down each leg. Looked like he'd got his clothes back from the drycleaner a few hours previously, and perhaps he'd just showered as well. He smiled at Katerina. He said the thought of going to work today was a twenty-year prison sentence served in a day. "Would you help save me from so infernal a fate?"

Katerina didn't return his smile. "How might I save you?" she asked. She was curious what he meant. He told her that in three more stops they'd pass the best hotel in Mexico and they could get off and go to the finest room on the top floor. They would overlook the entire city and no-one would be able to see them. The linen was clean, smooth and cool. They could have the restaurant bring them up anything on the menu. Or they might order the entire menu, eat what they wanted, and throw the rest out the windows to the poor masses below like Roman aristocrats.

She didn't respond, so the man said, "Or I can go to the bank and lose a little more of my time in the same meeting we've been having every day for twenty years. I find that the days don't get crossed off a calendar, as I used to think. The days are drops of water in a balloon. They fill and stretch the skin, yet the balloon will not tear. It gets heavier and bigger every year until it begins to push aside every organ in your rib cage. Until it's unbearable and all you want to do is find a way to tear a hole in your soul, to let your days run out into a muddy puddle."

Katerina didn't know how to reply and he looked away. He wasn't smiling anymore. She stood up at the third stop when it came and stepped down from the tram. The man didn't say another word to her until they'd gone up the elevator to the room with a breathtaking view down Paseo de la Reforma to the Angel of Independence.

Whistling draws her attention. She notices a man dressed as Matejko's red jester. He has three fishing rods, one over the edge of the ship, and two in a bucket beside him for the catch. He's whistling happily, looking over the edge expectantly, and then back at the passing passengers. A girl dressed as Little Miss Muffet, spider dangling from her bonnet, tells him he can't catch anything all the way up here. She points out that he'll need to go down to one of the lower decks if he wants a fish.

The red jester places his forefinger to his lips, not so much to hush Little Miss Muffet as to ask her to keep a secret he might imminently reveal. The man is missing most of his fingers besides forefingers and thumbs, and the girl takes a step away. Passengers gravitate towards them, watching and waiting, so despite her revulsion the girl doesn't leave.

The way some of the jester's fingers are cut off precisely at the middle joint, beyond the knuckle, makes Katerina think of twenty-eight-question interrogations she's heard about—ghastly gossip in embassies. A question would be asked, and whether wrong or right, the interrogated would lose a segment of his little finger on his left hand, and with the second and third questions be avulsed at the next segment of that finger, and then at the knuckle. The cuts would proceed to the right hand, until both little fingers were gone, and then back to the left hand for the ring finger, alternating hands all the way up to the thumbs. The first six questions didn't matter. More significant was the demonstration of implacable resolution.

A hero might cope with the idea of losing the little finger on each hand but the closer to the thumb, the less likely the hero was to wait for further questions—for all twenty-eight—divulging anything and everything that might be of use to the interrogators.

More probably the red jester was another veteran from the Great War, mutilated by a booby trap in the trenches, or nothing more extraordinary than frostbite.

The jester jiggles the fishing rod over the rail excitedly and then the two rods in the bucket beside him. He has enough of his fingers left to hold a rod and to reel in a fish, but Little Miss Muffet is right. It would be impossible for a man to catch anything from the boat deck. Too far down for the reel of a fishing line to reach.

When Katerina leans forward on her bench she notices he has no fishing reels, and the rods are broom handles. The line is made from thin white cotton ropes he might have stolen. The red jester has tied the ropes to the ends after sawing off the broom heads.

The jester dances gleefully, the bells sewn into his costume jangling and tinkling. His arms are extended to indicate how large a catch it will be. A huge fish that will fill everyone's stomach. He rubs his stomach with closed eyes and points to the little girl's tummy with a demonic smile. When he goes to the rod on the rail he's excited by a bite at the end of the line, struggling with his mutilated fingers to keep a hold of the fishing rod. A truly immense fish has taken his bait and his leg comes up to brace against the railing. He stumbles and fumbles as his fishing rod is cast out into the ocean.

Little Miss Muffet might have laughed at the jester's antics. Instead she is afraid of the way the jester's mouth opens wide with surprise, and then grief. Soundless and all the more frightening for it. The passengers who have stopped at the spectacle don't laugh either. One of them calls out that there are plenty of fish in the sea. The jester responds with a smile, perhaps expecting just such an obvious comment, rushing to the two other rods he has in the bucket of water. Jittering and hopping from foot to foot. He lifts the two rods and parts them with great care. There's no mirth in his face now. Very much the Stańczyk expression.

From between the cotton cords hanging from the broom handles, which he lifts and extends, emerges a long, slithering shape, a dazzling moray eel, five metres long and massive, spreading outwards in glassy iridescence, moving directly for the little girl who backs away from it, stopped by a lifeboat at the end of the deck. The gigantic bubble makes contact—bursts over the girl in a glittering sprinkle of droplets.

"My name's Kurt Greener." The chatty man has sat next to Katerina on the bench. He's having another one of his quick cigarettes. Pulls up the collar on his pea coat and shrugs when he sees that she continues to hold her silence. He is gaunt, with a cancerous emaciation about him. Robust and quick enough in gesture. The kind of fellow who gets all his nutrition from coffee and cigarettes. Smiles. A wide diastema at the front of his yellow teeth.

They watch the jester make more giant, elongated shapes with his bubble wands. Many of them burst instantly and he soon leaves. They are pretty enough but there are many merriments and entertainments on the ship tonight. Some passengers are going below decks for dinner and some are retiring to their cabins to get dressed in evening wear or costumes. Fewer and fewer passengers wander the decks. Kurt Greener blows warm air onto his bare hands and shivers. He is hatless and his thinning grey hair offers little protection from the evening ocean breeze. He tries to light another cigarette. It's become too windy for his matches.

"This time of year can be awful. A storm came close to sinking *Aquitania* in 1930. Mountain-high waves tumbling down, destroying the windows and portholes everywhere, even the captain's bridge at the very top over there." He nods in the direction of the bridge. "Eighty-foot waves for twenty-two hours. Can you imagine such a thing? Rooms and decks were flooded with seawater and broken glass. And then there's the kind of crossing where not a ripple is felt through the ship for the entire duration."

Kurt Greener wiggles his pinkie in a hole he has found in the wooden backrest they're leaning on. It's an odd place for a hole to have been drilled. No carved letters as she's seen on other benches.

"Twenty-two calibre, I'd say." Kurt Greener has bent over to look at the hole and is very near Katerina. "Would have been close range."

"Maybe a cowboy from the last time they celebrated New Year's on this ship," she says, smiling and leaning away from Kurt Greener. Eyelids flickering as another swell of opium moves through her brain. "You should leave before the Keystone Cops come back around. And I have an idea for a costume, so I should leave as well." Standing isn't easy. She'd rather close her eyes and listen to the harmonium player. Realises he's gone and there's no more music. Surprised she didn't notice it stop.

"Would have been from the war. Well, not much chance anyone fired on the boat deck outside of the war, so that's not a genius supposition. There would have been more bullet holes around the ship but the refitters must have missed this one. Neat. As clean as a drillhole. Didn't flake or splinter the wood."

"Didn't flake or splinter," she murmurs. Soon he'll let her close her eyes and drift away again.

"Are you feeling seasick?" he asks and comes near enough that she can feel his breath on her face. She had closed her eyes. She blinks them open now.

"No, I'm not seasick. A bit light-headed. It's been a very long day already and it's only dinnertime. I should eat. I think I'm hungry."

"You can lie down before dinner. Have a little rest. Would you like me to help you to your cabin?"

"No, I'll be OK."

The man's face is as close as the Keystone Cop looking through the keyhole of her eye, yet Greener is not looking for truth. "You're warm in that fur. Perhaps a little too snug." His breath makes her feel nauseous. So near she can't focus on his face.

"I need some air. Need to breathe. I'll be all right. Give me space, please. Get away from me!"

"Oh, you would fit me like a calfskin glove," he says. He has lifted the earflap of her ushanka, and his lips are pressed into her ear, his face moving in her hair like a pig searching out a truffle. "My sweet girl. You would be so warm and snug."

His right hand pushes through the two sable folds of the long coat she is wearing, a loose button easily torn away. Katerina has leaned her head backwards to breathe. She gasps as the cold hand finds her breast. She can feel his fingernails against her chest as he pushes.

He shifts above her, a knee over her hips, opening his mouth wide enough to cover both her nose and mouth because she is moving, needing air, wanting a moment to refute Kurt Greener. Surprised that it is beyond her will already. She feels him pressing his groin into her thigh, his erection barely detectable through his pants. It is the insistence of a splinter to be buried in flesh.

He has moved her fur out of the way and she takes a couple

of deep breaths through her nose. Another few moments and Kurt Greener might resolve his desire in his own pants, grinding against fabric, while his hands reach down looking to feel the warmth of her body with his fingers, seeking her cunt with his sallow fingernails, his desire making him tremble.

Fear rises through her body, threatening to become a storm. She does not let it sweep her away. Knows she will find a place in her mind where she can be sharp and clear and cold.

This is not a monster looking to drive the annihilating violence of his sex into her. This is a lonely, declining man, weaker and more pathetic year by year, rattling the gates of a garden that will never again allow him admittance.

Pointless to scream. The scream would be part of the pleasure for him. His left hand has come up to cover her mouth. Finds there is no sound to suppress. No fight to subdue. Instead his fingers find rose-petal lips ready to part at his touch. That she would suck his thumb as though to taste a sweetness in him. And she would then take his cock into her mouth as well. So he is whispering rapidly, "We must find another place, all of what I want can't happen here and now, we'll find a place where we can indulge ourselves, free ourselves, let's find a place, dear, sweet girl."

He hasn't said as much as he intended, breathing out his words in a rush, feeling himself already near ejaculation. Kurt Greener then finds that her rose-petal lips are a camouflage for a beast's jaws. Animal teeth that bite down to the bone in his thumb. Grind down above the joint. Grind down near the knuckle. And her head jerks side to side, hauling away from him, from his wrist. Her savage teeth cracking the bone as if to suck out the marrow.

❖❖❖❖❖

A gentleman carrying a cane and whistling "A-Tisket, A-Tasket" walks towards Katerina. He bumps into the wall of the corridor as he passes. A bungled attempt to doff his hat. Likely he's wearing the silk topper with its crimson grosgrain ribbon for the first time.

He doesn't delay Katerina with conversation. An early drunk, murmuring his embarrassment. Lurching forward. A clumsy twirl of his cane as he attempts to recover his nonchalant progress along the corridor. She's grateful that he stumbled into the wall and not into her. Heavy, broad, and well over six foot tall—a shoulder bump from him would have sent Katerina sprawling to the floor.

When leaving the water closet on this corridor, he struggled to coordinate closing the door with the cane and the top hat in his hands. He's too tall to walk through doorways wearing the hat. Hair plastered to his head with perspiration. Sweat beading on his face as he walks. Whistling the Ella Fitzgerald tune to appear unflustered.

Always ridiculous when drunks pretend to be sober, Katerina thinks as she strides to the door of the water closet—relieved that she need not see anyone else before she can wash her face and look in a mirror. She kept to the shadows while on the boat deck and moved with her head down, hair veiling her face, through two overly bright corridors.

Her ushanka is up on the deck, wherever it fell. She isn't going back for it. She only barely remembered to grab the handbag. Darting away before the questions came. Leaving that son of a bitch to explain his wailing to the gathering passengers and crew, as wordless as the jester, jittering and hopping from foot to foot. She smiled when she left the boat deck.

Katerina imagines a red-toothed grin. She finds a handkerchief in the handbag to clean her face and smother that gleeful ghoul. She needs to settle herself. Is desperate to wash out her mouth before she speaks to another person on the ship. She doesn't feel nauseous yet she might make herself vomit anyway. The thought of having Greener's blood in her stomach is sickening.

She locks the door to the bathroom behind her. Flicks the light switch. Illumination is not instantaneous. There's a gradual increase of electrical current until it's too bright in the room. A dripping washbasin outside a single stall. Cologne fills her nose. The gentleman with the cane left the same displeasing smell in his wake along the corridor. The vent above is quietly buzzing and there's a hum in the light fixture above the basin.

The toilet door isn't fully shut. She has already taken off the fur and thrown it onto a chair next to the bathroom door, so eager is she for soap and water, when she realises that she's not alone. She can hear the sole of a shoe sliding across the floorboards.

Too late to put Anne's sable back on and look for another bathroom. Her cabin is two decks down and there would be too many people along the way. Fellows like the one she just passed in the corridor, or Kurt Greener. Almost as bad would be bumping into Querida and Allegralita. How would she explain? She can't understand it herself.

A sense of ferocity had gone through her when she sent a porter tumbling to the ground after leaving the Argentines' cabin. And now an exhilaration she doesn't want to feel, coursing like panic from the centre of her chest to the tips of her fingers and toes. She winds her hair around her arm to form a cord and ties that into a loose knot at the back of her neck. She won't look at the reflection in the mirror.

She runs the hot water into the basin after fitting the plug into the drain. A minimal turn of the cold tap. She sucks the almost scalding water into her mouth and spits it out. "Rinse and spit, rinse and spit," Audrius would say when she was a child learning to brush her teeth. She washes her face with the hot water and the small circle of scentless soap that gives her no foam.

The door to the stall closes. It doesn't lock. After a few seconds it swings ajar again, not enough to see the person inside. She stops and listens. She can hear the occupant inhale sharply.

Greener's saliva on her face, around her nose and mouth, from that smothering kiss. Leaning back for air. Roused from an opium daze and wanting another moment to take in air. She breathes deeply, face up towards the vent. His tobacco-stained thumb between her teeth and on her tongue, worse than the notion of swallowing blood. Not the first time today either. A nosebleed like the one she had with Blackshaw always comes with a tablespoon of blood. She soaps her clean fingers and uses them on her tongue. Doesn't make herself vomit. She might have done that over the toilet bowl. Not the basin. And not with someone liable to leave the stall at any moment. She pulls the chain fastened to the plug and waits for the water to run down the drain. A slow pink swirl down clogged plumbing.

She looks into the mirror, sees her face is fever red. Eyes swollen, the right worse than the left one, as though she's been crying. She murmurs to her reflection that it's all the rubbing and the hot water. She turns the cold tap on and rinses again without the plug. Washes her face with a gasping chill of water.

Flakes of ice swirl down the slow drain. It reminds her how the ship has trouble this time of year with water pipes freezing and bursting. The Atlantic in winter—must be rushing just beyond the wall of this bathroom. She leans towards the wall to hear it through the plates of *Aquitania*'s hull.

A shuffling noise in the stall. And a groan that is quickly subdued.

Katerina dries her face with the roller towel on the wall, which is already damp from previous passengers using this bathroom. Normally she'd be repulsed by a public handtowel, wet from use. She closes her eyes, brings the damp fabric up to her face and rubs at her nose and her eyes and her mouth and her chin.

She decides she will leave the sable here. Her feet are overly warm in the valenki. And they look ridiculous along the glittering corridors adorned with festive decorations, especially as more and more people are dressed for the evening. The front of the long coat will have soaked up droplets of Greener's blood. She goes back to the mirror to look at her shirt. Still clean, if a little wrinkled. Missing a button. Not a problem for Katerina, Anne would point out with a chuckle.

Anne has often told Katerina that by the age of sixteen she would have been able to breastfeed a fat baby on each breast— breakfast, lunch and dinner. She says this when Katerina is naked. Laughs, though she's said it many times before, as she tells her daughter that she, poor girl, would barely be able to feed one starving kitten a saucer of milk.

When she looks in the mirror again it's only aspects of her father she sees. None of her mother's voluptuousness. Anne is a blonde, peroxide-assisted from her twenties on. She says Katerina has Indian hair. And her father's height, his athletic build. A strapping man until a fall from a horse ruined his back. Anne tells her she has an olive complexion. She isn't as rosy as Anne, but she understands "olive complexion" to mean that Katerina would always be fundamentally foreign to her mother.

Katerina turns to the bathroom door. She reaches out a hand to unlock it, is startled by a forceful knock before she does. The handle rattles in her fingers. Another vigorous rap on the door. Beyond the wood she can hear a sonorous voice say, "God-fucking-damn it!"

"I'm hoping, Miss, that you might want to keep that door locked. If only for another few minutes." An Irish accent from within the toilet stall.

She turns to the voice. "Hello?"

"Hello." It's a boy's voice. "I'm not able to do more than talk. Might have been hiding but that's on account of fear. Not being rude."

"Why are you afraid?" she asks. Takes a step closer to the stall.

"That's a story, Miss." The voice trembles. "Doubt you're in the mood for a story through a toilet door."

"I could get you help." She steps back and turns. There's no reply. She leans down and can see a crumpled body on the floorboards through the narrow gap between the toilet door and the deck. "Do you want me to get help?"

"Might you stay for a few minutes? Awful being alone in

this room." She hears a movement within the stall and a groan. "Please leave the light on if you must go."

"Someone else will come along soon." Katerina decides against leaving the fur behind. A few drops of blood are as unremarkable as a nosebleed. She turns it inside out and unlocks the bathroom door. "Someone else will know what to do with you."

"That very thing worries me, Miss." He talks haltingly and has a bad lisp. It's a speech impediment that makes Katerina lean forward and listen carefully to make out his words. "The knocking on the door before, and that hard voice that followed, all put a stamping monster of fear into my heart."

"Are you afraid of someone?"

"Anxious that he'll come back, Miss," he says, speaking as though Katerina were a teacher or an elder who required his best language before she'd treat him kindly.

"Who are you afraid of?"

The boy doesn't answer. She waits. Hears him moan and move again. She leans to the side and can see the worn-out sole of his shoe and his sockless ankle around the edge of the door. The Irish lad is cowering on the floor of the toilet.

"The gentleman with the cane?" she asks.

"Nothing gentle in that man. Brutal. Purely brutal," he says.

Katerina has her hand on the bathroom door, ready to leave. For the last few minutes she has felt Greener diminishing to a small thought. Flittering around this small room, easy enough to ignore because of this odd conversation with a boy in a toilet stall. Beyond the bathroom door there is a broken hive of thoughts waiting to swarm her as soon as she steps into the corridor. The opium has evaporated to nothing since the boat deck.

"Excuse me," she says. He's murmured words that she can't decipher. His speech impediment is getting worse. "Can you speak more clearly?"

"Don't turn off the light, Miss," he says. Easier to understand now. Not so much a lisp as the thick tongue a slow child might have.

"OK. I'll leave the light on," she says. Doesn't move.

She takes her fingers off the handle and checks that the door is locked.

"The dapper fellow with the cane is on his way to a ballroom. I'm sure he's meeting a sweetheart. He's dressed for a great celebration. You can still smell his enthusiasm in this room—cologne he must have bought from a pedlar on the wharves. So there's little chance he'll return. Likely it won't be long before he's collapsed from drink. Little reason for you to worry."

There's no response. She listens to the noise he makes as he tries to move to a more comfortable slump on the floor.

"Did he do something to you?" She can hear the heels of his shoes on the floorboards. Weak, ineffectual movements.

"What happened?" she asks. "I saw him leave the bathroom. Whistling, bumbling along, twirling his cane. Appeared to be one of those fellows the English call a jolly giant. Certainly not the type of chap to inspire panic."

"Thanks for taking the time, Miss. Talking is a good distraction from pain. Even when it causes pain." He stops. A rasp in his breathing. "All I ask is that you leave the light on when you go. Without the light I feel everything inside me grow. Becomes as big as a nightmare."

"Don't know what I can do for you," she says. "So I'll go. Is that all right?"

"Wonder if you know any sweet words, Miss?" She has no idea what he wants. Does the Irish lad have lewd hopes as did Kurt Greener?

"Sweet words?" With a harsher tone she asks, "What are you talking about? What do you want?"

"My ma was a tough lady. Had the sharpest tongue in the world but she had a way of finding the sweetest words when you was desperate to hear 'em. Like in the middle of the night, if you couldn't break out of a nightmare. She'd always have something sweet to put into your mind instead."

"A method for breaking out of nightmares sounds lovely. But I don't have anything to help you. I wish I did." She could point out that it wasn't a magic formula anyone might provide him if they were generous enough—that he was a son, and the woman who spoke to him in the dark crisis of a bad night was his mother.

She looks at the toilet door. He's quiet. The taste of poison is all she can find in her mouth. *We will drink our oblivion from cut crystal.* Anne sang those words like a lullaby in her letter to Katerina. Was the boy calling out for his mother, as many children do when they are in pain? When he asked for sweet words, was that his silent wish?

She opens the handbag. It's occurred to her that Anne carries a toothbrush and a thin tube of toothpaste in a silver travelling container. She digs around, pushing aside reading glasses and sunglasses in their cases, rummaging among hairclips and barrettes, blank *Aquitania* postcards, safety pins, a purse and travel papers, a clean floral handkerchief, notebooks and pencils, an unopened deck of playing cards, black, grey and white spools of cotton with needles stuck in their sides, coins from different countries at the bottom of the bag, two hairbrushes dense with Anne's hair, the letters from Kornél, an array of cosmetics and even a posy of lavender.

It's only when she has the toothbrush and toothpaste in her hand that Katerina understands she can't brush her teeth. She blinks her eyes in disbelief. What a callous act that would be! To brush her teeth while the Irish lad lies crumpled on the floor of a public toilet.

Wouldn't there be the usual droplets of urine, dry and fresh, from *Aquitania*'s male passengers standing above the bowl of the toilet, shaking their flaccid dicks dry? He wouldn't be lying down across that sticky awfulness if he had the choice of getting to his feet.

She looks at the door again. Wants to give him a few sweet words. Beads of dried paint line the top of the door. She has an impulse to run her fingertips over the beads as though reading a message in braille.

She imagines a jar of fireflies beside the boy's bed at home. On a nightstand near his pillow. When they faded they were nothing more than a small heap of dead black insects. Some evenings his mother would catch him a jar full of bright fireflies. And then his dreams would fill his soul with flashing angels. An agreeable little image she might work into a poem in her next letter to Kornél. Come the groggy morning, the boy wouldn't notice that the shrivelled black remnants in the jar were nothing but burned matchsticks.

"An emperor of Rome once wrote a poem." Shortly before he died. No need to mention that detail. "It's sweet. To me, it is—not sure you'll find it sweet," she says. The Irish lad doesn't speak. He attempts another movement and moans at the effort.

"His name was Hadrian. Do you want to hear his poem?"

"If you know the emperor's poem by heart, Miss. Yes, I would."

A passenger rattles the door handle from the corridor without knocking. Katerina waits to see if there will be another attempt on the door before speaking.

"Dear little soul,
Why wilt thou roam?
Long has thou found
In me a home.
Numb, pale, and naked, whither fly
From my companionship, and why?
Thy merry jests no more shall ring—
And must thou leave me, little thing?"

No response from the boy. She's been intending to write Kornél a letter but it's now clear to her it is a foolish idea. She'd see her brother before *Aquitania*'s mail could be received. A telegraph is the only practical way to deliver the dreadful news. Kornél will have to find Audrius. Despite Blackshaw's optimistic prognosis, immediate arrangements for Anne will need to be made in France.

"I could listen to your voice forever, Miss."

"I'm going to have to go. I need to see my mother. She's fallen ill. And I've left her down in the belly of the ship the whole day. Didn't mean to be so long from her side. When I get down to the ward I will send Doctor Blackshaw up to you. And there's a pretty nurse called Flora you might meet soon."

Katerina raises her hand to her mouth and closes her eyes. Kurt Greener would no doubt be down there, getting his thumb sewn back on by Doctor Blackshaw. She squeezes her cheeks until she can feel the ridges of her teeth through the flesh—the way she saw the woman do to her child over lunch today to stop him from giggling.

"Would you have a cigarette, I wonder, Miss? Before you go." It takes her a moment to work out what he's said. His speech impediment has grown worse.

"I'll leave you the packet. I'm not much of a smoker." She opens the handbag again and finds Anne's cigarettes and her lighter. She intends on tossing them into the stall. When she moves closer she nudges the door open enough for her to see the boy's broken body spread across the floor. She moves in further to see his face.

"Brutal. Purely brutal," she says. "You're not wrong about that."

She lights a cigarette and passes it to the Irish lad. He's barely able to reach up an arm to take it.

"Doubt you could light one for yourself," she says.

"You'd be right, Miss." Twelve years old, fourteen at the most, yet he smokes as though there're few pleasures in life sweeter than tobacco. The cigarette stays between his lips at the corner of his mouth. An ash cylinder grows and crumbles onto his neck.

"I want to get cleaned up before I go back to my cabin. My da and brothers will be waiting for me. They'd be stunned to see me in this ragged condition."

"They would be horrified. It's distressing even for me and I don't know you."

"But I've seen you, Miss. Perhaps you've seen me in the corridors. You and your mother have stepped around our marbles. Your mother was never happy to see us. Maybe she wouldn't be distressed by how I look. She'd say good riddance."

"I saw your friends on the boat deck not long ago."

He smokes the cigarette down to the ember and spits it out when it's too hot. It sticks to his lip and Katerina is quick to take it away from the boy before it burns him.

"Sorry to hear your ma has taken ill," he says. "She looked to be in fierce health. Mine didn't last long when she went into the hospital. Doctor Rawson said it'd been eating her up for years, so when she went to the hospital it was the last bit of her to go."

There's a knock on the bathroom door. A woman's voice asks whether the lavatory will be free soon. Katerina tells her, "Sorry, the bathroom is engaged." The woman asks her to hurry up, please. The last word is heavy with petulance. Katerina tells the impatient bitch to fuck off and find another goddamn lavatory.

"Easy to be rude through a locked door," she tells the Irish lad. He attempts to return her smile. It's such a sad expression she wants to apologise for provoking it.

"Do you think the fireworks will be going off soon?"

"Fireworks?" she asks.

"Should be a wondrous event, Miss. My favourite thing in the world is a fireworks show. When they're right above your head you can lie down on the ground and it's like all the stars are shooting and exploding at once. I have a place picked out on the sun deck for a clear view."

"Maybe they should call it a moon deck when it's night-time," she says.

Katerina has not forgotten the fireworks. She asked her question because it surprised her that the boy still thought he had a chance of seeing the fireworks tonight. The same type of impossible thought he had when he asked whether he might be cleaned up for his father and brothers. As if he'd had a spill on the playground. That he might be dusted off and sent on his way with a few bruises.

"The fireworks aren't going to be lit for another hour, I'd say. I'm not sure of the time. My watch is in cargo with the rest of our things. I never need my watch when I'm with my mother. She wears a wristwatch and keeps the day to a strict schedule. I'm rarely wondering what the time is before I'm being told to hurry up because we're due for breakfast or dinner, a walk, or a visit to the library. I can't imagine her watch has been of much use to her today." She stops at an image of her mother trying to see out of her one good eye—glasses in the handbag. "Time becomes different when you're hurt or ill."

"Good that we have another hour to get up to the sun deck—the *moon* deck. I'll just need another few minutes to catch my breath," he mutters through his ruined teeth.

"My name's Katerina," she tells the boy after a long silence. "Call me Kate."

"You can call me Farrar, if you ever have a need to call me."

"I have a clean handkerchief. You can keep it. Use it for your mouth. You're bleeding."

"Yes, you shan't want it back after I use it." He reaches up as far as he can, Katerina leans down and places it in his hand.

"Much appreciated, thank you," he says, barely intelligible.

He sits up a little, slides down again when the new position brings on too much pain. He lifts the floral handkerchief to his nose instead of his mouth and then his eyes, to take in its lavender smell and to feel the softness of the fabric. He is soon crying into the cloth.

Katerina waits. She puts the half-finished pack of cigarettes and the lighter beside him. His paddy cap has not quite come off his head but it's badly askew. She adjusts it for him without moving his head too much.

"I've lost some teeth. I don't want to feel around yet to find out how many are gone. I might have swallowed a couple."

"I think you might have a few broken bones as well."

"My ribs. It's not easy breathing, especially when I try to sit up. And there's a hot tingling in my feet I wish would stop. I think I will need to see Doctor Shaw. Or perhaps you could send Flora."

"I have something for pain in my handbag."

He moves and winces at the effort.

"You're already in the right position to use this. Hold the pipe bowl over the lamp. Inhale the vapour as deeply as you can." She helps him hold the pipe steady. "The pain will go away quickly. Like moving from a bad dream to a good dream in a breath." It's difficult for him to take deep inhalations. Katerina sucks in the last puffs of the opium for herself.

There's space in the stall for a narrow shelf for parents to change their infants. She sits down on the floor opposite. Far enough from the toilet not to touch the scattershot of urine with the backs of her legs. After two or three minutes he has stopped sobbing and his face has become placid.

"When I was a baby …" Farrar begins but the opium

sweeps his memory away. Katerina nods at him as though he's told her an entire story.

"When I was a baby my parents put me in a suitcase," she tells him. "They took me out only when they needed to add something personal to the next furnished house they moved into for a few months, or the next embassy rooms they might occupy for a year or two. When they were ready to leave for the next city, often on another continent, they would put me back into that suitcase for a few months. Unpack me when we arrived. Or maybe a few months later, when they were ready to have a child again. The inside of a suitcase was like a second womb I could return to, and sometimes even when I was let out, I would return to my suitcase to rest. To be lost and forgotten for a while. They would need me for official dinners, so they would put the suitcase on top of the wardrobe and dress me up in royal clothes, and call me their darling princess, and then present me to real princesses, to real royalty. I never knew what to say to those esteemed girls and women, and I would long to be returned to my suitcase. The grander the ballroom, the more brilliant the lights, the more I would want to crawl away and find my suitcase, away from their gold, diamonds and crystal, all aglitter in the love of the world. And then we would move house again and my mother would let me stay in that suitcase for months. She would close the lid and I would never know what season or what country it would be when she opened it again."

"Would that I could," Farrar says. A vague thought adrift in a cloud of smoke.

"There was an old king in Africa who understood me. His name was Nxumalo. Different conditions, he said, yet he knew what it was to live in a suitcase. He had lost all his power in a revolution. The revolution buried everyone he loved. The revolution spared him while spilling every drop of royal blood not within his own body. Thousands were massacred in their homes for having his portrait on their walls. The new order let him live to show his subjects how thoroughly royal power had been subdued. A coffin was designed for him and made of ivory, pearl and the finest mahogany, big enough for a king and a queen to be placed together, shoulder to shoulder. They had killed the queen and there would never be another one. The coffin was made only for him. It was richly upholstered in ruffled silks and satin. The new order demanded that he sleep in the royal coffin every night. For months he slept on the cold stone floor instead of the majestic coffin they had made for him and it ruined his back. Every movement had become an agony. Eventually he allowed them to place him into the coffin. He closed his eyes, and when he did, he found the most restful sleep of his entire life. And so Nxumalo began to look forward to his evenings in his elevated coffin. He was 'dead to the world' and found comfort in that phrase. He didn't know a person could rest as deeply as he did when sleeping in his coffin. He found he could remember every dream he had, from beginning to end. And his dreams grew, became epics, as marvellous as mythological sagas. Deeper and deeper he went into sleep and dreams, until he was even able to cut away the anchor to his body. And then Nxumalo was free to travel under the night skies of the entire world, to any point in history or the future—settling upon the breast of a princess who lived in a castle surrounded by ice. As gentle as a caress from a phantom. Or he might visit a queen in a paradise pyramid in the middle of a jungle in the Americas. He crossed oceans so often he knew the waves the way a person might the silhouettes of children in bed at night. Nxumalo was born from generations of African kings and so he felt only royalty would befit him when he travelled the world in this way. These royal women would sense him, and his august blood, when he came to them, and they would welcome him into their dreams, and into their perfumed beds. He could choose the body most welcome to their embraces and the heart sweetest to their desires. There were many queens and duchesses, countesses and princesses he visited, even that most glorious of all women, Helen of Troy, but in the morning he always awoke in his royal coffin, enclosed by ivory, pearl and mahogany, softly enfolded in silk and satin. Oft of a morning his face would be wet with the tears of an aristocratic woman he had left, weeping over his face at his departure. Nxumalo wanted the lid to be hammered down, for his people to let him go, yet they often needed him for ceremonies. Many an evening there was an ambassador or a diplomat or a politician needing to perform a function before the eyes of the king so they might say it was enacted with royal approval, and therefore the will of God. The new order had become nostalgic as its final king grew frailer with age and closer to death. Nxumalo said that I was more fortunate than he because I could spend as much time in my suitcase as I wanted to, that I need never come out at all. He didn't understand that I couldn't travel at will across space and across time, as he could, moving as swiftly as a thought beneath the night sky and across oceans—that I slept in a dead womb living on the paper of books, travelling only where and when an ink-stained notion could offer me transport. We finished dinner at his palace and were alone for hours. My parents had been taken out into the gardens and subsequently returned to the embassy for an ongoing negotiation between our governments. He told me of all his travels, and then he patted my hand with his old bejewelled claw, and whispered that one night, soon, he would die, but it would be a slow passing away. He would take the last moments of his life to travel once more over the lights of the night sky, and he would find me dreaming, and then he would make me his queen and we would lie together in his stately coffin for eternity."

Farrar coughs and blood bubbles from his mouth. He grips the wet rim of the toilet bowl with his left hand. He spits into his right hand and finds one of his teeth in the pink froth. He tells Katerina that only a few years ago he lost all his first teeth and his second teeth all came through. So it hasn't been that long since he got them and now some of them are already gone. Isn't it strange that there will be no more teeth to come? Why can a person make two sets of teeth yet never a third?

Katerina asks Farrar what happened to him. The boy looks into his hand, wipes the blood from his mouth with Anne's floral handkerchief. Farrar has had his two front teeth knocked out, and perhaps a few more she can't see. The dapper gent stomped him with the heel of his boot. Stamped his face and body when he fell to the deck. Before that, the elegantly dressed chap had punched him in the stomach, the chest, and the shoulders and head as Farrar went down. Farrar had never felt full-force blows from an adult. A giant of a man at that. It felt like the massive stone of a crumbling building collapsing in on him. When he closes his eyes he feels as though the rubble is still covering his body and he might suffocate at any moment. He tells Katerina that he has been beaten before in school fights, but when a lad curled up on the ground it meant the fight was over. There might be one or two more kicks if the victor was especially savage yet falling to the ground was a clear surrender. Everyone understood there was nothing more you could do when a lad had given up. The giant in his top hat was not satisfied with outright victory and the punishment he'd already inflicted. He kicked and stomped down on Farrar until his arms and face could not protect him, and then he drove his heel down into his body and face.

Katerina asks why the man was so violent. The Irish lad confesses to Katerina that he's a thief. Farrar steals whatever he can, because it's the only way he's likely to ever have anything at all. That's no excuse. He wishes he could be humble, find Christian humility, as his mother told him. Farrar never suspected that God's punishment for sin could be so swift and relentless. The boy had come into the unlocked bathroom and found the drunken giant with his pants around his ankles and a cane across his hairy thighs. The top hat askew, about to fall from his head. And there was a gold watch hanging out of his waistcoat, down by a naked hip. Farrar thought he could steal it quite easily. He has quick, dextrous fingers. And the watch was in plain sight. There it was. The pocket watch had a chain, of course, and when Farrar tried to free it he found the clasp was not as easily detached from the chain as he had hoped. The fat fellow slumping over to the side with his idiot mouth half-open woke up, instantly awake or shamming sleep.

The word "thief" was growled from his throat with ferocious hatred, as though it were ranked equally with "murderer" and "rapist". The man's rage was incomprehensible. He was God's angel of annihilation sent to destroy the sin in the boy before it could fully flower. To destroy sin as it came to bud.

Farrar says he wants to get up now. His eyes are fluttering open and shut as he talks. He will be able to walk, he says. She tells him that it's not likely. And not at all necessary. The doctor will come with crew and they can carry him to the infirmary the way they carried her mother this morning. Farrar insists, and struggles to get his feet under him. Katerina might guide him, as though nudging a somnambulist along, down to the ward.

She comes around, hunches beside him, to help Farrar stand. She has her arm around his back and can feel him tense, grappling with the walls of the toilet stall, his legs below him refusing to respond the way they always have before, and then his whole body goes limp as the havoc of damage done to his body forces him unconscious.

She puts the opium pipe back into her handbag and wishes she had more. The tow-headed ukulele player was at the cockroach race taking bets, so perhaps he wouldn't be hard to find. She's had only enough of a taste this time to want to fully lose herself. She'd go back to her cabin and smoke enough to see an end to this dreadful day and when she awoke she'd smoke again so she wouldn't have to think or feel anything until *Aquitania* steamed through the New Year. She had money enough to glide through smoke rings all the way to Calais.

Farrar comes back to consciousness a few moments later, eyes flickering with a smile, as if the world is a pleasant dream drawing him back with an unshakeable embrace. Coughing, and the extreme pain it generates from his broken rib cage, reminds him where he is and what has happened.

Katerina begins humming a song to soothe the boy. It pleases him. He wants to find a way back into the pleasant numbness of the opium. Hums along with her. Murmurs words she can't understand.

"Don't try to talk," she says. "Forget for a while."

"What is a tisket?" He looks earnest. As though there might be some kind of importance in knowing the answer. "What is a tasket?"

He's shivering. She lays the sable coat over him. Tucks some of the long coat around Farrar's head as he continues to hum the Ella Fitzgerald tune.

Katerina has noticed that his clothes are spattered with blood but she can feel the stickiness of semen when she touches him. The fluid had gone clear as it seeped into the rough fabric of his clothes. There is a white drop of ejaculate on the flesh, near his open collar.

The theft of a gold watch probably isn't the only motivation for the beating he's had, if there even was a gold watch. Maybe there was, yet the gold watch would have had to be earned, rather than stolen. There would have been an agreement and then a disagreement.

The whistled tune began out in the corridor, as the dapper gent made his way to a celebration. Farrar goes on with "A-Tisket, A-Tasket" until Katerina tells him to stop humming the song, speaking so loudly in the stall that Farrar agrees with a raised palm. As if she might strike him silent.

She washes her hands at the basin. The small circle of soap doesn't seem to have shrunk for all the use she's made of it. Yields up so little foam she doesn't know that it can clean her hands at all. And then she wonders whether the angel of annihilation, with his top hat on his head, cane placed on the chair by the bathroom door as he cleaned himself up, used the roller towel to dry off his hands after his righteous work.

"Could you tell me the emperor's poem again before you go?" he asks. Katerina shakes her head. The boy already has his eyes shut.

Humming "A-Tisket, A-Tasket" again.

"How did you fare in the race today?" she asks him, to stop the tune as much as to know the answer.

"Was I in a race today, Miss?" Farrar opens his eyes. "I don't know what you mean."

"I'm sure you were one of the Norwich boys on your hands and knees in the corridor. The race with those cockroaches. I recognise your patchwork cap, though otherwise you're all the same to me. Usually I'm just trying to get through your fields of play without becoming a toy for your games."

She closes her eyes and washes her face and then continues to wash her hands in the warm water. She'll have to dry her face with the sleeves of her shirt.

"I wish I could kiss you," Farrar says when she unlocks the bathroom door and pulls it open. No-one is waiting in the corridor. Katerina expected a line of angry passengers.

Farrar would have been on the boat deck as well. Stopping at the first water closet along the way down to the same deck her cabin was on. She considers asking Farrar whether he still has hopes of "seeing fireworks" tonight. It'd be in keeping with the word play he and his fellows enjoy when they talk to Katerina.

He would have been on the boat deck when one of his friends kissed the Mam-zel. Might have been there when

Kurt Greener made his advances. And would have continued to watch with pleasure in different circumstances. Certainly would not have come to her aid.

"What a mess of blood and pain that would be," she says.

"I'm too young anyways," he mumbles into his chest. "I know that."

"Too young." She turns off the light before stepping out into the corridor. "Not for long. Soon you'll be stomping on faces for yourself."

❖❖❖❖❖

No more views of the ocean—the evening has turned the two portholes into discs of black glass. She pulls the curtains across them so she won't have to see herself contorted in the reflections of her cabin.

The bath she requested before going to the Palladian Lounge has been wheeled in while she was out. A wooden bathtub that resembles a large whisky barrel cut in half. The water is shallow and has gone cold. It's fresh water, and that appeals to Katerina, as does the bar of Pears in a wrapper. Soap that should foam easily. And it will be fragrant. A spotless white bathrobe and cream-coloured towels that smell freshly washed are on a towel rail beside the bathtub.

Katerina locks the door. Checks it three times. She puts a chair under the handle to make sure even someone with a key cannot enter.

She places what she's wearing into an *Aquitania* laundry

bag and throws the whole bundle on top of the dusty wardrobe. Pushes it to the back, where it will not be visible, using the ceremonial sword Kornél would have adored wearing at his graduation ceremony. Now it's only useful as a broom handle might be to shove something out of the way. She tosses the unsharpened sword onto Anne's bed.

Katerina has no intention of sending the bag to the laundry. The clothes inside it smell of sweat and seawater, bad cologne and opium. Her stockings are a dark grey and her skirt is black—she chose not to search them for stains. Easier to get rid of everything that makes her think of Greener or Farrar. She'd have incinerated the clothes if she were back at the embassy.

There is a bowl of chocolate coins on the dresser, colourful foil bright under the lamplight. The porter she'd shoved to the ground must have wanted to make amends for his rudeness because there's also a small vase with pink and purple paper carnations beside an unopened bottle of Drene shampoo.

She washes her hair first and then steps into the foamy water. The tub is uncomfortably cool at room temperature but she finds herself enjoying it within minutes and soon drifts away in the bath as though she's in a steamy hotel bathroom.

She'd spent minutes, petrified, at the windows overlooking the traffic moving down Paseo de la Reforma. Durrant had kicked off his shoes and lain down on the bed. He didn't call her over. Didn't ask her to "get comfortable" or demand they satisfy an agreement. He asked her if she was hungry and she told him the menu sounded wonderful but she didn't have an appetite. He let her stand at the window as if all she wanted was to escape the heat of the tram and she was mesmerised by the view of the city. Durrant took off his clothes behind her and she could only just see the pale reflection of his naked body behind her own indistinct form in the broad hotel window. Yet he still didn't move towards her or ask her to remove her clothes.

They'd already kissed in the elevator and he'd crushed her against the panelled wall as they rose to the top of the hotel—surprised he'd released her when the tinkle of the elevator announced their floor. A delicate sound after the muffled roar of his lust against her body. She followed him down the hallway with dizzy steps, quietly counting down the room numbers to their door with a jubilant dread.

He said he would take a bath and she could join him or she could leave; that he knew how young she was. She'd told him she was nineteen years old so that wasn't true. He'd made it clear Katerina could freely choose what she wanted, and when she felt that choice offered to her again, she decided she did want to be the woman in the reflection of the glass. She dropped her clothes to the luxurious carpet around her and became translucent—thick veins of traffic driving oil-stained life through the stone and steel heart of Mexico.

Katerina hears rolling explosions firing in the distance and tries to ignore them. She is desperate for sleep. The din wakes her enough to make her realise she has been in a contorted shape within the whisky barrel bathtub. She is naked and shivering, hair soaking wet and cold across her face, wrapped about her neck. For the brief time she was asleep she'd tried to squirm below the water level as though trying to get underneath a warm blanket in bed. The explosions do not stop after a few seconds. Detonations peter out into occasional bursts and suddenly build to a crescendo, gathering up a violence of noise in one long eruption.

When her teeth start chattering she shakes herself awake. She keeps her eyes closed as she stands up and steps out of the bath onto the dusty floorboards. Dries herself with the towel; wraps it around her head. Puts on the bathrobe and collapses onto her bed. Lower than she remembered, so she bounces awkwardly. Durrant would have seen how young she was in that silly, ungainly mistake.

Katerina is ready for sleep to come as a total oblivion. Unavoidable in the bath and coy when she is in bed. A constant trickle of adrenaline keeps her on the surface of her mind; not asleep and not conscious. An agonisingly slow movement of time that feels like the ever-restless pull of tides in an eternal oceanic night.

I have come to the borders of sleep,
The unfathomable deep.

Only the first two lines remembered from a poem she once knew by heart.

Notes of jazz come through the cabin door. The music moves closer and becomes more distinct until she can identify Louis Armstrong's version of "When the Saints Go Marching In". She goes to the keyhole to have a look. Opens the door a few centimetres to see a New Orleans marching band passing by her door. Four men in blackface playing a trumpet, a clarinet, a trombone and a banjo amble along, followed by singing passengers carrying bottles of champagne and saucer glasses above their heads.

Its silence I hear and obey
That I may lose my way
And myself.

A few more fragments of rhyme from a poem by Edward Thomas.

Katerina returns from the door and sits at the dresser. Picks out one of the bronze chocolate coins. The bowl would have been enough for two people to enjoy for the rest of the voyage. She sits at the dresser. Sleep is going to be impossible tonight. She peels every coin until she has a stomach full of chocolate.

The porter was lovely despite her anger and petulance. He'd not been rude enough to deserve being shoved to the ground. She did not intend to hurt him; she wouldn't have thought to do such a thing. He'd already been off balance and the push was a burst of anger that caught both of them unawares. There is no reason to feel regretful—it occurs to Katerina that the porter no doubt discovered that while the Klovas are travelling modestly, they are an ambassadorial family. And that it might not be in a porter's interests to offend passengers of influence.

The message Anne sent through Flora is sitting near the jadeite lamp. During the day Katerina thought her mother was unconscious, sleeping or sedated, and that her presence in the infirmary wouldn't be of any benefit, yet that message is a clear indication that Anne has been awake and conscious. Beyond the go/stop code, what is also clear is the summons. Anne has been waiting for hours now for her daughter to come and give her solace.

Katerina stands up and begins to dress herself to leave the cabin. She will be required to help her mother return through the ship's celebrations, back to a cabin which feels small with only one person in it. The first thing Anne will do is ask Katerina how she enjoyed her bath. And then how she enjoyed her day freewheeling about an ocean liner.

Katerina has to think of a way to explain her absence to her mother. It didn't feel awful as time passed but it will clearly be unforgivable when Anne stands in this room again with an endless series of questions, accusations, threats.

This cabin will become a cell again. The two porthole windows, black with the lightless sea, will keep them small and deformed in the contorted reflections they make even behind the curtain.

There's a knock on the cabin door. A gentle tapping as though Katerina might not answer it if she isn't in the mood for a visitor. She is almost dressed for the evening. Needs only to lace up the boots that go with the Saint-Cyr uniform.

She stands and looks in the mirror. Lifts her face. Raises the revolver.

More knocking on her door, as if the person in the corridor is searching for a melody through the wood.

Katerina points the revolver at the reflection in the oval mirror above the dressing table. Moves the gun barrel to the door, to the persistent knocking.

The boots are too big but the rest of the uniform fits well enough. *Klova* is embroidered on the chest so she will be able to say it belongs to her as much as her brother. Especially now that Kornél will not be able to use it.

She feels the spring of the trigger. Difficult to resist the temptation to pull it back. The revolver produces a heavy click and she sees herself grimacing like a soldier in a war film. Katerina moves the chair away—unlocks and opens the door.

"Oh, hello. I'd given up hope." He's walked down the corridor. Turns back when he sees her emerging from the cabin. "Thought you must have gone off celebrating." He's wearing a mask yet she recognises the midshipman's voice; can't remember his name for the moment.

Katerina notices a piece of paper at her feet.

"Hi," he says, with a smile that looks silly with his Phantom of the Opera costume.

"Hi," she replies, picking up a page that has been torn out of a Bible.

"Should I salute you, Sir?" He has an admirable snap to the movement.

"Did you put this under my door?" she asks, holding up another page from the Book of Job.

Let that day be darkness; let not God regard it from above.

"I didn't put anything under your door," he says. "What is it?"

Let a cloud dwell upon it; let the blackness of the day terrify it.

"I'm only guilty of knocking incessantly." Smiling behind his half-mask again. He has his hands up, as if under arrest. She's holding the revolver in her hand. She lifts the weapon to his chest. Pulls the trigger to hear the metal click. The stewards had taken the bullets when Anne and Katerina boarded.

"Erik is dead," she tells him.

"What?" he says after staggering back from his bullet wound. Suddenly so sincere it makes Katerina laugh. "Who's Erik?"

"You are?" She returns the revolver to the holster. "You're Erik."

"I don't understand," he says, lifting the mask from his face as if she might be mistaking him for another man.

"The Phantom's name is Erik." She crosses her eyes at him.

"I've only seen the posters," he says through a wince.

"It was a book first," she tells him.

"Yes, of course." He slaps himself on the forehead. His mask falls from his head and he scrambles to pick it up, delighted to play the fool for Katerina. "Must learn how to read one of these days. I know you're bookish. You could teach me."

"This wasn't here when I came back in tonight." Another passage circled in thick pencil.

As for the night, let the darkness seize upon it, let it not be joined unto the days of the year, let it not come into the number of the months.

She crumples the paper without reading all of it. "Or I might have missed it." Remembering the state she was in when she returned from the boat deck. "That's certainly possible." She steps back into her cabin.

"I had hoped you'd find this costume dashing. Wasn't cheap either, but you've put me to shame, Kitty. Very handsome in a French uniform." He tips his hat to Katerina, then drops his head, pretending that he's chagrined.

"Wait there," she tells him. Cypress, she now recalls, though she's still not sure what his first name is. A name he's not fond of. They'd agreed to use each other's surnames but he heard Blackshaw call her Kitty in the restaurant.

"The mask was the thing about this costume. Fraternising with the guests isn't allowed. I'd lose my job. I thought maybe they wouldn't recognise me as the Phantom of the Opera." He lowers the mask again, and pulls his cape about his shoulders dramatically.

"OK, but that's about the worst fellow a girl could imagine knocking at her door. You should know that before we go promenading."

"Just as well you're not a girl then, Monsieur."

The handbag will stay in the cabin. Katerina can't carry it around wearing the uniform. She removes Kornél's letters and places them in an inside pocket of the jacket. Looks around, wondering what else she should bring with her. Lifts her arms and lets her palms drop to her hips. She puts the peaked cap on her head. She'd planned on pinning her hair up but doesn't want to do that with Cypress in her doorway so leaves it loose around her shoulders and down her back. Katerina locks the cabin door and rattles the handle to make sure.

The corridor is busy with passengers walking along slowly or stopping to talk, wishing strangers a happy New Year. The Norwich boys scamper up the corridors dressed as ghosts. The cheapest, easiest costumes they could make. Holes cut in sheets. Their singing is outrageously clamorous. They bump into a group of aged passengers as though the boys can't see where they're going in their sheets. They sing "We're Off to See the Wizard" before crashing and merrily dance away from the pain they've inflicted, singing "Ding Dong! The Witch Is Dead". Katerina has little doubt they've done it before and will do it again. The Norwich boys will send passengers tumbling to the floorboards if they can manage it.

She left the ceremonial sword behind on Anne's bed and considers going back for it. Even blunt it might be useful. Not only for the ghosts having their fun. There are other men like Greener out and about tonight, and there are those not as chatty or as weak as he is.

She notices that the Argentines' cabin is wide open. No-one in the room from what she can see. Strange that Querida and Allegralita wouldn't keep it locked, whether they'd decided to stay in or not.

"The last time I saw you standing outside an open cabin there was a dead man inside it. What's happening over there?" She nods to the door opposite.

"I have no idea, Kitty. I've come for you. I wanted to see if you felt like dancing tonight."

"Haven't we already agreed to call each other by our surnames? You can call me Kate or Katerina but I'm not a little fucking cat." She wants to swear in a manner suited to men talking in boisterous camaraderie—real anger escapes in her voice.

"OK." He's gritting his teeth in another wince. Nods. Shrugs. "What about Four Leaf, as a nickname?"

"No," she says. Can't help smiling. "Isn't it a bit late to come calling?"

"I was first here hours ago. I've come by more than once. It's not a flattering image of me—haunting the corridor outside your door."

"And yet appropriate for a Phantom."

"Yes," he says and lowers the mask, ominously. Then with a jaunty expression raises it to keep speaking. "I did try to give you up and have a night for myself. Heart wasn't in it. I found myself sad, wandering about, looking for you."

"I won't be dancing tonight," she tells him. She remembers the lovely thing he said about laughter at lunch, about the crystal bell of a soul ringing out. "But your company is most welcome."

"Maybe you won't mind if I dance along by your side if a song is played that sets my feet going in the style of an Irish jig."

"And you don't know why the door to Querida and Allegralita's cabin is open?"

"Open doors everywhere tonight. You might have noticed there's a great celebration ablaze all around us." He begins walking down the corridor. "We might go to the ballroom …" He stops when he notices Katerina is not following him.

"Would you mind having a look in there for me? You're only a Phantom by night." She's seen no movement within the Argentines' cabin in the time she's been talking with Cypress. "Querida and Allegralita are cautious, practical ladies. Not the kind of women to dance about those fires."

"I can have a look but there's little chance I'll be able to pronounce those names." He walks to the open door. This time his knocking is forceful.

"Pardon me, ladies. Please, I do hope you will excuse me." He knocks again before taking a step inside. "I'm one of *Aquitania*'s officers and I do not mean to interrupt your festivities tonight." He walks into the cabin. Returns a half a minute later. Closes the door behind him.

"As I was saying, we could go to the ballroom. There's no reason we'd feel obliged to dance at all. We could watch everyone else having a lovely time and have that joy sweep over us. We need not be set alight."

"Querida and Allegralita are all right then?" she asks as they walk down the corridor.

"I don't know. There was no-one in the cabin."

"So why did they leave their door open?"

"The doors on this ship can be warped from the weather. It's humid down on these decks when we're in tropical waters. I'd guess they forgot to lock the door before going out." He tilts his head away from where he's just been. "I closed the door. So there's no issue. Let's go and see the splendid world frolicking."

"Go ahead. I'll come along soon," Katerina tells him. She places a hand on his chest to assure him. "I will. I'll see you in the ballroom in a few minutes." Katerina walks back, opens the door, and steps into the Argentines' cabin.

❖❖❖❖❖

Katerina's eyes water in the high-noon brightness. All the overhead lights and the many lamps are switched on. She blinks and uses the thick sleeve of Kornél's jacket to dry her eyes. Smells a trace of her mother's perfume in the military embroidery. Anne put care into every thread, using Katerina as a tailor's doll for her brother's uniform. Occasionally a pin would prick her skin yet she enjoyed her mother moving her arms; the way she half-embraced her, a needle between her lips, to move her torso instead of telling her to shift position—so immersed in the process Katerina might have been a moveable upholstered wooden frame.

Katerina blinks—disorientated and overwhelmed by fatigue. "Kitty" was sweet coming from Cypress's mouth. She regrets shooing him away. In this moment she could curl up in a corner like a cat and sleep in a spot of sunshine. No windows this far below the water on *Aquitania*. Sunlight has never found its way down to this deck. There's a grandfather clock beside a closed door that tells her it's a quarter-past one in the morning.

The infirmary reception is unattended. Katerina expected the dim lighting she's seen hospitals employ at night to give their patients the best conditions for sleep. Every chair in the waiting room is occupied. Some are sitting on the floor rug. Passengers that are not in too much pain are trying to sleep. Whenever there is a moan, the rest of the room shushes angrily and loudly—a serpent chorus far more disruptive than any sound of suffering.

Nobody speaks above the most discreet whisper. It strikes Katerina as remarkable that so many people in need of medical attention could be clustered together and yet be so quiet. A few are dressed in costumes. The Red Baron rests his head on the shoulder of a bullet-riddled Dillinger, who checks his wristwatch every five minutes.

Katerina stands at the reception desk. She takes the latest page of the Book of Job from her pocket and reads it twice. Time passes without anyone coming to attend to her or those in the waiting room.

She approaches a fellow sitting on a stool in the corridor leading to the men's ward and asks where the nurses and doctors are, or whether there are any attendants or stewards about. They can talk without the shushing in the waiting room.

He's dressed in a drab suit and tie, a Victoria Cross pinned to his breast pocket. He's playing a game of chess. When he's made a move for white, he turns the board around and considers the move he might make for black. The chess set is on his lap, magnetic pieces on a metallic chequerboard. He's in his socks, shoes beneath the stool. He doesn't respond, even after she says excuse me three times.

She notices that he's been making slight shrugging gestures ever since she started talking to him and he's blinking as though whispered words might have the physical force of hail. There's a trembling in his neck and limbs as he tries to stay focused on his game. Katerina suspects he's doing everything he can simply to keep himself together. Desperately waiting through every minute of the evening for help—and now waiting into the morning.

Further along the corridor there's a prayer room. Passengers have filled this area too. Many have opened Bibles, lips moving noiselessly as they trace fingers across the pages. One or two of them are rocking back and forth with the rhythm of their silent song to God. Katerina can see a modest altar from the arched doorway. She wonders whether there is only the one priest on *Aquitania*. If so, he might emerge at any moment, drunk and with a cigarette in his mouth. She imagines him surprised by the need in this room, walking himself backwards out of the prayer room as he did from Katerina's cabin.

Above and around all of them here in the infirmary, on *Aquitania*'s ten decks, over a thousand passengers are raging ever deeper into their revelries. Katerina has never seen such celebratory ferocity. There's as much desperation as there is happiness in their welcome of 1939. Passengers are dancing along the corridors, singing "Auld Lang Syne" over and again, skipping past those that have fallen to the floor, inebriated and exhausted. Katerina imagines that eventually all of them will stumble and fall, and crew will have to come tend to them in the morning, as though to war wounded.

Katerina walks to the women's ward and pushes open the door with its sign informing her in red letters that there's strictly no admittance to visitors after nine in the evening. The nurses' station is also unattended. The lights have been dimmed here. It makes the quiet and stillness all the more suffocating. Katerina finds the door to her mother's room open. She remembers Flora telling her Anne had been moved when they put her in a straitjacket.

Within the tiny room there's a balding woman with an auburn wig next to her pillow. She's sitting beside the bed in the chair Katerina used this morning. Her forehead in her left hand, her right hand lifting a cup of tea to her lips, sipping. Her ribs and a nipple show through the thin fabric of her nightgown. Her bare legs are shapely, younger than the rest of her.

"Hello, Madame. I'm sorry to bother you."

The woman does not lift her head. Continues to drink her tea.

"Are you bothering me?" she says into her teacup. "I'd be glad to have some company."

"Is there anyone about who can help me? I've come to visit my mother."

"She's bound to be sleeping at this hour."

"My mother's not much of a sleeper."

"I was always a good sleeper. Can't say that's true anymore. My husband envied me. Said listening to me would often lull him back to sleep. Said he could listen to my breathing for hours. Never slept for more than an hour at a time after the Somme."

Katerina lifts her hand to apologise again for the bother, ready to quietly leave the woman to her tea when she laughs and says, "Just as well I wasn't a snorer."

"Her name is Anne Klova. You wouldn't know where they have moved her, would you?" *Aquitania* has all the features of a city, from tennis courts to libraries, so she wonders whether the ship also has a discreet asylum.

"I don't know the name." Intent on drinking her tea. Has trouble swallowing. "Was there a queen with that name? One of Henry's wives?"

Katerina shakes her head and realises the woman has yet to raise her head. "Anne Klova was in this room earlier today," she tells her.

"I'm the occupant now, I'm sorry to say." She puts down the cup to pick up a biscuit. Takes a small bite and chews.

"Where are the nurses? There's no matron or doctor around either."

"I woke up and nobody was about. Don't know where anyone is. I can't help you. Unless you'd like a cup of tea. I made a pot myself." A Canadian accent from the way she pronounces "about". Her head is still in her hand; she's nibbling on the biscuit as though it were sinew in a piece of tough steak.

Katerina glances around the darkened women's ward. Considers opening the closed doors and turning on the lights to find Anne. She could be quick enough that the patients within would barely notice, and yet Katerina would find different kinds of despair and illness within each room. Awful being here as it is. Difficult to resist the urge to scurry away from the torment of this place.

She's already too late to be visiting her mother. Better to go and find Cypress and get swept up in the ship's New Year joy. In the Argentines' room it felt imperative for her to talk with Anne. Not sure now what's vital to the moment. She's struggling to see anything clearly in the radical shifts of light and darkness in this infirmary.

To Cypress, the cabin had looked untidy, the two passengers having left it after preparing for their grand evening. Trying on different dresses and leaving them strewn over beds and chairs. Getting drunk before leaving. There were bottles and glasses on the table and beds, a couple of spills on the rug. The ashtray had been overturned and a lamp had fallen to the ground.

Among the papers on the floor Katerina found one of the Trotsky messages that had been in the cherry-wood box. The envelope was empty but it had Audrius's name on the front, so there was no doubt about it. Katerina couldn't explain what it was doing in the Argentines' room. It is likely that none of the letters had been in the box when she threw it from the sun deck this morning. She hadn't thought to check, yet they must all have been removed beforehand.

Anne has to be told that the response to her go/stop message has changed. Katerina looks around the ward. The clock above the nurses' station tells her it's almost 2 a.m.

"We could share tea while we wait for someone to come help us. I'll need my medicine soon." The woman scratches her thin scalp delicately with her ring finger and pinkie. "My heart is on the fritz. My stomach and nerves have also been giving me trouble. Some nights I do worry I won't find my way through."

"There will be a nurse along at any moment," Katerina assures her.

"The celebrations tonight would keep the nurses and the doctors hopping, if not dancing."

"I'm sure that's what it is—the celebrations," Katerina says, looking up and down the darkened corridor. "It's not a hospital. I suspect their duties are fairly easy to cope with generally. This must be the most hectic night of the year for the ship's medical staff. And maybe this year's party is unusually boisterous." The image Katerina has in mind is of a hive getting louder and noisier until the whole thing is rocking back and forth on its branch.

"Up there it's music and dancing. A whole world smiling and laughing. All I can do is keep a hand on my heart, waiting for it to pop like an old light globe on a cord hanging from the ceiling. Going out. I imagine my chest as a tiny dark room after that. I'm in there, small and quiet and cold, as grey as used coal." She takes a sip of her tea without opening her eyes. She doesn't lift her head to talk to Katerina. "Asleep in my small bed but never waking up again. So I think to myself, Mary, up you get. You're alive yet. Make some tea, dear. A little milk and a little sugar with your tea."

Screwed onto the wall opposite the bed is a tapestry in a large frame. Katerina didn't notice it this morning and it makes her wonder if it is the same room after all. One of *Aquitania*'s many passengers might have left it as a gift to the ward. A sunrise over the sea. The rising sun is at the top of the frame so most of the tapestry is of soothing blue water. Fine work that must have taken weeks or months to complete. Started before a voyage perhaps. Or it could be the work of crew. The ocean is placid, words in foam-white worked into the tapestry:

*Be Still, and Know That I **AM** God.*
Psalm 46:10.

Katerina isn't sure why "am" is so important to the message that it needs emphasis. "Be still," she mouths to herself. "Be still, or you will not know that I am God. Be still, or there's just the dead water. Earth without form, void. The face of the deep a reflection of stars and nothing more—no great spirit. Be still ..."

"Anne of Cleves. That's the name I was thinking of." It takes Katerina a second to understand that the balding woman is referring to one of King Henry's wives again.

"Your pills are here, if your name is Mary Alford." There is a trolley near the door with Mrs Alford's medical file. The woman's drugs have been prepared for her—a number of pills in a paper cup. Katerina checks off the box on the file indicating that the medicine has been administered, as she saw Flora do earlier at the nurses' station. When the woman looks up she's surprised to see Katerina wearing an officer's uniform. Mrs Alford leans back in dismay and puts on her wig. A moment later she offers a wan smile, reaching forward for her medicine.

"Lester would have had something to say about that uniform," Mrs Alford says, eyes to the ceiling.

"It's a costume. Not a uniform." She removes the cap from her head and hangs it on a hook on the wall. "Who's Lester? Was that your husband's name?" Katerina asks.

"Les *is* my husband. They're looking after him in a nice place I found for him in Vancouver."

Mrs Alford swallows the pills, one at a time. She shakes her face and neck to help them down, the way some birds drink water. Katerina lifts a blanket that has almost fallen to the floor and pulls it across the bed. She picks up Mrs Alford's slippers and carries them over to the side of the bed she's on for her tea—bare feet going blue on the cold linoleum floor.

"I believe they're killing my appetite," Mrs Alford says as she swallows one final pill with her cup of tea. "Saving my heart at the cost of my stomach."

She reaches out for Katerina's arm as she climbs into bed, vertebrae visible through her nightgown. Settles herself on three pillows, a hot water bottle placed on her belly. Keeps her wig on, for warmth as much as vanity. She holds Katerina's right hand in her dry palms. Closes her eyes for a few seconds. Mrs Alford opens hers eyes again before Katerina can wonder if the woman is saying a prayer.

"Have some tea," she tells Katerina. "It's still warm. And I have cookies my son brought me. Help yourself. He'll bring more when he comes to visit again."

Katerina sits down beside the bed. Finds the back of the chair as uncomfortably low as it was before. She pushes it back so that she can lean against the wall and still reach the bedside table. Pours herself a cup of tea and is pleased to see it steaming. The last cup, so it comes with the dregs. Katerina's favourite because it is also the strongest tea in the pot. A little sugar and milk. The plate of digestives is also welcome.

She says thank you to Mrs Alford. The woman already has her eyes closed. She murmurs an acknowledgement in her sleep. Katerina might go through the women's ward opening doors and turning on lights but she'll wait for now. They are identical to the cabins on other decks. Not like rooms she has seen in hospitals where the doors are sliding glass and there's a sense that privacy is not a priority; someone is expected to slip in and out, to examine a pulse or check an instrument. These are shut cabin doors. They could be locked. And surely a nurse or a doctor will show up soon. *Be still*, she tells herself again. Hard to settle herself when she feels like running. She has a disorientating thought that she's been running all day, running the way she would if she were up to her chest in water.

She's not sure what the news will mean for Anne. Or what change it might bring. The letters have not been destroyed but nor are they in her possession. Katerina's urgency is part of a growing panic—a need to understand how their family circumstances have altered; she has never been shown the entire picture. Anne wanted the letters destroyed if she could no longer get them to Audrius.

She reaches into her jacket and brings out Kornél's letters. All of them addressed to Katerina. Anne has always read all of Katerina's correspondence, just as she reads her journal. She would read Katerina's responses to letters as well. Katerina got into the habit of writing and sending them off before her mother could get to them. Anne would have been eager to read her son's letters, regardless of whether they were addressed to her or Katerina.

Her mother also withheld or destroyed letters, as she did one from Durrant that Katerina never got to read. Maybe more than one. Katerina had felt the need to tell him of the abortion before it happened. She didn't doubt he would have been easily reconciled to the procedure. No need for his life to be disrupted, yet Katerina never knew how he had felt about the wriggle of cells in her womb. She could assume it was a problem to be resolved efficiently, but that wasn't the same as knowing in his own words what he felt about their chemical accident. Katerina has wondered ever since whether he was perhaps a person looking for precisely this particular disruption.

These letters from Kornél would have been lost in the jumble of Anne's large handbag and forgotten as her distress grew in the days before the voyage and as they set out across the Atlantic. Likely she would have remembered them; handed them over during a spell of boredom. Anne enjoyed the kind of surprise that made you angry as well as elated. The more of both extremes, the better.

Katerina is pleased that Kornél is writing about their father. The lamplight isn't bright enough to read comfortably. It will be sufficient for one letter, if not all of them. Katerina suspects that she might need glasses. She takes the last sip of her tea before reading, plucking tea leaf pieces from her lips.

She glances at Mrs Alford as the woman wriggles down deeper under the blanket and sheet, turning away from the bedside lamp. Her breathing is steady, soothing. Katerina imagines the veteran lying beside his wife, listening to the sounds of her life, gently drawing him on, through one moment of the night to the next.

Katerina yawns and rubs her eyes against her sleeve. Lets them stay closed as she remembers a conversation she had with her father shortly before he left for Europe. They had started to play chess in earnest after she turned sixteen. Before that she'd been too easy to beat for him to bother, but she'd played Kornél a lot, beating him often, and then she'd managed a stalemate in one game with Audrius. It had stunned him. Made him declare that she had a fine mind. She'd set herself the goal of defeating her father once and then never again playing. She could tease him with that victory for years. She found that if she distracted him she could get closer to that win, so was strategic in what she chose to talk about during a game with her father.

"I occasionally read fantastic books or find a story with a miracle in it. Some magic that dazzles the narrative. A fabulous happening that alters a character's soul. And there are horror stories everyone at school reads with all kinds of monsters in them. Children hear ghost stories when they are little. They tell the same ghost stories when they get older, to their own sons and daughters. There are millions of incredible things in all the mythologies, and every religion still conjures angels and devils. We spend years of our lives having trouble going to sleep because we worry about those demons and vampires, spectres and ghouls. As time goes by, we find that there are no monsters and no ghosts. If we have trouble falling asleep at night, it's not because we're worried the fantastic will materialise but rather that reality will get harder and more brutal. So I find myself longing for a miracle. Nothing grand. I don't imagine a flying carpet or an angel singing for my soul. I don't need a Lazarus raised from the dead. A vase of dead flowers coming back into full bloom with a lovely fragrance—that's a kind of miracle that wouldn't mean anything to anyone else. No-one would believe me that the vase of flowers had once wilted and the water smelt awful with decay. Yet it'd be a consolation that might last a lifetime. I would know, no matter what else happened to me, that the fantastic wasn't solely a thing of the imagination. That we hadn't wasted thousands of libraries' worth of imagination on the purely impossible. Built countless temples, churches, mosques, all of them to be filled with nothing but empty prayers. That reality isn't a cold thing of stone that can never be made to flower again after death. That at its core, the laws of existence can never be broken, not bent, not even touched without the flesh disintegrating at the moment of contact. A divine being will never drift into the world from paradise. No magic will ever happen. Every bit of the fabulous an illusion, a dismal trick. No miracle, never. Despite billions of stories. Despite the world's ceaseless prayers. All our hopes for a way through the stone—nothing, not the slightest crack. Never. Ever. Is that the bedtime story no-one ever tells their children?"

Months went by without the one victory Katerina wanted. Her father's end game was unshakable, no matter how much trouble she could occasionally give him from a good opening. She would continue to try to distract Audrius with ideas he might find compelling but she was never able to beat him. More than a disruption for a potential win, she enjoyed seeing the face and voice of her father fall away. With the right kind of thought posed to him, another man emerged, a buried self that was never seen at the embassy, long locked away and out of sight even at home. Anne Iverson had fallen in love with that hidden man two decades before, that's what Katerina saw as she watched him emerge from thoughts of escaping a loss to respond to her provocation.

The game was precariously balanced for Audrius after Katerina managed to shock him with a vigorous Stonewall Attack. He looked at the board a long time with a troubled expression and then glanced up at her with a smile that showed he understood her—the desire for a miracle. He could see Katerina as no-one ever could or would again. And what he saw pleased him enough to bring tears to his eyes. She could hear him suck his air in, with what sounded like a sob. He removed his glasses, wiped at his eyes with a handkerchief, settled back into his chair. No longer interested in the game of chess. Another stalemate of a kind, because they never finished it.

"My darling girl, I think you've become too used to the cracks. You dance across them with a nonchalant jeté or fouetté. The miraculous is so commonplace that you no longer see the miracle beneath your feet. If you look around, you will see that we are surrounded by a spectral audience. A vast theatre of ghosts. We are all ghosts. The only difference is the stage. We can still thrill with our words and delight with our dances. A ghost need not float about a dilapidated mansion wailing over an unjust murder. We see ghosts in faces we pass in the street and hear their voices in the books we read. They sing in our electricity and they play in our lights. The dead built our roads and our bridges, constructed our cities and created our histories for us to dwell within—together, those of us that breathe and those that did breathe. The air is ever made stale by us, and then returns to us fresh, and we do not see that it is the same air since the first man breathed. The air belongs as much to the dead as to the living. Listen to the words I'm using. I found them all when I was a child. I didn't come up with any myself. None are my invention. Do you see how the dead designed me through words? I breathed in their thoughts and their thoughts became my own. I breathe them out and they become yours. Our language is the history of the dead. We carry the entire evolution of thought as lightly as a child holds a balloon. Every other animal carries their history in their bodies—we have found a way to also carry it in the air so that we can illuminate ourselves and the world. That balloon is as bright as a star. Our sun also moves through the darkness of the cosmos with a string of fabulous balloons. There is no Great Father. I don't believe in a divine power. So this not a sermon. This is only a series of words. Thoughts and more thoughts. Stars and more stars. Sentences strung out as constellations to be switched on or off as though they were nothing more than light bulbs in a room. These eternal lights are given such mundane and functional purposes. No grand author in those stars. And I think, my dear child, that was the point of the miracle. It freed us from the dull truths of the stone. It showed us a way into a great story in glimpses through the fractures. And a peek is enough for the inborn genius of creation to flow into the world. The most miraculous thing you can imagine has already happened. It is happening right now and who knows what it will turn into because it isn't at an end. Let me tell you what the miracle looked like when it first emerged. There was an animal and it had been running for its life from the time it was born. Threat was the world so all it knew was fear. It wasn't a predator animal like a tiger or a bear, which might know little fear, motivated only by hunger. This animal was prey and its existence depended on its speed and whatever intelligence it could muster to stay ahead of the next threat. That second part was important because it wasn't that fast and it wasn't that nimble, not like the monkey cousin was, and it didn't have the furious power of other apes, although it bore a resemblance to both. Yes, it was a hard reality and it was getting harder, brutal from birth to death with barely a moment's pleasure or peace in between.

Then the hard rock cracked and something that had been impossible became possible. The greatest miracle in billions of years of life, in all the time since our sun spun out its planets. This pathetic creature, nothing but prey, took pause from its fear and looked into the still surface of a puddle, saw its face reflected in the water. There are other creatures that recognise themselves in a mirror. It's been proven that even a magpie can understand that it is looking at a reflection. The miracle was something a little more incredible. That creature saw itself as a man, and then through that obvious image saw deeper, beyond its actual vision, saw in itself Man. It was looking into the eyes of its own life and into the eyes of its species. The collective presence. A shared soul. That creature said, 'Eye am eye, I am I,' and understood that this was a mirror it could share with brothers, sisters, daughters, sons, mothers, fathers by putting that mirror into their minds as well. The miracle was small to begin with. A bunch of flowers in the fist, wilted and dying, suddenly coming into bloom. Nothing but a whisper in the brain of a weak ape plucking flowers. The miracle was so small it could easily have been forgotten, and it would have slipped away and that creature would have fallen into the entropy of all other forms of life. It wasn't fast or nimble enough. Didn't have the right combination of power and rage to stand its ground. The only escape from being prey, running from birth to death, was to look into the reflection and understand not only the face as a breathing, real presence in the world, which was obvious to the dumbest ape or monkey, but to breathe into that reflection and see the ghost behind the face. The ghost in the eyes. And we made all kinds of names for it—soul, mind, spirit, psyche, God—yet it's really a ghost. A monster or an angel, something that could destroy the world and eat it all up, or something that could recreate the whole of existence and make paradise. We're still animals, of course, and we do not control the miracle. We're just parts of it—the wilting flowers in a fist—distracted by the falling petals of our individual lives. The fist is ever the same one. The single hand of a species holding onto creation's genius at the roots, murmuring 'I am I' into a mud-puddle reflection. And it doesn't matter if we forget because forgetting is the secret of the flower. The secret, my darling girl, is that we are already dead, already cut from the ground. And many of us prefer life on the cracked stone anyway. Ghosts whispering into each other's ears, listening to the noise of the miracle. And to me that is the loveliest sound in the world. Look at the way we've turned the air in our lungs into so many different ghost songs."

Katerina blinks in the lamplight. Audrius's voice had filled the room but it had not woken Anne. She is no longer murmuring, "My apologies, my apologies." Finally sleeping. Slipping from the tentacles of her fear and anger. Soundly off and away.

The hazy bedside light makes Katerina squint. Hard to see anything. She wonders why she's wearing her brother's uniform. Anne will be furious when she sees. Katerina yawns with her eyes closed. Anne will want to go back to work on the precisely detailed jacket so it's perfect for the graduation. Her mother's boundless love. No. All of her love—bound up in darling Kornél. Maybe that's why she is dressed in Kornél's uniform. That's how she'll answer Anne's fury when she wakes. Katerina recalls dressing before a mirror, a revolver in her hand, pulling the trigger to hear the explosion in her chest.

She doesn't want to go back to the forsaken world beyond that reflection.

She'd rather stay here, where she can smell Audrius—his pleasing body odour mixed with cigars, aftershave and brandy. Lovely of him to visit them both now when they needed him. He would have shown Anne there was no monster by crushing her in his own arms. Making her cry out and beg for an octopus. Never a question of his love, no matter how long he'd been kept away—no doubt at least for Katerina. His heart has only ever been a safe place for his daughter.

She tries to come up with another provocative thought for him so that they might continue to talk. Finds she can't think clearly enough to ask anything other than if he would stay with them this time. "Without you, nothing works. Do you understand? Without you, all that's left is fear and fury."

An angry whisper in her ear. A hand on her shoulder. She's jerked forward. The back of her head bounces against the wall when she's released.

"What are you doing in Mrs Alford's room?" Katerina opens her eyes and sees Anne's face, that familiar mask of rage, dissolving from second to second. An unfamiliar nurse in a uniform—close enough to make Katerina lean back into the wall again. She wonders whether she is dressed in a costume. A nun's veil on her head, made of a sheer white cotton. *Looks like curtain fabric*, thinks Katerina. Two martial rows of bright silver buttons down the sides of her chest, from shoulder to waist; more bright buttons sewn onto thin epaulettes.

Katerina whispers, "Be still and know that I am a ghost." Dazed. Blinking without being able to clear her eyes. A joke for her father.

"This is a sick woman's room. She's not to be disturbed. Certainly not at three o'clock in the morning. Why are you here?"

Katerina can only blink at the woman. The nurse takes Katerina's wrist and yanks her to her feet. Drags her to the doorway. The grip is on the wrist where she was bitten by one of the borzoi. Makes her gasp. She recalls being roughly shaken awake by her mother as a child—carried over her father's shoulder up a long staircase, feeling every step jerk her limp body, head swaying loosely, unable for all that to fully wake up. The same sensation now.

"What have you done with her medicine?" She is looking at Katerina with a doctor's eye, forming a diagnosis. Katerina wants to ask the nurse where Audrius went. Feels a sob waiting in her chest with the question. She lets them both dissolve, swallowing, holding her breath for a moment.

"Have you taken all her medicine for yourself?" It's a reasonable question. Katerina doesn't know. She glances over at the bed and sees Mrs Alford sleeping, her wig on the floor by her bed. She moves to pick it up for her, so she can put it back on the woman's head. Or she might put it beside her pillow. It shouldn't be on the floor, as if a part of her head has been hacked away. Katerina doesn't take more than a step before she is yanked back to the doorway. And then pulled into the corridor; a misbehaving child taken aside to be rebuked.

"You're the matron," Katerina says, wanting to find her way back to a clear mind. "Not here this morning … I mean, yesterday morning. Flora was the only nurse on the ward at that time of the day." Katerina is rubbing her wrist, trying to speak clearly; can hear she's still slurring her words. "Midshipman

Cypress tells me you had to look after the old fellow with the pornography."

"You are not in your right mind." The matron might spit in Katerina's face, she's so exasperated. "I'm not sure what pills you have been taking. I need to know whether you stole her medicine for yourself. Mrs Alford has already had two heart attacks in the last year. She doesn't need another one because of you and your grotesque appetites."

"I just drank her tea," she says. "Mrs Alford was having trouble sleeping and I helped her take her medicine. There's nothing wrong with my heart. Why would I take her pills?"

"Goddamn it!"

Katerina flinches.

"All of her medicine at once? Is that what you did? Every pill in one go?" The matron walks into the room and checks the woman's pulse. Mrs Alford stirs awake. Tells the matron she's fine.

Katerina takes her hat from the hook and waits for the matron in the dark hallway. Gathers her hair and puts the officer's cap back on, brim pulled down. She stands to attention. Wants to look sober. It occurs to her she might appear as though she's mocking the matron when the woman strides out into the corridor.

"You're still here?" She is appalled. "Why are you standing in my way?"

"I didn't come here to cause a disturbance. There was no-one to help me. It's urgent that I speak to Anne Klova." Katerina can't find resolve in her voice. "My mother. She had an awful turn this morning. Yesterday morning, I mean. And she was a danger to herself. She hurt her eye."

"If I could physically remove you, I would. I'd carry you out of my ward in pieces." The matron grits her teeth. "I don't have the time or the energy for outrage. You've wandered into a place where lives are in genuine crisis. Searching for *thrills in pills*. That's what the youth call it, isn't it? Don't speak to me of what's urgent to you—a girl dressed up as a soldier but looking for her mummy."

The matron turns off the lights in Mrs Alford's room and quietly closes the door behind her. Turns off another light in the corridor and hurries away to the waiting room to deal with a male voice crying out for help.

Katerina's head is ringing as if the matron has been raging loudly, spittle flying from her mouth. Clear-eyed, sensible and whispering. The only real emotion showing in her clean white teeth. An admirable working woman.

Katerina turns around and gazes at the closed doors of the women's ward. "At least … tell her I was here," she mutters down the empty corridor. "That I didn't leave her here alone all day and all night."

She follows the matron to the reception area. As she passes the nurses' station it occurs to her that Anne Klova's room would be listed in one of the files on the desk. If Anne is sleeping soundly, Katerina will go back to the cabin and return when the ward opens again for visitors. She'll leave a response to the message sent by Nurse Flora. A fragment of a song or a piece of poetry using the word "love". Anne will understand then that Katerina didn't make an irreversible error.

She finds a faded blackboard that lists all the rooms and their occupants, none of them with the name she's looking for. There's an open logbook on the desk that tells her Anne was released from the infirmary at 10 p.m. *Anne Klova* is printed in sober handwriting, placed in the *Checked Out* column, as though Anne had been staying in a hotel and decided to leave early. Katerina looks up and down the corridor as if her mother might come along at any moment and ask what she is doing here so late at night.

A drop of blood falls to her sleeve. Soaks into the embroidery. She watches the descent of another drop, past the dark blue sleeve and onto the red of her pants. Light-headed; a few seconds go by before she understands that she's having another nosebleed. There's a box of tissues on the nurses' station desk. She sits down and leans her head back. Unlikely for it to be as bad as the one she had at lunchtime. Months or weeks might go by between bleeds yet it is not uncommon for her to have two in a day. The first one didn't quite release all the blood that needed to come out.

The officer's cap is too large for her head so it falls off and her hair spills out around her shoulders again. She'll be ready to walk in a minute or two. Just a few tissues spotted for this bleed. When she feels it's done she turns on the bright lamp on the desk and takes out the letter from Kornél.

> *I should have gone to London ... deeply regret that I didn't accept Kip's invitation. Distance to this news would have been a great blessing. I had no choice when I heard Daddy was unwell. That he'd been very ill for some time and not told anyone about it ... least of all his family. Ashamed not so much of his condition as his situation. He is living in an awful hotel near the Montparnasse railway station, which was meant to be temporary, a month or two while matters in Moscow were*

resolved, so future and past could be dealt with, but months and months have bundled up into a year in this hotel. The sound of the trains passing back and forth is the least of it. The revolting folk here shout obscenities at each other with drill sergeant voices, and not only in their rooms, they follow each other down the halls, pushing, tumbling down the stairs, pulling at each other's hair and biting, punching and kicking out into the street below his window ... where they go on and on ... at every hour of the night and morning. The police are called. Yet even the police are reluctant to come to this neighbourhood. They would be here every night if they were dutiful so they hardly ever come at all. A murder might bring them out. That's about all. The noise comes through from everywhere, the thin walls and the door to the corridor and the windows. That's what Daddy hears morning, noon and night, and he does not leave his rooms ... barely leaves his bed. This is where he lives. Under house arrest. He's been told in no uncertain terms that he's taking his life into his own hands should he leave this hotel. Hard for me to write this letter, Katie. I know I should concern myself with your feelings about a man who is your father as well, but my own feelings for him, of rage and disgust, pity and love ... it's a toxic cluster of thought I do not want to transmit through this letter. I don't know if I can help it ... and you are no longer a child so I think I will tell you the truth. I should attempt to simply report the reasons for his situation. Mexico was a failure for him, a small misstep which he compounded with a whole ragged dance of missteps, making a bad situation worse, and then worse again, until somehow he'd managed to effect the end of his career without decisions or declarations from anyone. His rooms are filled with papers and letters. Piles of books on the carpet, many of them open as though dropped to the floor in disgust. There are newspapers and there's cigar ash covering his dining room table and everything is filthy with the food he's been eating and the brandy he's been drinking … I suspect he's rarely sober now … there's a broken clock on the wall, glass shattered by a thrown bottle … this pitiful clock hangs askew in his small living room, the minute hand motionless, the hour hand trembling and hesitating with every movement forward. And Daddy is always busy shuffling through his correspondence, the books he needs to consult, and yet he says his eyes have become weak and he no longer knows what to write. Not even a sentence.

Katerina hears a door being unlocked. A few seconds later the door to the dispensary opens. Katerina sees Blackshaw emerge from the room. He drops his keys in the corridor. Places a bottle of pills in the pocket of his white doctor's coat. Glares at the keys on the linoleum as if they have fallen through the grating in a city street. He rubs his eyes. Stretches his neck. Hair on the back of his head mussed from sleep. Farts when he bends down. He picks up the keys and tries to place one of them in the lock. He gets the right one on the third try.

Blackshaw turns around and finds Katerina standing before him. He draws in a breath. He thought he was alone; jangling the keys and not hearing Katerina walk towards him. He doesn't recognise her in the darkness of the corridor. Sees the uniform and doesn't know what to make of the sudden apparition.

Katerina knows that if she speaks, she will weep. A year already under house arrest. Montparnasse station might never shut down for the evening. France and the rest of Europe arriving and departing outside Audrius's window. His life in his own hands should he leave. How far from those metal tracks might he be sleeping? And then those voices. Those desolate, desperate hotel guests—their endless footfalls up and down the halls. Anne has known where he is living, no doubt. Keeping it to herself; breaking down under the pressure of this catastrophe. Katerina folds the letter and places it back in the pocket with the rest of Kornél's letters. Buttons up the jacket again. Presses the dog bite on her wrist the way Blackshaw did at the barber's, wanting the pain to push away thought.

Blackshaw reaches out a hand. Katerina won't be able to hold herself together for another moment if the doctor tries to console her. He does not offer her a soft touch. Doesn't bring her in for an embrace. He is pointing at her as if to determine where she is in the shadows of the hallway. That pointed finger finds her shoulder, pushes until she makes a noise. Only then does he blink. Takes a deep breath. Relieved.

"You'll have to come back," Blackshaw says in a hoarse voice. Clearing his throat to little effect. "Make an appointment with Matron tomorrow." He nods at the bloody tissues in Katerina's right hand.

"I'm not here for a nosebleed. I'm here for my mother. There's a crisis in the family."

"Another crisis? I can't see her now." He looks at the keys in his hands as though he might want to duck back into the dispensary. "Can't see straight," murmuring as he walks along the unlit hallway to his office.

"You don't need to see her," she says, following behind him. "I want to know where she is."

"Why are you asking me?" He scratches the top of his head—bald but for a few wisps. He wasn't bald in the Louis XVI restaurant or at the barber's for his shave. During the day he must wear a toupee. Along with his obvious fatigue, he looks twenty years older than he did only a few hours ago.

"She's in your care." Katerina says, bringing her last clean tissue to her nose to make sure she's stopped bleeding. There's not enough light for her to see if it's clean or whether there is still a smudge of crimson in her snot.

"In *my* care? I've done all I *can* for your mother. I put her back on her *feet*. You're aware that I'm not a psychiatrist, so I don't know what else you're asking from me." The pills in his pocket have been rattling with every step. He stops at his door. "Soon you'll be in Europe and will have any number of experts. There's a thousand *geniuses* in the field. You might go and see Freud himself, with your family connections." He begins looking through his keys. He raises them for Katerina. "I can't see with so little light. Might you find the brass key with an end that resembles a chess king?"

There's a light switch on the wall. When Katerina reaches for it, Blackshaw catches her wrist. Shakes his head. Nods to the waiting room apprehensively. Hiding from his patients. He's been sleeping in the locked dispensary. Maybe he was woken by the movement around Mrs Alford's room, next door. He might have heard the hiss of the matron's rebuke and waited for her to have walked away before venturing out.

"The logbook says she's been discharged." Katerina takes the keys, about twenty of them on three links. "That can't be correct."

"Of course it's correct." He nods at the keys, urging her to find the one that will open his office. "It's a log. Matron keeps it absolutely accurate at all times."

"So where is my mother?" Katerina steps towards the weak illumination reaching her from the nurses' station, finds a key that resembles the top of a king chess piece. "She didn't come back to the cabin."

"How could I know the answer to that question? I really am very tired. Please find the key to this door. I need to regroup."

"That logbook says Anne Klova was released over four hours ago."

"And so it must be," he mumbles and shrugs. So utterly pathetic; she struggles to recognise in him the man who commanded the centre of the Louis XVI restaurant.

"My mother is not herself. She's been very ill. I was expecting to see her medicated, perhaps bound for her own safety. Am I to imagine her walking away, as though about to take a promenade on one of the decks?"

"Exhaustion scrambles the mind." He lifts his hands to his face as if to say, *Look at me*. "Exhaustion is not an abstract concept. There's a quick degeneration of the faculties when there's not enough rest. As basic a contact with reality as there is. Your mother is not mentally ill. Not in the profound sense. Some days I wonder what mental health looks like, but Anne Klova is fully functional. We forced her to sleep for six hours. I've prescribed sedatives for the rest of her journey. When her friend came to pick her up we were glad to have another room."

"She doesn't know anyone on the ship. We're travelling alone. My mother and me—there is no friend." Katerina holds the key to the doctor's office. She glances at the light switch as though she might illuminate the entire hallway. Blackshaw reaches into his pocket and brings out the bottle of pills. He swallows one of them. When Katerina puts her hand out he shakes out a few into her palm as if they were sweets.

"You're not a child. So you must know how friendly passengers get on a cruise. People don't often have time to make new friends, but what else is there other than time when crossing an ocean? Passengers can make a friend for life, and sometimes the association lasts only a night."

"She has not met anyone on *Aquitania*. It's been three days and nights and we've been together every minute." Katerina swallows two of the pills Blackshaw gave her. "Until this morning … yesterday morning."

"Then she already knew the chap before boarding." He breathes out an exasperated noise. Pointing to the door. "Would that be remarkable? Thousands of people crossing the Atlantic together. Matron might have got his name. You'll have to ask her. All I can tell you is that I saw your mother talking with him and she certainly knew the fellow. She was glad to leave with him. A dapper Englishman, so not a word of French between them. A first-rate gentleman, I assure you. They might yet be somewhere above, enjoying the New Year," he suggests, scratching at the dense facial hair that has returned to his jowls since Alder Gideon's blade. She opens the door for him and he waves her away as he enters.

"I don't have the optimism for celebration," he says. "All I want is sleep."

❖❖❖❖❖

A.S. PATRIĆ

Katerina finds herself before the door of her cabin. Doesn't recall walking from the infirmary. She's been thinking about how useless Blackshaw's pills have been. Even so, she stands gazing at the door in a stupor. Not sure which way to proceed—bewildered by a simple sign hanging from the door handle: *Do not disturb*.

Silence beyond the door; light along the floor below it. Katerina stares at the sign on the door handle for minutes before she knocks. She takes a breath. Prepares herself to endure the tirade to come. With any luck, her mother will also have taken Blackshaw's medicine. The floorboards creak as Anne moves towards the door. The handle does not turn.

Katerina waits. Minutes go by.

She knocks again. Has a moment when she forgets where she is and why she's waiting—thinks, *Poor Mrs Alford. Two heart attacks already and now she can barely eat a biscuit as she waits for the third and final one to come knocking.* Katerina murmurs, "Do not disturb," as she places her head against the door. Closes her eyes.

Anne decided they would go to the Palladian for champagne the first evening on *Aquitania*. She even went down to the cargo hold to fetch high heels for them both. When they arrived at the lounge, the ships's official photographer told them they were the loveliest women he'd seen on the ship the whole day.

Anne wouldn't let him take any photos. She was adamant, reaching out for the camera before he could take a quick shot. The flash exploded near Anne's hand but did not burn her.

The amiable smile on his face disappeared. He apologised with a pout, explaining that at the end of the voyage he would have had a series of photos for them. Passengers like to buy a sequence of images in a book as a memento of their grand trip across the Atlantic. He would have nothing to offer the Klovas when they reached France. Not a single framed photograph.

Anne had no intention of smiling for anyone. Their first night on the ocean liner made it difficult even for her to keep to the confinement of a small cabin but she wasn't interested in socialising. While they were dressing, Anne pulled out a white-gold pendant Katerina hadn't seen her wear since Portugal. A heart-shaped locket Audrius had bought when they were married—the two frames within containing wedding pictures of husband and wife.

Anne hadn't thought she'd need to keep her good jewellery in the cabin, just as she hadn't thought they'd require more than practical shoes. Most of her precious clothes and jewellery had been sent ahead by secure shipment, and she wasn't going back to the cargo hold a second time, so her choices for the evening were limited. Katerina couldn't imagine those two youthful pictures still within the locket. An empty heart now, or perhaps Anne had put other photographs inside it. Katerina was curious but Anne was in a vicious mood despite the perfume and a dress she'd bought in Cancún—an exquisite floral mosaic decorating the bare-shouldered gown made of gauze and multicoloured guipure.

Katerina thought about the photo album that would not be available when they arrived in Calais. The crestfallen expression on the photographer's face had amused her but she found the notion of such a book interesting—that their family might find itself set out in a sequence of photographs. Moments in Warsaw or Lisbon, Moscow or Mexico, with one or two more to come when they were reunited in France in the new year. She thought about which images she might want to include. And she wondered how many significant moments in their lives had already slipped from her mind. Such a book might help them find a new perspective, see the story of their lives together, see that very moment in the Palladian Lounge—Anne in another wonderful dress, Katerina wearing the off-the-shoulder featherprint dress she had bought the day she met Durrant.

"Did he break your heart?" she asked. "My father?" Katerina pointed to the locket at Anne's throat.

The waiter had left another bottle of champagne. They hadn't ordered it—a gift from a nearby smiling group of gentlemen. One of them bore a resemblance to Durrant and Katerina was thinking about her own heart—how it was hard to tell where the fractures were, how many missing pieces or chipped corners she had in her chest. A heart was much like a bust in a public garden, she thought, exposed to the weather, discoloured by seasonal extremes, defaced by any disgruntled visitor strolling past.

Perhaps the moment on the tram in Avenida de los Insurgentes might be included in the end-of-voyage book, though no-one had taken a picture. There was a restaurant near Bosque de Chapultepec to which Durrant had taken Katerina one evening, where a mariachi band had played and they had danced together for two hours after eating their dinner. Eight violins playing for them, four trumpets, and guitars of different sizes; so many she hadn't been able to count them. Durrant and Katerina had been soaked through with sweat and could taste pure life on each other's lips. That's what Durrant had called it—*pura vida*. Kissing again when they could stop grinning to let their lips meet. No photographs that night either.

Also none of the Klova wedding day. An apartment building fire in Leningrad had claimed every picture except for the ones Anne carried around her neck. So the impossible album in Katerina's imagination might contain a sequence of images including the wedding dress and the suit Anne had made with her own hands, which had otherwise only been caught within the tiny halves of a white-gold locket.

What would a series of photographs of that marriage show them now? It wasn't a question Katerina asked herself in her pleasant champagne nostalgia. She could not then imagine a sequence including a broken clock in a dismal hotel room near a train terminus or a pretty woman clawing her eye out of its socket.

"Did he break your heart?" she asked Anne again as she pulled the bottle of champagne out of the bucket of ice to pour them both another glass.

"A romantic fool." Anne stubbed her cigarette out in a fruit plate, embers spilling to the table. "Is that what you are becoming, you silly girl?"

Katerina had surprised herself just asking the question. The situation confused her. Alone with her mother, drinking champagne, surrounded by pleasant people—an expansive generosity filling the luxuriously comfortable room. For a few minutes Katerina had felt the friendliness also belonged to them, as if they were companions on an exciting journey over the ocean after all.

There were not many words between them for the next hour in the Palladian. Anne glared at the people moving about her, commenting on what she saw, as though they were all pitiful caged animals in a zoo and she was appalled to find herself in the same enclosure. The champagne gentlemen were drawn to the voluptuous ease they saw in Anne as she leaned back into her couch—none attempting to speak with her when they saw the profound contempt on her face.

Katerina regretted asking the question. She'd made an already strained mood worse. She knew Anne instinctively: that her mother would not open herself up to certain areas of thought willingly; not to her daughter and maybe not to herself. There might be nothing in the locket now, yet Katerina knew Anne's heart was not empty. Audrius was never far from Anne's thoughts. Neither was fury.

When they came back to their cabin from the Palladian, Anne said the two glasses of champagne had gone straight to her head, and she was dizzy. She rarely drank. Didn't have a tolerance for alcohol. Katerina had finished a third glass—there had been a plate of strawberries she'd enjoyed with each sip. She had her father's constitution and would have enjoyed a whole evening in the Palladian Lounge. She felt like dancing with the taste of strawberry still in her mouth, head full of exploding bubbles.

Anne lay down fully clothed on the small bed and closed her eyes, breathing so deeply she might have gone to sleep. Motionless for twenty minutes. Her hat was on her chest, the only thing she'd removed before lying down. Katerina put it away in its box and then took off her mother's shoes and her silk gloves, with no indication that Anne was conscious. The locket had slid down her throat and Katerina lifted it and placed it delicately back on Anne's chest so as not to wake her.

"Such a romantic fool. Must get that from Audrius," Anne said loudly, eyes still closed. Maybe she had slept but it was hard to tell. Anne could lie motionless for two hours and later insist she hadn't slept for a single minute.

"No, your father did not break my heart." A quiver of laughter in her sharp voice. "You can break a statue." She took a deep breath that settled her anger. "We're better at bleeding. We can lose a lot of blood over the years."

Katerina's knees buckle and she falls to the floor. "Sorry. Excuse me," she says as if she has bumped into another passenger walking down the hall. It might be as late as four in the morning. Few people are now walking the corridors.

Katerina takes a moment to work out where she is. Gets back to her feet and knocks on the door. Waits and knocks again. Minutes pass with no response. Katerina puts her key in the lock. Can't turn it. She steps back and checks the brass numbers on the wood. She has not made a mistake.

It's possible Anne is so sedated that she can't get up to answer the door. Katerina considers leaving. Finding somewhere else to sleep. She can't use Querida and Allegralita's empty cabin. The door is open but the two women might return. Even worse is the thought that they won't—that a violence befell them in the room when it was ransacked.

Katerina glances up and down the corridor. Where might she go at this hour? She hears a creak beyond the door and recalls those two loose floorboards, the ones she was so careful to avoid when Anne was trying to sleep. They gave away her mother's movement behind the door.

"Mother," Katerina calls out. "Please open the door. It's late and I want to go to bed."

Revellers stagger down the corridor behind Katerina, angrily shouting at each other and then hugging in a drawled reconciliation. One of them bumps into Katerina and apologises as though to a superior officer—one hand to his forehead in a sincere if inebriated salute. Perhaps a soldier in the Great War and so drunk he sees nothing but a uniform.

"Don't have a hard heart, *Maman*. I came to see you earlier today and they told me you'd done something awful to yourself. The nurse wouldn't let me see you. I left to find Doctor Blackshaw and he told me to let you be, that you were resting and recovering. And now I've come from the infirmary because I was trying to find you. Please open the door. I know you're there. I can feel your grip on the door handle."

A couple stagger down the hallway. It's the bearded fellow who watched the cockroach race from his doorway. His wife is the one barefoot now, high heels in her handbag. Both so intoxicated that they stop to rest every few metres, leaning on each other or against the wall. "Almost there," the woman says to the man. "Almost there," says the man to the woman. They continue to murmur the same words until they reach the door and enter the quiet darkness of their cabin.

"We have to talk about the letters you asked me to destroy this morning. I made a mistake but the mistake isn't irrevocable. The letters have *not* been thrown away as I thought. I found one of the Trotsky envelopes in the Argentines' cabin. Mother, please open the door. We can't talk about these things in the corridor."

She bangs on the door. Her left arm is sore from the dog bite, so she uses her right hand until she can't bear the pain in her wrist. She kicks at the door as if she might break it down. She's unable to coordinate her movements because of Blackshaw's pills. Kornél's shoes are too big for her and she stumbles sideways. A door down the corridor opens but Anne does not unlock the cabin for her daughter. Katerina must appear drunk to their neighbours. She does not look at them to see their anger or derision.

"I found the letters from Kornél in your handbag." Katerina is shouting now. "The ones he sent me after Saint-Cyr. He told me about Father being in that appalling hotel in Montparnasse. Are you hiding? What have you done?"

Anne opens the door wide. She is wearing her nightgown. A hairnet reveals vivid silver at the roots of her peroxide hair. She wouldn't usually leave it this long without attending to her colour. Anne doesn't look as though she's been sleeping—her good eye is as sharp as it's ever been. Behind her, beneath the jadeite lamp, are letters she's in the process of writing. There are telegraphs as well. She's wearing her glasses askew because her right eye bulges with a gauze bandage. None of the hysteria from this morning in her face. This is Anne in full possession of herself. Determined to drive forward after stumbling briefly. Lips pulled tight against her teeth.

Anne steps back, allowing Katerina to enter. Katerina is relieved that this terrible day might soon be done. Whatever angry words are to come, accusations and threats, none would matter because Katerina will get into bed and throw pillows and sheets over her head and wait for the storm of her mother's recriminations to pass.

Katerina takes two steps forward. Stops. Rocked by a blow. Staggers back. Eyes closed. Not sure what is happening until the second time Anne slaps her. Rings on Anne's fingers catching Katerina on the cheek. More force with the second slap. Absolute vehemence. The first stopped Katerina; the second moves her backwards. More blows will fall upon her if she does not step back through the doorway. Katerina is blinking, disorientated, unable to judge when the next slap will land. She raises her arms and shuffles into the hallway.

The officer's cap comes off Katerina's head with the force of the second blow. Anne bends down and picks up Kornél's hat. Dusts it with the back of her fingers. Closes the door. Locks it again. The *Do not disturb* sign swings on the handle and settles. The open doors down the corridor close quietly.

❖❖❖❖❖

Bubbles float to the surface
of the brawling black river
foaming rage white in rapids …
hovering above—almost free
of the surging current …
my soul
such a tiny
perfect
bubble.

The poem was folded around a strip of photo booth pictures of Kornél in a new uniform. The poem had been pinned to his bedroom wall in Saint-Cyr. Written by Aleksa Alimpich. Sent to Katerina in one of her brother's letters. A printed page cut from a literary journal he bought in Paris last year. She blinks and corrects herself—the year before. Hours into 1939 now.

There's one more letter she needs to read before she finds the telegraph office. She's been walking, trying to settle down after crying in a stairwell; she'd held herself together until she was out of Anne's earshot. She doesn't know what she can tell her brother in a telegraph about what's happened on *Aquitania*. She will sit down in the telegraph office and try to sort out her mind. And if she can't do that, she will remind Kornél that there are powerful family friends he should appeal to. Audrius will have been frantically trying to save his own career but it could be time for his son to search out clemency, even if Audrius's political life is over. The kind of begging only a son can do for his father. If she's lucky she will receive an answering telegraph from France within the day.

Kornél's letter might show Katerina he's effected some change already. She couldn't read it—mind swimming just trying to take in the short Alimpich piece. After looking over the poem she returned all her brother's letters to the pocket of her jacket and realised that aside from a screwed-up page from the Book of Job, she has nothing—no passport, no money and no place to sleep. She threw the key to her mother's cabin down the stairwell.

Katerina walks about the ship, avoiding the parts of it that are noisy with the persistent joys of revellers. She finds herself on an unfamiliar deck, lost until she catches sight of the boatswain backing carefully through a narrow doorway, a metal tray in his hands. She rushes towards him before he can disappear beyond the door, which has a sign on it informing her that there is strictly no admittance to passengers.

He's wearing a bathrobe. The heel of one slippered foot holds open the door. Most of his body is through the doorway and his balance is precarious. There's a spring in the hinges that could knock over the tray. He's carrying Turkish coffee in a copper pot, steaming in the cool air.

"Excuse me, Mr Deering," she asks. "I'm looking for the telegraph office."

"Won't be open for another hour … at least." He attempts to look at his watch but can't turn his wrist enough because of the tray.

Katerina feels the chill of open water and can smell the ocean. They must be close to an exit. His corridor leads deeper into the ship.

She remembers his voice from when he dressed down Flora, telling the nurse he would fix her dancing eyes. Tones rising from his belly, slow and insistent. Katerina doesn't pay attention to his convoluted directions to the telegraph office. As fickle-headed as Flora. Just listening to his pleasing voice. Every word is a rich sound in his mouth. Already shaved and showered—his hair damp. Wide awake after a good sleep. Katerina feels only the endless evening yet she sees the morning in Deering.

Katerina shrugs. "I'll find it eventually."

"Near the wheelhouse on the command deck." He sees she hasn't taken in his previous, more detailed directions.

"I should let you go," she says with a tilt of her head down the narrow crew corridor. "Thank you, Mr Deering."

"I wouldn't search for it. You can't expect the telegraphist to be open on time. Not *today*. Likely the Italian fellow who runs it had a very late night. I'd give him until noon to have it all up and running."

"I should let you go." She doesn't look away, step back or

allow him to leave. She is very still, her eyes clearing, finding focus on his mouth, as if waiting for his next words though he has nothing more to say to her.

"Is there anything else?" he asks. Done with Katerina and everything about the present moment. The tray in his arms is perfectly level. The coffee in the pot steady. No tremble beneath the bronze-coloured foam floating on the black liquid. Strong wrists at the bathrobe's cuffs. Even with a light tray the muscles are taut at the open fold of fabric at his chest.

"Anything else?" he asks in that same hard voice he used with Flora. One that brooks no foolish answers, doesn't allow for soft, uncertain responses.

"Yes, there is something else, Mr Deering."

"What?" he demands. Not willing to waste another second on Katerina. Looking past her shoulder to a raucous burst of music coming from the foyer and back at her face. "What?"

She steps towards him into the crew corridor, her body touching the tray. He retracts it a centimetre. When he takes a step backwards, the door closes and she moves forward. Touching the tray with her stomach. She reaches out a steadying hand. The bare silver of the tray is warm from the coffee and his body heat.

"Me," she says, unsure whether it is an adequate answer to his question. His eyes move from her face to her stomach against the tray, to her fingers on his wrist. They rise and search her eyes. When she sees doubt cross his mind she finds a tone of voice that rises from her own belly, and tells him again, "Me."

"Fine." He blinks. Refocuses on her face. "Yes, fine."

"Perhaps you'll share some coffee with me as well."

"Do you drink Turkish coffee, Mademoiselle?" he says, remembering her from the infirmary.

"It's Katerina," she tells him. "Don't call me Mademoiselle."

"Katerina," he says with an unforced pronunciation, unusual for an Englishman. He leans his head to suggest they start walking.

"Where are we going?"

"I was returning to my room. I can't take you anywhere special. I can't give you anything special."

"I'm not looking for anything special. Where's the room?"

"Not far."

He carries the tray before him, walking slowly, so as not to tip the copper pot. She follows behind, as though hypnotised by the trailing ribbon of coffee steam. He does not look around or talk to her as they walk the drab corridors of *Aquitania*'s working men and women. Deering will not be an affectionate man, she knows, yet she is drawn by the thought of coming into contact with him, feeling the warmth of his flesh thump into her flesh, his body entering hers, if only briefly.

A few doors are already open with crew preparing for the day ahead. Triple bunks within the rooms. A man brushes his teeth in a doorway and spits foam into a small tin cup as they pass. In another room, a fully dressed waitress with an unbuttoned shirt breastfeeds an infant as other women jostle about her—all of them smoking and laughing as though they were in a bar. Katerina kicks a spotted rubber ball that has rolled into the corridor back into the room. The women look up at her but she doesn't wait for new expressions to form on their ruddy faces.

Inside his cabin, Deering places the tray on a semicircular

table folded out from the wall. It reminds Katerina of a wall-mounted ironing board. An oil heater is turned to full. It's a tiny room so they breathe the thick heat of it into their lungs.

"Should have turned it off," he says, moving to the heater. "Made a greenhouse with nothing green."

"Leave it on, please," she says. "I've been feeling cold for hours. I need to thaw my bones."

He stops at the heater, nods as if taking a command. Removes his bathrobe. Hangs it on one of five hooks on his door. Much of his uniform is ready on the other hooks. He's wearing a collarless grey shirt, half-unbuttoned, and faded blue pyjama pants. Pours the coffee into silver Ottoman cups he might have bought in the Near East—porcelain within intricate, hand-wrought metal holders. She recalls Cypress saying that the boatswain had travelled all over the world. Deering brings her the cup of coffee—doesn't look Katerina in the eye.

"Do you want to sit?" he asks. Turning around the one kitchen chair in the cabin for her.

"It'd be odd, me seated, while you continue to stand."

"I'll sit on the bed. You can use the chair," he says.

Katerina is by the door. Deering hasn't locked it—giving her, perhaps, the option of fleeing. She locks the door and turns to him. He's drinking. Eyes closed for the full taste of his coffee. Before drinking he'd taken in the aroma with a long inhalation.

Not much space in the cabin. He's sitting on the narrow bed. Instead of a bedside table he has a small shipping box with *Rolleiflex* stencilled on the side—a clock and a harmonica sitting on top of it. A cupboard at the end of the bed and the table with the chair opposite the door. No books. No pictures or paintings. A Victorian cast-iron lamp with a gleaming glass-beaded fringe in one corner—surprisingly pretty for the spartan cabin. Burnt orange, gold, deep pink and olive green silk velvet panels with clusters of flowers and embroidered vines, all aglow.

"Can I sit beside you on the bed?"

"If you want." He holds his silver cup in both hands. He keeps his gaze before him on the darkened porthole low on the wall. She sits near him, her spine surprised at the jolt of the hard bed below. No springs under the thin mattress. Likely he's placed planks of wood beneath it.

She has a taste of the viscous liquid in the cup. Katerina has never enjoyed Turkish coffee before—isn't sure if she does now. The heat of it is welcome, as is the growing warmth of the room. She can feel a pleasant flush moving through her fingers and toes, her neck and face. Deering doesn't attempt small talk. Drinks his coffee. Tiny circular marks of sweat forming in the fabric of his shirt, on his back and at his chest.

"Not much of a view," she says.

He nods and doesn't say anything. Katerina understands that it was a mistake to come to Deering's room. He's bound up within himself, barely able to speak to Katerina, let alone touch her. She drops her head, thinking about having to walk down the crew corridors and back out onto *Aquitania*'s grubby post-celebratory decks.

She takes another sip from the silver Ottoman cup and sees the metal glinting back at her from the black circle of the window. The tall lamp, which might have been found in an aristocrat's reception, casts an opulent illumination around the small, bare cabin. Katerina notices the gold buttons of her uniform are also caught in the porthole glass. They resemble a constellation in a night sky, trembling as though reflected on water.

"It'll be a while before first light," he says. That voice, thrilling her again. "There's early sunshine come summertime. And here, we're low, right on the rush of the waterline. It's a sight, the steady way the sea moves. That sense of momentum it imparts as easy as your own breathing. The planet rolling you along. As it does every day. The ocean crosses right over the window during a good storm. And then you get to see the occasional fish passing through. Nothing for us this morning, sorry to say."

"Sunlight can't be too far away now." She unlaces the uncomfortable boots she's been wearing. She stretches her feet and toes. A pleasure to be barefoot in a warm room.

"As late as eight in the morning this time of year."

"This isn't bad." She raises the cup.

"Don't drink all the way down. There's coffee sludge at the bottom of the cup that's only good for fortune-telling," he tells her.

"My grandmother drinks this kind of coffee," she tells him. "So I know about the sludge. She didn't read fortunes but I used to make coffee for her every morning when I was a child." He looks away from the porthole. She senses him glancing at her. Can feel the weight of that last word.

She takes another sip and hands back the cup. Stands up. Turns to face him, stomach close to his face. Between his knees. She leans her back against the wall. Undoes the top button of her jacket. The second, third and fourth buttons. He places the cups on the *Rolleiflex* crate beside the bed. Straightens up his back, lifts his head, and looks at nothing else now but her. She removes the jacket and throws it towards the door, the gold buttons sounding like scattering coins on the floorboards. She pulls the suspenders off her shoulders, unbuttons her pants and lets them fall to her bare feet. She picks up the hem of her shirt and lifts it over her head, drops the fabric into his open palms.

Deering's hands come around as he takes hold of her whole body, rising, lifting her up, allowing her to slide down through his tight embrace when she reaches the ceiling. Turns and lowers her down to the bed. Takes off his shirt and his pants.

He picks up her foot and lifts it to his mouth—kisses the soft arch of her foot. He lifts the other foot and kisses the ankle. Kneels between her legs and watches for a moment as she moves on his mattress, to make herself comfortable, to ready herself for him.

Deering does not rush into that preparation. Leans forward on all fours, above her as though not sure where he will begin devouring her, deciding upon her waist at the curve of her hip—mouth wide, his teeth gentle. Hands stretched up to her breasts. His face moves below her navel. Breathes her in. His mouth opens again. Lips and tongue dwell upon her, and then stop, taking hold of her hips and roughly pulling her down the mattress to his own hips, pausing above her, looking at her face.

A look of violence in his eyes yet all he does with it is to move his cheek to hers, delicately resting there like a child greeting another wordlessly, while beneath she feels him open her body and pause. He lingers on the threshold. Another movement will bring him inside. She trembles, up and down her legs. Remaining ready, savouring this pleasure before it races to completion—until she bites him on the shoulder, moans and says please. He finds her at her deepest point with a slow shove, and investing himself to that depth, more rapidly, driving relentlessly now, into her every moment and movement.

When she opens her eyes again, her breathing becoming steady, she notices the swaying fringe of clear beads on the lamp. She watches the movement, expecting it to subside. Deering is motionless beside her. His breath has settled. Near sleep. A moment later, he inhales deeply, stretches and blinks. The beads have continued to sway all the while.

"I wondered why you had such a pretty lamp," she says. "It's the fringe of glass beads, isn't it—the way they catch the light as they move with the ship?"

He doesn't reply. Lifts his head to look at it as if seeing the lamp for the first time.

"I've barely felt the motion of the sea since we left Veracruz," she tells him. The two zigzag rows of beads cast a scintillation of light over the bare walls as the liner makes its progress across the Atlantic. Katerina closes her eyes to see if she can feel *Aquitania*.

"A ship has a balancing point. Low and in the middle." Deering shifts onto his side, to look at her again. His hand rests over her navel. "A couple of decks above this point and you'd feel her movement in your own body. The higher you go, the more you'd feel her as she sashays—the closer to prow or stern, the more you'd feel her seesawing through the water. The ocean has been placid. You'll feel her making her way soon enough. Winter is rough. And there's likely a storm coming down from the north already."

His mouth moves to her breasts, he takes a nipple between his teeth. A moment later gets out of bed to go to his cupboard. Picks up Kornél's jacket so he doesn't trample it. Before he can hang it on one of his hooks she asks Deering to bring her the letters in the pocket. She reconsiders reading him the poem when he does. Probably not a literary person, but to Deering it might also feel juvenile.

"Is that your boyfriend?" She had not put the photo booth pictures back into the envelope with the poem. "Handsome fellow." He opens his cupboard and removes a knife and a cloth bundle.

"That's my brother, Kornél."

Deering comes back—indicates with a motion of his knife that she's to move to the side against the wall so he can sit on the edge of the bed.

Katerina looks at the four photos again. A basic uniform now for her brother. No more gold buttons. On the back of the strip he has scribbled a message for Katerina to contact him in future at the 507th Tank Regiment, under Colonel Charles de Gaulle.

"Kornél is wearing a new uniform. He's enlisted as a regular soldier but I don't know why. Kornél was going to have a political career, and it was supposed to begin with him becoming an officer. He topped his class for most of his time at the academy. I was wearing the uniform he should have worn at his Saint-Cyr graduation." She takes a breath as she realises that her brother's troubles began when Audrius found himself under house arrest in Montparnasse. "Things have gone awry."

"The coffee leaves a stale taste in the mouth." Deering unwraps a couple of oranges and carves the thick skin from one of them. He cuts out a segment and offers it to Katerina. "Fruit will give you back your sense of taste," he says. "And it's good for you."

"Do you have children?" She takes the piece of fruit and sits with her back to the wall.

"It's possible. Not intentional, if a fact."

"You never wanted a child?"

"Seems simple, doesn't it? Have a child and love surrounds you like in one of those Pears adverts. What I received from my dad wasn't like that and kids won't make for anything sweet in my heart either. My dad saw nothing but a rival in me. A rival for the love he already had, from my mother, from his children—my siblings, from God, and I don't know what else. Might be little reasoning in a head filled with rage and fear. A rival for everything, a rival for his life as well, because a helpless child is sweet, but as that child grows strong, the father weakens with natural mortality, so his rival is the ultimate reminder of death. No matter what you do to that rival, he wins, unless you kill that rival before he can replace you. You see—not a pretty place inside my heart because of all that, so I thought I'd better stop things with me. Let others make the world bustle with their children."

"Can you get me a glass of water?" she asks.

She places the photographs back in the envelope, empty except for the poem. Kornél told her in a previous letter that he'd been given the nickname "Bubble" after another cadet noticed the Alimpich poem on his wall at the academy. Katerina puts her palms to her eyes—Kornél has recently gone from wanting to leave for art in London to signing up for service in a tank regiment. A grim face in each of the four images and the only other thing written on the photos is: *Apologies … I have no more words. k.* It is the last message Kornél sent Katerina. She opened it hoping to find the latest news about Father. There is another letter for Katerina to read, earlier to this one; written after Montparnasse.

"Katerina," he says. "Should I leave you to sleep?" Asking because she's closed her eyes. She enjoys the care he gives her name. Awkward to ask for Deering's given name now.

"I wouldn't sleep. Can't find a way to turn off my mind." She opens her eyes and takes the glass of water. Drinks it down in three gulps and gives him back the glass.

"Your revelries haven't yet exhausted you?"

"Revelries? The uniform was more camouflage than costume."

"You'll sleep well tonight," he says.

"Do you need to go to work?"

"The ship will be a disaster today but there's no rush to fix that disaster." He yawns without putting his hand over his mouth. Missing a couple of teeth. His hair is cut very short, thick and combed forward, reminding her of a Roman bust— white and grey mottling with the natural brown of his colour. "Better to let the dust settle before racing about trying to get anything clean."

"No trouble for you otherwise, last night?" She pushes her hair from her face as she eats another segment of orange.

He tells her he used to be a drunk. Was well on the way to ruin. Nothing but despair before him. Found another way forward—across the seas. And ever on the water since then. He left his wife and the post office job he had in Manchester. Now he lives a simpler existence; a cleaner life. Savours an orange the way he used to enjoy scotch. And avoids the New Year and all such celebrations. Had his head buried beneath a pillow early last night. Goes to bed before ten every evening if he can possibly manage it.

He wakes early, today a little earlier than usual because of all the havoc on the ship. He makes a point of seeing the sunrise every day. Takes a pipe with him to smoke up on the sun deck. Always brings with him a camera: his Rolleiflex. He has accumulated a long sequence of sunrises from all around the world. In every season and all weather. Shame he can't capture the colours but that early light is the thing. One image of the sun rising after another. He imagines putting them all together in a book. He likes to catch the moment the light moves into the sky—that instant when darkness begins to dissolve.

"Can I see the photos?" Katerina asks.

Deering lifts the crate from beside his bed and opens it for her. Within it are a great many film canisters he says he will develop one day. He unrolls wide lengths of negatives for her to look over.

"I love God and I love my soul. Most of the time these words mean nothing to me. They especially mean nothing to me when there's a priest in a church talking about any of it as though he has any idea what God means or what a soul is. Every priest I've met is an idiot or a liar. You see, in a church I'm the worst kind of atheist, so I rarely enter a church for any reason. But I feel the truth of the great light of God illuminating my soul in that moment when I look out across the wide waters and sunlight lifts into a radiating glory, illuminating the entire dome of the sky and constructing me a cathedral anew every morning. In that moment there is no separation in divinity. God takes a breath in me. Takes another breath as creation dilates in my vision. Not most mornings, yet there's that chance of an ecstatic moment. And nothing else matters. I wait there on the sun deck. Rarely a passenger about that early, especially when it's wintertime. I take my photo. I finish my pipe. And then it's back to work. But through the whole day I feel it in my soul, that glory coming out of the darkness."

The Rolleiflex is a box with two lenses on the front with dials on the other sides. The viewfinder is above the box. Deering shows her how it is used. And then stands, gazing downwards, the camera resting on his stomach. He takes three photos as Katerina rests on the warm bed—her hand reaching across, long fingers playing with the fringe of the glowing lamp.

"Your camera reminds me of a story I was told at the embassy in Mexico City," she says. "About how everyone had to carry a passport box in the Aztec world. Imperial officers would ask to inspect the box routinely and it was an offence punishable by death to be without one, especially in the capital. An egg-shaped piece of emerald might be within one, a wooden spool for thread in another, a one-of-a-kind gold coin, an acorn with an abnormality, a seashell, a volcanic rock—they were all meant to be different, and small enough that they could fit into a box that could be carried around the neck on a strap when travelling in the capital. One day, a prince destined to rule the empire was asked as a joke to open his box and display the peridot pallasite he was known to carry. Since he was the heir apparent, his face easily recognisable to everyone in the capital, it had been many years since he'd been asked to display his soul. That was what the identifying item in the passport box was also called. The prince laughed, but there were laws relating to the soul. Even the highest of aristocrats had to carry around their passport boxes. The prince opened the container. The peridot pallasite he'd carried with him since he was an infant was gone. A man who had lost his soul was a man who was dead for all eternity, so the prince was executed after searching high and low for his lost soul. There's more in the story about how he lost it, and who hid his soul from him. I always thought it an interesting idea, the notion of a box that we carry around with us, because it isn't a stretch of the imagination to think that the body is a type of box—and then I can't help wondering what kind of object I carry around with me. I used to imagine all kinds of fantastical objects. We never get to see our soul. I came to think that perhaps what I'd been carrying around within myself was a casino chip. A colourful piece of plastic that only had value for a game of chance. But I like that you've found a way to fit the sun in that container around your neck."

Angry voices, snatches of abuse, feet running up the hall—violent noises getting louder outside Deering's door as Katerina speaks. The boatswain puts away his camera, repacking the crate and placing it beside his bed again. He's fully dressed in his uniform in minutes. A knocking on his door before he's got his boots laced up. Thumping now. The handle is rattled to see if it will open. More thumping with a hoarse voice calling through the door.

"Bosun! Bosun, you're fucking needed out here. A brawl has broken out! An engineer has a steak knife in his belly. Bosun! Are you fucking in there?"

"Stay here. And lock the door when I leave," he says in a voice of command that resonates in her head for minutes.

He leaves with one boot unlaced. Throws shut the door as he exits. Kornél's jacket falls from the hook to the floorboards again. She can hear Deering's voice booming down the corridor as he hurries to deal with the awful fracas. Katerina gets dressed as fast as she can manage and then stands at the door, listening to the turbulence beyond—swelling, simmering and swelling again. Sounds of boots and shoes running up and down the corridor. Men and women call out names, warnings and instructions to each other. It makes Katerina think of the Montparnasse hotel Kornél described in his letter.

She locks the door and sits on the kitchen chair at the half-table. Two ribbons of orange skin lie on the table in unbroken spirals. Both can be held up to resemble the oranges they were before Deering cut them open.

She opens the final unread letter from Kornél. Postmarked shortly before they boarded *Aquitania*. It is brief. No introduction. It doesn't have his name or his usual *k.* at the end of the letter. No poetry or literary quotes. Just a page of his handwriting raggedly slashed across the paper. Every dot from a full stop or *i* or ellipsis pushing through the thin paper so the letter reminds her of a spray of bullets into a wall.

Tragic news … News beyond the word "tragedy" … a meaningless word for me until this moment. My apologies, my deepest apologies for having to put it in a letter. You must know what has befallen us and there's no other way for me to tell you. I know Mother won't give you the news herself. I can't tell yet how much she's had to do with this catastrophe. The worst day of my life. Soon to also be the worst day of your life, Katie. I apologise again. My deepest apologies, dear sister. I love you more purely and dearly than anyone else in the world ... you must know this, believe this in your soul, before I break your heart. Please know, if there was any way to tell you myself, I would. Our father is dead ... he has been shot. Police reports and newspaper articles declare ... Tawdry headlines. Robbery in Montparnasse station. Murder unintended, but desperate people make desperate mistakes. Common enough this year. Audrius Klova. No longer gainfully employed. A dilettante. They say he resisted the robbery. Wouldn't give up what he was carrying. A pathetic suggestion of blame ... as though if he were less proud he would not have been shot down. A former Russian diplomat, travelling around France ... as reported ... at his own leisure. In the public convenience at Montparnasse. More suggestions in that regard ... that he had his own sordid pleasures. A tawdry death no government wants to touch. His body is in the morgue. I must decide what to do now ... even if everything in the world is undone.

❖❖❖❖❖

Katerina walks out into the falling snow. Thick, heavy flakes move like swarms of bleached bees. She steps back to stand beneath the cover over the bulkhead hatch. Finds she's holding her breath. Inhales deeply with a hand on her chest. Breathes again, shifting her palm to her belly.

The snowfall creates a sense of silence despite the

ceaseless susurration of water on the metal hull. The sea keeps rolling, black and empty as space, swallowing every fleck of white—all the starlight of the cosmos easily gulped down, the endless bits and pieces of light falling into the eternal deep. The ocean rolls on into a forever-black past, present, future.

The four funnels above pour out immense clouds of steam. They do not plume away into long smoke ribbons as they did when Katerina was on the boat deck. The icy pre-dawn air swallows whatever heat the engines can generate. A falling flake of snow gets caught in the lashes of one of her eyes. She blinks the tear away.

Aquitania's progress feels relentless. The liner drives off the snow as she races along, radiating white nimbuses around the electric lights dotted over the sun deck. Katerina notices flashes of light around a crewman's cupped hands near the railing at the back of the ship as he lights a cigarette.

Four passengers talk beneath the shelter of an awning. Two couples. A muffled quality to their voices, as if Katerina's ears are below water, the way they are sometimes when half-submerged in the bathtub—only her face above the waterline. They draw out bidding each other goodnight, tiredly going over amusing details from an exhilarating evening in the ballroom. The men shake hands. The women embrace, though they barely touch each other.

Katerina notices that one of the wives also has a hand on her belly. Just a slight mound. Katerina thinks perhaps it will be a summertime baby. The two couples are ready to retire to their cabins, talking about how they'll sleep the entire day away, passing Katerina as they re-enter the ship. They each nod to her, all four of them wishing Katerina a happy New Year. She nods, unable to speak. *No more words.*

She is still carrying the heat of Deering's cabin and the frigid conditions out here are not yet unpleasant. The discomfort in her exposed hands and face is a welcome distraction. Blackshaw's last couple of pills have already dissolved in her stomach. His chemicals ease through her blood. Slow down her heart until it feels full of mud. Her mouth thick—tongue like a slug resting behind her teeth. She knows that pain is racing across the ocean with the storm from the north Deering mentioned; that when it hits, nothing will help. For now, she can breathe and nod mutely at people as they pass.

The snowfall eases and she walks to the railing with the same poppy-red umbrella from the amphora. She wants to throw away Kornél's letters as she did the cherry-wood box. Holds the letters over the water—she will be relieved to see them scatter and disappear. She grips the paper, crushing the letters. Nothing will destroy the message, but she will lose a part of her brother if she discards his words, so she returns them to her jacket.

I was yet the invisible seed. First in the womb and then in the brain. I could feel it as much as know it, but it was very distinct ... A seed. One so small it was as made of particles of light, and it could flicker like a candle flame near an open window.

The wind sends her hair flying around her head. She plucks strands out of her mouth and eyes. She can feel *Aquitania* moving as if the ship is climbing and descending a vast landscape of travelling hills. Eyes adjusted to the darkness, she looks out now and can see the ocean is carving out valleys of water, pushing up mountains that foam white at the breaking tops where the wind catches them.

Snow is swept off *Aquitania*'s railings; bundles accumulate in corners of the deck and on some of the benches. Katerina sees a bundle move and realises a man has fallen asleep. She walks over to the bench and prods him with the sharp end of the umbrella.

"What?" he says, as though he has been rudely awoken in his own bed. "I'm resting. Is there a law against resting on a bench?"

"You should find a warmer place to sleep." There is a bottle of champagne beneath the man's arm. Vomit on the deck. The smell of piss and shit in the air, so he's probably relieved himself in his own clothes, unable to get to a toilet, let alone his cabin. He places his face back into his arm, as birds do into a wing, used to sleeping outdoors. She pokes the drunk in the ribs.

"Leave me be, you cunt," he says in a guttural voice. "I'll get up. When I do I'll beat you senseless. Leave me to rise in my own fucking time."

If he did manage to get to his feet, he'd barely be able to stumble after Katerina, let alone hurt her. Katerina has the urge to beat him with the umbrella. She pushes the end of it into his ribs and pulls it out of his weak grip when his hand takes hold of it.

"Get up," she says. "You reek and you're too fat for me to carry you back inside."

"What? I don't understand you!"

She doesn't want to talk to him. She needs to find a space in her mind to understand Kornél's last letters. Is there a chance that the newspapers misreported what happened at Montparnasse? No room for misunderstanding, is there? Where is her father now? There might still be the possibility of seeing him before the earth covers him over. Or is she never to see the face of her father again?

"I don't fucking understand." He turns his face up to her, blinking at her in befuddlement. "Don't understand what you're saying."

"Get up," she says in Russian, poking him in the thigh with the umbrella. "Go find a place to collapse where you won't die in your sleep."

He takes off his hat and scratches his bald head—surprised by the snow that falls from the brim. Nods at Katerina and lifts a palm as though to thank her rather than hurt her. He breathes, readying himself to walk as an athlete might before running.

The champagne falls to the deck; half-full, it pours out onto the wood with a hiss of foam. The bottle rolls along the deck, hits the railing with a hard tink of glass on metal, and rolls back to the bench—champagne bubbling out in a sparkling puddle.

The soused passenger lifts himself to his feet with difficulty, shuffles to the bulkhead hatch and hobbles inside. No doubt he will find a place to sleep on the first seat he comes across. *A broken animal*, thinks Katerina.

She hears a hacking cough from the other side of the sun deck and notices the German by the rail, looking out into the ocean the way he did when she first saw him. He's barely visible; wearing his long black jacket with a bomber hat.

Almost daybreak once more—this time he is not leaning over the railing. His body is on the other side of the railing. Heels on the base rail, left hand loosely on the top rail, right hand covering his own mouth as if aghast at something that has been said to him. Coughing a moment later.

"Could you give me a cigarette before you go away?" she asks.

He is surprised to hear her voice. Ducks his head as though she has struck him with the umbrella. His back becomes rigid, neck corded. Gripping the top of the rail with both his hands behind him, leaning out as he would to step off a tram at the next stop.

He speaks but she can't hear what he's saying, so she takes another step forward, raises her voice without shouting.

"Do you remember me from the morning? We shared a cigarette beneath a squabble of seagulls."

Ready to go. He breathes. Ready to fall. He breathes and stays another moment. A Jonah waiting for a leviathan to swallow his fear and pain whole.

"Daisy Miller, yes?" he asks, not turning to face her.

Katerina frowns and almost asks who she is, as though Daisy Miller might be a real person, a passenger on the ship.

"Yes." Katerina nods, within touching distance. "Daisy Miller." She might have stopped him from climbing the rail but with him already on the other side of the rail there's nothing she can do to stop him when he decides to step out into the Atlantic. "And I'll call you Ishmael—if you're still looking for that whale."

"I cannot give you a cigarette. I have dropped the silver case for my cigarettes into the ocean. Awful for me because it has been with my family since the time of Bismarck. When I was a child I put *Süssigkeiten* inside this case and I daydreamed about being a man and having tobacco inside. So it hurt me very much to lose this case in the waters."

She doesn't point out to him that it was about to be lost to the sea anyway. Little difference if it dropped by itself or with his body. And yet perhaps it's his Aztec passport box and he needs it more in his next moments below the waves than he did when he was a child filling it with sweets.

"My name is Katerina. Will you tell me your name?"

"Heinrich," he murmurs. She strains to hear the rest: "Heinrich Wilhelm Krake."

"I don't want a cigarette, Heinrich." She pulls her hair into a cord and holds onto it as though it were a rope. "I found talking with you this morning pleasant. I think you did as well. I wanted to talk with you again. I do understand this is not a good time for conversation. Terrible for both of us."

Glancing away from the ocean for the first time. Looking at her. He removes his hat and pushes it towards Katerina. His fingers glisten with moisture as they did when he lit the two cigarettes in his mouth for both of them.

"Katerina, take this for your warmth," he says.

She doesn't take it. He shakes the hat at her—only one hand on the wet railing. She accepts the bomber hat and ties the straps below her chin.

"The snow is easing," she says, unsure whether he is casting off a final item of unnecessary clothing before departing. "I've been told that there's a storm on the way but *Aquitania* is likely to skip right past it." He shakes his head, disbelieving that forecast.

"I have Ritz crackers for you," he says, "if your belly is empty. I bought them just today when I went to the cinema."

"I've thought of going to the cinema. I haven't been able to get away. What did you see?"

"I watched *The Wizard of Oz*."

"I haven't seen it," she says. "It's a film for children, isn't it?"

"It was the only picture they were showing in the cinema. And they were showing it again and again. I watched three times."

"I've heard music from the film on the radio. Did you enjoy it?"

"There is a moment when a witch is killed. The witch dissolves in water." A response to that will lead Heinrich into the ocean, so Katerina tells him she is hungry and she would enjoy the Ritz crackers.

His right hand fumbles with the buttons of his jacket. Trembling, hands shaking. The cold is bitter but he's also becoming more frightened as he delays with idle talk. Two hands on the railing, his grip made out in jagged knuckles.

"I'm sorry," he says. Coughing so hard he's gasping for air at the end of the fit. "Mine fingers are not well. This body is also not working very well."

"I can find the crackers if you will allow me to touch you?"

He nods. She steps behind him, her mouth near enough to his neck she has an impulse to kiss him. Katerina reaches through his arm and around his waist with her left arm. It isn't easy even for her to unbutton the wet leather. Inside the jacket she can feel Heinrich's body radiating heat and his adrenalised heart beating a desperate rhythm on his rib cage. Katerina leaves her hand there a few seconds to keep him present. He will not lean back against the rail at her pressure. She is careful not to encourage him to push forward.

She finds paper in one of his pockets. Wonders if he has letters as she does. When she removes the papers she finds that they are not letters; that they are torn-out Bible pages—the same thin paper as her pages from the Book of Job. She still has the last one she found slipped under her door when Cypress visited.

"'Let that day be darkness; let not God regard it from above, neither let the light shine upon it. Let darkness and the shadow of death stain it; let a cloud dwell upon it; let the blackness of the day terrify it.' That was you?" Katerina asks.

"They are not my words," he says, attempting to rebutton his jacket, returning both hands to the railing behind him before he's managed it. She can't see his face.

"No, not your words. The words of Job? 'As for that night, let darkness seize upon it; let it not be joined unto the days of the year, let it not come into the number of the months. Lo, let that night be solitary, let no joyful voice come therein.'"

Shaking his head as Katerina spoke. "Those words have been in the world for so many generations the children forgot the parents who decided first to keep them as sacred. Whose words are they this day? Not mine alone."

"'Let them curse it that curse the day, who are ready to raise up their mourning. Let the stars of the twilight thereof be dark; let it look for light, but have none; neither let it see the dawning of the day.'"

"Please stop. They are a great agony of words."

"You slipped a great agony under my door to get away

from it. Placed these words at my feet. You don't want to hear them now?"

"I did not bring this book with me. It was already in my cabin when I found myself in crisis. And there was no solace in these pages. I found only my own pain and I tore it from the spine. I have been throwing it out into the ocean for hours."

Katerina opens her hand—the rest of the pages from his Bible flutter down, along with her page from the Book of Job. She places her hand above the letters she has inside her jacket, as if Kornél's pages might follow if she is not careful to keep them safe.

"I have heard people say the war is done. War is finished for us after the great conflict," he says. "They do not understand what they are saying. They do not see, we *are* the war. The war is *us*."

Katerina is still holding the umbrella with her right hand, though the snow has eased. A flew flakes are borne up by wind, rising with the rush of the water below. She leans forward and lets the umbrella go, watching it float down like a parachute. The floral pattern illuminated in flashes of red as it passes the bright windows of the decks below them—flipping over as the wooden handle touches the water, then floating for a few seconds, upside down. The umbrella founders and disappears.

"I have found myself thinking that death is nothing but a passing thought," she says. She leans near him, so she can speak without raising her voice. This close to his ear, she can whisper. "Death flitters through my mind and I think why not float away with it? Leave body and mind behind. It's all just a passing thought anyway. And when those thoughts are gone, no matter. The same as when you lie down at night. Released into shades less substantial than shadows. It's as easy to forget a life as it is to settle yourself down to sleep. For a few hours or eternity, little difference. You can release yourself from your pain so easily, more easily than tearing pages from a book."

Katerina reaches out her left hand, to prod him as she did the drunken man on the bench. To push him away from the ship. Expecting him to tumble forward. Without resistance. Ready as he has been a whole day and night to find his way down to the water.

Heinrich does not drift from her hand as the umbrella and the Bible pages did. He turns to his right with a twist—a dog snarling after its tail has been stepped on. His left hand comes away from the railing at her push but he turns adroitly so the same hand can come about, back to the railing as he turns to face the ship. His feet lose purchase on the deck in the movement yet his right hand darts out to her wrist and takes a hold.

Horror explodes in his eyes. For another moment she thinks she might stop him falling and bring Heinrich to her if he's intent on living. His left hand releases the tenuous grip it has of the railing and takes instead a good handful of her embroidered sleeve.

The full weight of the German pulls her to the railing. Ribs break on her left side. Ligaments in her shoulder tear. And the ocean is roaring with agony as his face fills with the death below her.

"Please," she says, "please let go." She can't speak over a whisper. "I'm sorry." She can't get enough air into her lungs to make herself heard. "I'm sorry. Please let me go," she mouths noiselessly. "I'm sorry."

Both his legs pendulum below him, entirely loose until he moves his feet to the side of the ship. He intends to climb back up. His feet slip on the slick hull metal. He drops and swings. Kicking the side of the ship in an effort to climb again. Her ribs are hauled sideways against the railing and downwards with greater force. Grinding into the railing until splinters of her broken bones begin to tear at her lungs.

She lifts and allows herself to be dragged over the railing to release the weight that is threatening to crush her chest or tear her arm away at the socket. He releases her when he feels her coming down and she is able to catch hold of the bottom rail with her right hand. Doesn't have the strength to keep her grip. Barely has time to take a breath before her feet hit the water.

She won't be able to swim fully clothed so she pushes off her oversized boots, slips away from the heavy officers's jacket and trousers. She kicks towards the surface, but he gets a hold of Katerina once more as she breaks the surface. Catching sight of her white shirt, her pale limbs. This time he takes her ankle, and then the other ankle with another hand. She kicks him away. He swims upward. Gets a grip of her wrist. She shakes it loose. He takes hold of her long hair, turning his hand within it—binding her hair around his fist. His other arm wraps around her shoulders, and his legs go about her waist. He releases her only to be able to move downwards. Not trying to drown her so much as embrace her.

Aquitania's propellers make an awful noise as they come close. Terrible to feel the metal cut them apart and tear up their bodies with those immense blades. They aren't close enough to be pulled into the vortex. They tumble over and over in the wake and deeper into the ocean.

The lightless water washes her eyes with pure winter and the taste that rushes through her mouth and down into her stomach is of black salt. He will not let her go back to the surface. Her lungs heave for air, wanting to breathe despite being full of water. Spasms of movement because her lungs have been finding air every moment of her life. Heart thumping as though racing her to a destination.

There is more life in Heinrich; she can feel that as she gets nearer to her last moment. He has air in his lungs. His arms pull her tighter to him, crushing her body into his. His legs wrap around her as well. Her eyes are open and through the water she can see the brightly lit-up glass of the many decks of *Aquitania* as she moves away.

Katerina reaches her arms around Heinrich. Pulls his body to hers, pushing herself into the heat she feels in him. He will let her go when he feels Katerina begin to drift downward to the bottom of the ocean. Then he will understand that he does want to live. He will never again move towards his death willingly. Will do whatever is necessary to continue breathing. In future Heinrich will not make the mistake of dawdling so near the edges of his life.

She closes her eyes. Pushes her face into his neck, feeling pulses of warmth in his body. She opens her mouth. A kiss to bid him farewell. She uses her teeth instead. To find a way into his body—to suck the air right out of his lungs. She finds a deep vein through his soft flesh and a thick rush of blood.

She is released from his embrace. Pushed away violently. Kicked upwards with force. She floats to the surface. Only her face above the waterline. Heinrich does not come up for air. His body is tugged away, downwards into an ever darker black.

A few flakes of snow drift down to Katerina as she continues to loll with the current. Her face above the deep—placidly taking in the movement of an entire ocean. A smear of blood across her mouth. Eyes open as if she is waiting for daybreak.

ATLANTIC OCEAN, 1 JANUARY 1939.